SEASONS OF CHANGE

*Featuring Hauptkommissar Müller
and his sidekick, Pappenheim*

In Australia following the trail of an important informant on the shadowy organization threatening German democracy, Müller is disturbed by troubling memories, and a puzzling sense of déjà vu. But he must keep his wits about him, as he knows he has been followed, and those he is trying to uncover have already sent one sniper to put an end to his investigations...

Julian Jay Savarin titles available from
Severn House Large Print

A Hot Day in May
Winter and the General
Romeo Summer

SEASONS OF CHANGE

Julian Jay Savarin

Severn House Large Print
London & New York

This first large print edition published 2010
in Great Britain and the USA by
SEVERN HOUSE PUBLISHERS LTD of
9-15 High Street, Sutton, Surrey, SM1 1DF.
First world regular print edition published 2005 by
Severn House Publishers Ltd., London and New York.

British Library Cataloguing in Publication Data

Savarin, Julian Jay.
  Seasons of change.
  1. Muller, Jens, Hauptkommissar (Fictitious character)--
  Fiction. 2. Police--Germany--Berlin--Fiction.
  3. Suspense fiction. 4. Large type books.
  I. Title
  823.9'14-dc22

  ISBN-13: 978-0-7278-7875-5

Severn House Publishers support The Forest Stewardship Council
[FSC], the leading international forest certification organisation. All
our titles that are printed on Greenpeace-approved FSC-certified paper
carry the FSC logo.

 **Mixed Sources**
Product group from well-managed
forests and other controlled sources
www.fsc.org Cert no. SA-COC-1565
FSC © 1996 Forest Stewardship Council

Printed and bound in Great Britain by the
MPG Books Group, Bodmin, Cornwall.

One

'A change of season,' he said quietly, looking out upon the greenish blue of the ocean. His remark was not in English.

Above him was an impossibly dark blue, clear sky. Beneath his feet, the bright white of the beach; and behind him soared the dark red of the pindan cliffs. It was a landscape like no other on the planet.

'After today,' he continued, 'nothing can be the same again.'

The incredibly white beach was at Cape Leveque, at the tip of the Dampier peninsula in the Kimberley region of Western Australia. It probed its way into the vastness of the Indian Ocean. Only two people were on that beautiful and otherwise empty beach.

Not far from where they stood was the red gash of an unsealed airstrip. A single small aircraft, with no one in it, waited in the dry heat of the day. The aircraft was unusual in design. Looking for all the world like a pregnant guppy, it was in such excellent condition, its red coat with white side stripes so gleamed in the heat of the day, that it appeared to have the sheen of sweat.

The Cessna 337, a centreline push-pull twin-engined piston aircraft with twin tail-booms, possessed an unexpected agility. Originally designed to carry six, including the pilot, it had been extensively refurbished to give a roomy capacity of four, including the seats at the dual controls. Richly upholstered in black leather, the reclinable high-backed seats were both functional and comfortable, and perfect for long flights. The general interior was itself upholstered in light, neutral material that enhanced the impression of cool space.

Instruments had been updated with the latest gear, many of which were in the form of multi-function displays. The Cessna had been fitted with a navigation suite – including GPS – that would not have been out of place in the latest private jet. It even had a traffic avoidance and collision-warning display. It had also been fully rigged for de-icing. De-icing capability had not been standard on the 337 Cessnas

Its engines had been so thoroughly refurbished, they might have been brand new. Turbochargers – not on the original aircraft when they had bought it – had been added to the engines. The 337 was now able to cruise at 25,000 feet with ease, and, on occasion, they had taken the pressurized Cessna to 30,000. For an aircraft that had been built in the late 1970s, it looked barely a year old, a testimony to the care lavished upon it. It was fast, and looked remarkably sleek, despite its shape.

When they had picked it up after the work had been completed, he had looked at it and had said, 'A plane built to flee.'

And she had understood.

The man and the woman were both fully licensed, accomplished pilots, with years of experience.

'We were always afraid this day might come,' she now said. Her voice carried the sadness of years.

He nodded. 'Yes.'

The radiophone in his hand crackled. 'Jacko?' a familiar voice, anxious, called. 'You there?' The voice spoke Australian-accented English.

He raised the phone. 'We're here.' He spoke with the same Australian accent.

'And where exactly is that? I tried your plane. When there was no answer, I reckoned I'd try your phone.'

'We're at our favourite place.'

'Stay there. I'll be right with you.'

The man called Jacko frowned briefly. 'Is there a problem?'

'Stay where you are, Jack. Over and out.'

As the transmission ended, he looked at her. ' "Jack" this time. Not "Jacko". Business-like. Now what?'

About forty minutes later, the four-wheel-drive police patrol vehicle pulled up at the airstrip and stopped a short distance from the Cessna.

7

A police inspector with short, white-blond hair, tanned by years of police work in the sun, wearing dark, mirrored shades and in bush uniform of khaki shirt, shorts, and sturdy boots, climbed out. He reached into the 4WD to pick up his long-serving police-issue bush hat, and put that on too. Then he got out a hand-held radio. Tall and athletic, he went over to the aircraft and gave it a cursory check before looking towards the beach, a five-minute walk away. Two people, also wearing bush hats, were sitting on the sand at the far end of the white beach, waiting.

'Have I got some news for you two,' he said quietly, and began walking towards them.

Graeme Wishart was in his forties, but looked much younger. Despite some tiny lines near the eyes from almost as many years of squinting in the bright sun, his face was itself remarkably unlined. His eyes, were he not wearing sunglasses, would have been seen to be a very dark green. He had known Jack and Maggie Hargreaves for a good twenty years, and the couple were close friends of his.

He made his way with purposeful strides.

They got to their feet as he approached and, when he had stopped before them, surveyed him with curious eyes, noting the grim expression upon his face.

Wishart shook hands with them. 'How're ya doing? Awright?'

'We're fine,' Hargreaves replied, eyes watchful.

Wishart paused, gave a heavy sigh, then said bluntly, 'Jamie Mackay's dead.'

'*What?*' they exclaimed in unison. Their shock was genuine.

'But how?' Jack Hargreaves demanded. 'We spoke to him today. Not so long ago, in fact. How could he be dead? How did it happen?'

'Shot,' Wishart answered.

That shocked them even more.

'Jamie Mackay, dead?' Maggie Hargreaves said in horror. 'You can't mean that.'

'With respect, Maggie,' Wishart said, 'I'm not in the habit of joking about one of my officers getting killed.'

The tone of his voice brought her up short. She looked at Wishart as if anew.

Hargreaves simply stared at him.

'Sorry to be so harsh, Maggie,' Wishart told her in a voice that was only barely softer. 'But this has knocked the sails right out of me. It's not every day...' He paused again. 'Jamie was an old mate, as well as a colleague. Jamie's survived being bitten by a snake in the middle of nowhere, chased by a saltie looking for breakfast, had his head cracked open by a man he arrested, and shot by the wife of another man he went to arrest. People like Jamie just don't get killed. I expected him to reach his nineties, at least. Thought he'd outlive the lot of us. Now this happens.'

'Jamie was our friend too,' Hargreaves reminded him.

Wishart nodded. 'Which is why I need an explanation.'

'From *us*? Surely you don't think...'

'Jack, if I thought for one minute you two were responsible in some way, I would not be talking to you now. Friendship or no friendship, I'd have had a few of the mob with me to take you in. Jamie, from what I can gather so far, was in the wrong place at the wrong time. So, right now, I'm just looking for some answers.'

'And you believe we've got them?' Maggie Hargreaves suggested.

Wishart looked from one to the other. 'I don't know. And that's the truth. But I have many questions. Let's talk about secrets.'

Hargreaves looked at him closely. 'Secrets?'

Instead of replying, Wishart turned to look out upon the ocean. 'I have always admired what you two have made out of the old abandoned Woonnalla station,' he began, eyes fixed upon the far horizon. 'The place had been derelict for years when you bought the property. The agents responsible for it were so glad to get rid of it, they thought you were both crazy, even as they took your money.

'The Kimberley has been my beat for the last twenty years. When I first met you, I was a young constable. I was fascinated by this amazing couple – who did not seem short of the folding stuff – who had decided to turn the Woonnalla into what has become an ecological Garden of Eden. In the beginning, people in the area thought you were as crazy as the real-estate agents believed. I don't mean *The* People, of course. *They* were curious to see what you would do with the land. In time, they came to admire you as well. You turned that barren piece of ground into a place that supplies organic food throughout the state, and beyond. The hotels in particular love your produce. You have a thriving, successful business. You have built a beautiful house that is furnished in a way that sometimes reminds me of one of those classic mansions in Europe.'

'We were lucky with the place,' Hargreaves said. 'We found ground water.'

'I think,' Wishart said, 'there was more to it than just being lucky. You must have done your research and surveys bloody well, when looking for a place to settle. The station had been abandoned for more than thirty years by the time you got to it. You had the technology, and knew what you were looking for. You found it where no one else had. The old Woonnalla station was sitting on a huge underground lake, deep down, and no one knew about it – until you came along to find it. The real-estate agents must have kicked themselves every day when they saw what you had done with the place. You've even put in solar power, which gives you more than enough for all your needs. God knows what the place is worth now.

'I have admired the way you behaved, and behave, towards the local tribespeople,' Wishart continued. 'You give them respect, and they respect you for not abusing the land. One day, two boys – twins – from the local

11

tribe came to you. Peter and Paul Lysert. They wanted to work with you. They stayed ever since. You treated them like your own. Now grown men, they have their own families. Sometimes their relatives even turn up to help. You taught Pete to fly. You trust him with the plane...'

Hargreaves, listening to Wishart's monologue with great interest, said, 'He practically taught himself. He had the aptitude.'

The policeman, still looking out to sea, nodded. 'I once asked him why he didn't apply for a commercial licence. He's certainly good enough. He asked what for. He enjoyed flying the Cessna, delivering orders to customers when either you or Maggie were not flying. For big orders, some customers either come in their own planes or trucks, or the Lyserts deliver special orders in your own trucks. Today, Woonnalla produce has a great reputation. A neat life, running very nicely at its own pace. If you ask me.

'In the early days, the policeman in me did wonder why two sophisticated people like you would want to hide themselves way out here, in the outback. Each time, I told myself it was your choice. Unless you did something that caused the law to take an interest, it was none of my business.

'Time came and I got myself a family of my own. My boy, your godson, was named after you, Jack. He was so keen to fly, you showed him the ropes early on. Today, he's an airforce pilot candidate. I'm telling the both of

12

you all this because the last twenty years have suddenly come to a kind of watershed. Which brings me to the secrets I mentioned earlier.

'My mother's Finnish, my father was of German descent, with a bit of the Irish in him. I have green eyes, and my hair is so blond, it's nearly white. What would you say if I told you that my great-great-grand-mother, on my father's side, was of The People?'

Wishart still kept his gaze upon the ocean.

Hargreaves suddenly understood why in all the years he had known Wishart, he had never heard the policeman refer to the native Aus-tralians as Aborigines. It had always been 'The People', which he had mistakenly be-lieved had been Wishart's vaguely politically correct way of referring to them. He felt embarrassed by the calumny.

'I won't deny it's a great surprise,' Har-greaves said, while Maggie just stared at Wishart. 'But that's about it. It's not a big deal, as your son – our godson – would say.'

Wishart made a noise that could have meant anything. 'My little secret. Not many people know of it outside my close family. My father was dying when he told me. I made certain I would not do the same to my son. I told him as soon as I could. He made me proud. "Great," he said, pleased. Part of our blood belongs with the ancient people. We are true Australians. Of course, history being what it is, I doubt my great-great-grandma had much choice in the matter. Secrets,'

13

Wishart repeated. 'What's yours, Jack? Maggie?'

'We're not sure what you mean, Graeme,' Maggie said.

Wishart glanced round. 'I think you do. Let's talk about a Berlin copper,' he said, changing tack, speaking to the ocean. 'I received a note on official paper, telling me that I will be visited by a policeman from Berlin. That note was signed by someone very high up. Although the cop from Berlin can't usurp my authority, there is no question of my obstructing him. That takes big clout.

'So he turns up with his ponytail, expensive clothes, and *earring*. "*This* is a copper?" I ask myself. He's very polite, speaks English like a public-school Pom, about ten years younger than me. I give him a second look, and realize this is no softie. A hard man in velvet, if you get me. He has a pretty young woman with him. Not a decorative accessory. *She* turns out to be American. Air-force lieutenant-colonel, at that. They both carry guns and are allowed to keep them. You can imagine the things going through my policeman's mind when this German copper asks me about one Jack and Maggie Hargreaves, whom he's come to question.

'He is at pains to assure me they are not fugitives from justice. He is on a case about which he believes they may have valuable information that might help him. That was all. Once he'd seen them, it would be back to Germany for him, and the States for the

14

lady. Simple. By now I'm asking myself what kind of investigation could be so important that an English-sounding copper from Berlin, and an American air-force officer, would come all the way down under just to ask my old friends the Hargreaves some questions.

'If it's that simple, I ask, why the guns? He is reluctant to answer. In the end, he says it's not because of the Hargreaves. Not because of the Hargreaves, I'm thinking. If they're not worried about the Hargreaves, then they expect trouble – or are being prepared in case of trouble – from another quarter.'

Wishart at last turned round from the ocean. 'They found it, at Woonnalla. Care to shed some daylight, Jack? Maggie?'

They looked at him, but did not immediately make comment.

'Let me help you some more,' Wishart said. 'I warned Jamie Mackay, who was in the area, to expect Müller – that's the copper's name – and his companion, Colonel Bloomfield. I suspect that after he met them, Jamie warned you. By the time Müller and Miss Bloomfield got to your place, you had already flown the coop. Literally. The Lyserts were gone too, which says you warned them to get out fast. That smells like an escape plan to me. You do see my problem, don't you? Why would you absent yourself from someone who was only coming to ask you some questions? Or was there something – or some*one* – else worrying you?

15

'Things get even more complicated after that,' Wishart continued into their silence. 'Someone else does turn up. Someone who was following Müller and Bloomfield and who, according to Müller, was hoping that he, Müller, would lead him to you two. Who was this mysterious person? A killer, no less. Someone who did his job by *sniping*. Someone who came to kill the both of you. And Jamie got in the way. He was shot at close range, with a handgun, by the sniper.

'The killer decided to kill all the birds with one stone. He started on Müller and the colonel, planning to deal with you two later. Müller believes that, as the killer had no idea you had a plane, he thought you were still in the house. Luckily for you, Müller and the colonel decided to go after the sniper themselves. Luckily for *them*, they had been allowed to keep their guns. They got him. Actually, a snake got him...'

'A *snake?*' Maggie Hargreaves said.

'Yeah. Big, speckled mulga. Couldn't have happened to a nicer bloke. Seems our killer enjoyed a bit of torturing. Müller and the colonel had come at him from two sides, each playing decoy. The colonel caught the killer off-guard. He had pinned the mulga to the ground with a big combat knife jabbed behind the head. He had his fun watching the snake die slowly.

'That was when Miss Bloomfield surprised him. They had wanted to take him alive, so she shot him in the leg. Bad luck for him that he startled a second mulga. It bit him, and kept biting.'

'Mulgas can get a bit cross,' Hargreaves said in massive understatement.

'Yeah,' Wishart said, almost absentmindedly. 'They found Jamie,' he continued, 'dead in his own patrol car. That killer was a pro, and used a pro weapon. According to Müller, one of the best weapons for the job, if not *the* best: a Dragunov SVDS. To give you even more of an idea how all this worries me, I have been ordered to let Müller take the weapon back to Berlin, because it is a vital part of his ongoing investigations. The sniper – who was a dirty copper – will be buried anonymously out here.'

Wishart paused at long last, and stared at each of them, switching from one to the other for a full thirty seconds.

'So many questions in my mind,' he said finally. 'Are you two going to give me some answers? Who are you, *really*?'

'Not criminals,' Hargreaves said.

'I've already worked that one out,' Wishart remarked, 'as I said earlier. And even if I hadn't, Müller did a good job of defending you. He tried his best to convince me that you were not fugitives from justice. If anything, he seemed very upset that he might have led the killer to you. Not what you'd expect from a copper hunting out hardened criminals. He still wants to see you two.'

Wishart paused again, this time for even longer. 'And another thing. If I didn't know better, I'd say there was a family resemblance. But that can't be right, can it?'

Berlin, same day. 1200, local

One of the phones in Pappenheim's smoke zone of an office cut into his enjoyment of his third Gauloise Blonde with a demanding ring. He grabbed at it before it had time for a repeat performance.

'You've got me,' he said into the phone. 'It had better be worth it.'

'Cheerful, as usual,' the voice of one of his many contacts said. 'How's life in the smoker's paradise on this fine August day?'

'So good, you wish you were here.'

'No thanks!' The shudder of disgust could almost be felt. 'Smoking is so ... You're a dinosaur, Pappi. Do you know that?'

'For creatures with low-performance brains, they had a good run. I'm not sure the same will be said of us when some inter-stellar scientist writes a history of the human race.'

'Good God. What's in those cigarettes of yours?'

'Something you're missing. As I know you did not call to chat about my bad habits, what's driven you to make this one?'

'Beware of Greeks bearing gifts.'

'And you should stay off the quotations,' Pappenheim advised. 'Bad for your health.'

'Where's Müller?' the other countered.

'That's for me to know, and you never to find out.'

'I can find out,' the other said. It was not a boast.

'Then why ask me?'

'Just testing.'

'You failed. Now do I get to know what this is all about? Or are we practising for a TV game show?'

'I've told you all you need to know – which is plenty. You're smart, Pappi. Work it out when it happens – which won't be long.'

'Well...' Pappenheim paused, killed the cigarette he was smoking, and promptly lit another. 'Well,' he repeated. 'Since I know you're not talking about our resident Greek philosopher, Hermann Spyros—'

'He's half-Greek. His mother's German—'

'Bad manners to interrupt ... and my mother was Sudeten. So?'

'Keep your shirt on, Pappi,' the contact said, a smile in his voice. 'Just remember the little warning. You'll work it out.'

The call ended.

'So many people wanting to be comedians,' Pappenheim grumbled as he replaced the receiver. 'Must be those talent shows.'

He leaned back in his chair and blew some more pollution at the ceiling, in the shape of perfect smoke rings. He squinted an eye as if sighting through them as they drifted upwards.

'So who's the Greek? And what is he bringing?'

Half an hour later, Pappenheim got an inkling when a knock sounded on his door.

19

'In!'

Berger, dressed in civilian attire like most of the members of the special Friedrichstrasse police unit, entered, a strained expression upon her face. A shoulder harness, gun in holster, was strapped to her t-shirt.

'You look ... how shall I put it ... strange, Berger,' Pappenheim said by way of greeting. 'A kind of dazed stare is pointed my way. Can't be my smoke. You should be accustomed by now.'

'Not your smoke, Chief.'

'Alright. Not my smoke. Finding being a day-old *Kommissarin* too much to handle?'

'That feels ... just fine. Wish I had my own office. Klemp is moaning on about how he was the senior sergeant, and should have had the silver star on his shoulders...'

'You just got your first silver and you want an office? Shame on you!' Pappenheim's dry comment wrung a brief smile out of her. 'As for Klemp, if his brain had a choice, it would leave him just to experience the sense of relief. Don't let him get to you. We need people like Klemp for the rough stuff. He's very good at that.'

'Cannon fodder, you mean.'

Pappenheim removed the cigarette from his mouth, pointed it at her, squinting along it as if through a sniper's scope. 'Don't you think there are those who look upon *us* as cannon fodder? Once you understand that, everything else falls into place.'

'Then you'll like this.'

'Why do I know you mean the opposite?'

Berger gave him another weak smile. 'The Interior Minister's wolfhound is here. He's got one of those Lanzarote tans, and a designer suit.'

'No cheap sun studio for our wolfhound. And designer suit. Goes with the territory these days, I suppose. What kind?'

'Am I his dresser?' Then she added, 'It doesn't look like one of the boss's.'

'Not Armani, then. Some people look like pimps no matter how expensive they dress. Tells you a lot about them. Jens, on the other hand, would look exactly what he is, even in rags: a *Graf*, no matter how hard he tries not to be, or how much he hates wearing ties. So? Does the wolfhound look like a pimp?'

'How should I know?'

'Hmm.'

'He's here to see you...' Berger announced with some drama. 'Well, to see the boss, really. But as he's not ... er ... here, I thought...'

'You'd set the wolfhound on me? Don't answer that.'

'Well...'

'And what does he want with me, or Jens?'

'He wouldn't say.'

'Of course he wouldn't say. Day-old *Kommissarins* are beneath the lofty *Herr* Melk. I'm surprised he allows himself to stoop to the level of a lowly *Oberkommissar* like me – a large, chain-smoking one at that. What is so important that makes him take the trouble to come all the way to the workers' compound?'

21

'If I knew the answer to that one, Chief...'

'Rhetorical question, Berger.'

'Ah. One of those.'

'Watch it. *Kommissarin* or no *Kommissarin*, I'm still your superior.'

'Should I quake?'

Cigarette clamped between his teeth, Pappenheim grinned at her through its veil of smoke.

The cigarette bobbed as he said, 'You could at least pretend to. So where's the minister's hatchet man waiting?'

'In the VIP conference room next to *Polizeidirektor* Kaltendorf's office. He's got two bodyguards with him.'

'*Two* bodyguards,' Pappenheim remarked as if he had never heard the word 'bodyguard' before. 'Doesn't he feel safe with us? And where's the Great White himself?' he added, using their nickname for Kaltendorf. It was not fondly said.

'Not here.'

'Small mercies. So I've got Melk all to myself. What have I done to deserve this?'

'Another rhetorical—'

'Berger.'

'Sir?'

'Don't push it.'

'As if.'

'Yes, if.'

Berger watched him warily.

Pappenheim did not shift off his chair. 'Wolfgang Melk. Do you know what he was before he became a political animal, Berger?'

'Well, I know he used to be a colleague of sorts.'

'"Of sorts" is a good way of putting it. Long before this unit of ours came into being, and when you were still at school, Wolfgang Melk was a *Polizeihauptmeister*...'

'Like Klemp.'

'Like Klemp, but not like Klemp. Nothing at all like Klemp in fact. Melk is a clever man. We've never worked together, but I've met him ... once, back ... oh ... years ago.' Pappenheim drew on his cigarette. 'Heard about him, though. Many, many times.'

'When did you meet?'

'And where. One of those police association conferences. It was about working conditions. Melk was a speaker. He's a very good speaker. At the time, someone told me he was about to get his first silver...'

'Didn't he get it?'

'Oh, yes. But he resigned soon after.'

Berger was surprised. 'Why?'

'Damascus.'

'What?'

'Saul – or St Paul, if you prefer. Melk found his road to Damascus that day, and I was standing right next to him when the revelation took place. Someone came up to congratulate him on his speech, and said he should be in politics. That man should have been shot on the spot for letting that escape from his stupid mouth. I thought he'd been half joking. Whether he was or not, a faraway look came into Melk's eyes. He resigned soon

23

after he got his promotion. I suppose he considered that entering politics as an ex-*Polizeikommissar* sounded better than ex-*Polizeihauptmeister.* He's done well. See where he is now. A VIP, no less. Some colleagues like to see him as "our" man at the Ministry. Fools. Who says politics doesn't pay?'

'Not me.'

'Nor me,' Pappenheim grunted. 'But there isn't enough money around to get me into that whore's game.'

'I can tell you like politicians.'

'Oh, I love them. I really do.'

Berger glanced at her watch. 'Sir,' she warned tentatively. 'He's *waiting*...' It was a sharp, nervous whisper, as if she expected Melk to suddenly appear. 'He's not a colleague any more. It's one thing with the *Direktor*...'

Pappenheim still made no move to leave his desk. 'Don't worry, Lene. The condemned man can have his last smoke. Tell him I've been told, and I'm on my way.'

'Ye-es, sir.'

With a last, uncertain look, she went out.

'Wolfgang Melk,' Pappenheim repeated softly as the door closed. 'So you're the "Greek". What "gifts" do you bring? Will they be poisonous? What do you really want? Doing your boss's bidding, or your own?' He remained seated, drawing slowly on the cigarette. 'I like asking myself questions. That way, I can refuse to answer.'

Pappenheim had truthfully described himself. A big, round man with a cuddly exterior and baby-blue eyes, he had for years – since childhood – successfully conned the world into believing his air of guileless innocence. This had worked so well, it effectively hid the very sharp individual beneath it all. At school it had kept bullies off his back; though one stupid enough to try his luck had been very painfully surprised. Result: Pappenheim had got suspended for slamming the boy's head against a school wall. Only when the truth of the matter had come out – the months-long goading that Pappenheim had first endured with patience – was his suspension lifted.

'But the teacher never apologized for his wrong decision,' Pappenheim now muttered. 'Those in power never do. As it was yesterday, so it is today.'

Pappenheim's rumpled clothing, ash-speckled, served only to confirm the impression of bumbling ineptitude that he had so assiduously cultivated. Yet despite the fact that whatever suit he wore inevitably seemed wrong, his choice of tie was always spot-on and immaculate; an apparent anomaly that should have warned the observant. That he succeeded in this camouflage was a testimony to his cunning, and throughout his career as a policeman this had worked wonders for him. His fingers, unexpectedly for a man who smoked so compulsively, were scrupulously clean.

Like Müller, there was also something of the predator – which had briefly appeared that day at school – hiding behind those eyes.

In his chosen profession, his prey were criminals of any kind, which he hunted mercilessly by any means at his disposal. Pappenheim also had the knack of ferreting out information from the unlikeliest of sources. His networking skills were phenomenal, and his network of contacts was itself a potent weapon which he put to use with consummate ruthlessness when need be.

At long last, Pappenheim stubbed out his cigarette in an already-full ashtray, heaved himself off his chair, half-heartedly brushed at the speckled pattern of ash on his crushed suit, then let himself out into the pristinely clean air of the corridor.

'God,' he shuddered. 'Poison!'

As decreed by Kaltendorf, the corridor, like every other corridor, lift, and public space within the building, was a rigorously defined smokeless zone. The plethora of no-smoking signs that adorned such areas would have been difficult to miss.

Pappenheim glared at them as he passed, imagining Kaltendorf's face framed like a target within the familiar logo of red circle and diagonal bar squashing the image of a lighted cigarette.

'I'm haunted by these things,' he said, scowling at one of the signs.

Like Müller's and Pappenheim's offices, the VIP conference room and Kaltendorf's office were on the top floor, but there the similarities ended. Kaltendorf's office would please a corporate CEO. A short corridor at the other

26

end of the building led to it. Save for the conference room, there were no other offices close by. The area was the inner sanctum – the exclusion zone, as everyone else in the building had dubbed it.

Pappenheim took his time making his way to the VIP conference room. The two bodyguards, stony-faced and in neat suits, were standing sentry on either side of the closed door.

'People are allowed to smile here,' Pappenheim tried as an opening gambit.

Dead eyes looked back at him. The faces remained stony.

'Or not,' Pappenheim continued. 'Let myself in, shall I?'

'Your gun,' one of the stony faces said.

Pappenheim stared at him. *'What?'*

'Are you carrying a weapon?'

'Is that a serious question?'

'If you are, you hand it over. Or you don't go in.'

Pappenheim looked at the man as if at a tick. 'Do you know where you are, *sonny?* This is a *police* building. *My* building. Carrying guns happens to be part of the job. You are in *my* territory; and if I have any more of your crap, I'll have *your* guns taken away. Did I speak slowly enough so that even you can understand?'

Two pairs of dead eyes began to look dangerous as the bodyguards, clearly offended by Pappenheim's tone, seemed as if they were going to do something about it.

Then the door suddenly opened. The Lanzarote-tanned, designer-suited Melk stood there, smiling at Pappenheim.

'Ah! The famous Pappi!' he beamed. 'Don't mind them. They take their job very seriously – as they should, of course.' He looked at his men. 'This *is* a police building. We don't give the orders here...' He paused. 'Not always.' He turned back to Pappenheim. 'Come in, Pappi. Come in!' he enthused, as if he were the host, and not the visitor. He had a strong voice that carried, well in keeping with Pappenheim's description of him as an excellent orator.

Pappenheim gave the bodyguards a cold stare, then entered the room. 'You need *two* bodyguards?'

Melk was a man of average height who looked extremely fit. His head, which had a distinct triangular shape, seemed just a little too big for his body. His eyes were like dark, deeply sunken pebbles.

He gave a deprecating shrug.

'Goes with the territory these days,' he said as he shut the door on the bodyguards. 'It's this terrorism thing. You know how it is.' He came round to give Pappenheim's reluctant hand an enthusiastic, brief shake.

Pappenheim said nothing.

There was the briefest of awkward pauses.

'I remember you,' Melk continued, 'from the conference. Do you remember?'

'I do.'

'A long time ago. Good to see you again.'

Who would have thought, back then, that you would become half of the famous Müller and Pappenheim team?'

'Who indeed?' Pappenheim said carefully, watching Melk as he would a highly poisonous snake.

'You've caught the attention of quite a few influential people.' Melk's enthusiasm was unabated.

I'll bet we have, Pappenheim thought, his mistrust rising. 'Have we?' he asked, all innocence.

'Oh, you have, Pappi. The two of you have been making waves. Big ones.'

'Just doing the job we were assigned to.'

'And very well you've been doing it, too.' Melk glanced out of the huge expanse of the armoured window. 'The boys of the Friedrichstrasse glass palace. That's what some people call you.'

'Do they? You never know with some people.'

'Oh, they don't mean it nastily. More a kind of admiration.'

'I see.'

Melk looked about the vast room that was furnished in a manner to rival even Kaltendorf's paean to the corporate boardroom. But even here, Kaltendorf's no-smoking signs had penetrated.

'The best for the best,' Melk continued.

Enough of the slimy praise, Pappenheim thought, scepticism continuing to rise by the second. *Let's hear what you've really come for.*

29

He waited to see what would be next.

'As I've just said,' Melk went on, 'many influential people have taken notice of your work.'

'Come up on the radar, have we?'

'You could put it like that. And they have reacted positively.'

'I like positive.'

Melk looked at him as if unsure how to take the remark, then smiled. 'Ah, the famous Müller and Pappi wit.'

'Müller's not here.'

'So I gather. Any idea where he is? He really should be here. This concerns him as well.'

'No idea where,' Pappenheim lied, his baby-blue eyes at their most guileless. 'But he's like that. He can be gone for days on an investigation...'

'But he keeps in touch, surely?'

'He does ... but in his own time. Drives me to distraction.' Pappenheim made a gesture of helplessness. 'But there it is. It drives the *Herr Direktor* insane, and I have to take the flak.'

Melk's brief smile was a flash that could have meant anything. 'I'm sure you can cope. What is Müller working on?'

'Following a lead.'

'Ah. That catch-all. Care to enlighten?'

'Not really. An investigation has to be kept tight, until it is over. With respect.'

Melk nodded, showing no offence. 'Understood. Well, can't be helped. I might as well give you the good news.'

Pappenheim raised a fleeting eyebrow.

'Good news. I like good news.'

'Don't we all. You've both been promoted.'

This was so unexpected that Pappenheim was stumped for a repartee – a rare thing indeed. He chose to say nothing, but felt alarm bells begin to ring in frenzy. The 'gift' was being presented.

Melk looked pleased by what he mistakenly believed to be Pappenheim's confusion. 'I can see my surprise is complete. It is true. You have been promoted. You get your third star to *Hauptkommissar*, and, as your unit does not have *Ersterhauptkommissar* rank, Müller goes straight up to *Polizeirat*. His first gold.'

'I think I'm going to faint,' Pappenheim commented after a long pause.

He seemed completely bewildered, but in fact his mind was racing. Where's the poison? he wondered. Everything has a price.

'Whom do we have to kill?' he asked.

Melk gave him a speculative look. 'You're thinking this is too good to be true. That there's a catch.'

'There's always a catch,' Pappenheim said. 'There are procedures for promotions—'

'Which have been bypassed – with good reason, and by those with the authority to do so. These are very special circumstances.'

'So? What's the catch?'

'You will still have your autonomy...'

'Here it comes.'

'... perhaps even more.'

Pappenheim allowed his scepticism to show. 'This sounds like someone's setting up a new unit. I like it here.'

Melk did not attempt to deny it. 'Müller would head the unit, with you as second-in-command. You would answer to no one except the Minister ... through me, of course.'

'Of course.'

'This would not be as bad as you seem to think. And you would be able to choose anyone you would like for your new team.'

'And now the icing on the cake.'

'Look. I understand your caution—'

'No you don't. Can we refuse?'

'You can ... but that could be a career mistake, in the long run.'

Pappenheim's eyes fixed themselves upon Melk. The lurking predator peeked out, surveying his prey. 'Is that a threat?'

'No threat. A reading of a possible outcome.'

'"A reading of a possible outcome",' Pappenheim repeated without warmth. 'That sounds like a threat to me.'

'Read it as you will. It's a good offer. A very good one.'

'The Minister's personal police unit? I don't like the sound of that. Too many echoes of the past.'

'I understand where you're coming from, Pappi. This is not what you believe it to be. These are dangerous times ... for the country, for Europe, for the world. We need to defend ourselves by all means possible, without the need to engage armies. What we do now can help prevent wars. God knows we don't need wars.'

'I agree on the war part. It's the rest that bothers me.'

Melk turned again to glance out of the window. 'I don't give in easily. '

'Neither do we.'

'Look. Tell you what. You have a word with Müller when he gets back; then both of you have a good think about my offer.' Melk fished into a pocket and brought out an embossed card, which he handed to Pappenheim. 'My direct number and my handy number are on there. You are now one of the very few people who know these numbers. This is both for you, and for Müller. That's how serious I am.'

'I'm honoured, and I'm certain he will be too.'

'Think very hard about it, Pappi.' Melk paused. 'I'll let myself out.'

Without another word, he opened the door and left.

'Let's go,' Pappenheim heard him say to his bodyguards.

Back in his office, Pappenheim leaned back in his chair and blew several smoke rings at the ceiling. Every so often, he would look down at the small card that lay on the desk. An exhibit to be studied.

He looked at it for perhaps the tenth time. 'The poison has begun to drip,' he said quietly.

With a sudden thought, he reached for one of the phones. 'Ah, Hermann,' he began to

Spyros, the *Kommissar* in charge of the unit's advanced communications department. 'Is she there?'

Spyros sighed. 'Why don't you just keep her? She spends more time with you and Jens than with us.'

'Hermann, Hermann,' Pappenheim said soothingly, 'don't be ridiculous. She needs to stay with you so that she can continue to invent all those crazy programs of hers, which we all benefit from.'

'Sweet talk,' Spyros countered. 'Here she is.'

'Thank you, Hermann.'

'I don't know what for.'

'Sir?' came the goth's voice in Pappenheim's ear.

'Ah, Miss Meyer. Can you spare some time to meet me in the Rogues' Gallery?'

'Of course. When?'

'Half an hour. Bring any new program you have cooked up that can kill even the most sophisticated attempt at intercepting a sat call.'

'Are we going to reach someone out of the country?'

'We are.'

'Haven't you already done so?'

'I have. But this time, I want even more protection. Just to be especially careful. Do you have anything extra?'

'I have a real killer.'

'Thought you might. Bring it.'

'Half an hour. I'll be there.'

'That young woman is a living genius,' Pappenheim said to himself as he hung up. 'Melk,' he continued, blowing more smoke rings up to the ceiling. 'I hate it when people who don't know me well enough call me Pappi.'

Two

Carey Bloomfield knocked on the door to Müller's suite in their hotel. There was no response.

'Müller?' she called.

There was still no response.

'Müller! You in there?'

When he still did not respond, she tried the door. It was locked.

'What the hell?' she muttered.

'Looking for me?'

She jumped. 'Jesus, Müller!' she said, involuntarily squeaking. 'Do you have to sneak up on people?'

'I did not "sneak". You were so preoccupied with the door, you did not hear me. Guard down. Not like you.'

She went on to the attack. 'Where have you been?'

'Just taking a walk. Pleasant, warm evening.'

'Hot evening,' she corrected. 'You went for a walk in the dark?'

'Take a look around you,' Müller said. 'There's plenty of lighting. Hardly in the dark.'

'You know what I mean, Müller.'

'Do you realize,' he began, bypassing her retort, 'that this town has no traffic lights? At least, none that I could see. Plenty of round-abouts, though. I needed that walk,' he added. 'Many things to think about.'

This softened her. 'You OK?'

'I'm fine.'

'As if you'd tell me. I know you, Müller.'

She barely caught his fleeting smile.

'Why were you banging on my door?' he asked.

'I wasn't banging! I was ... worried. That's all.'

'Thank you for the worry ... but I am fine, as I've said. Look, you must be starving. I should not have left it so late, but better late than never. All sorts of people here. Very international, or inter-ethnic, to be more precise. I saw many interesting places where we can have dinner...'

'First we talk, then dinner.'

'That could take some time. Why don't we combine both...?'

She shook her head vehemently. 'No, mister. Talk, in private, then eat. If we try in a public place, you'll have an excuse not to talk. So, no way, José.'

'You are determined.'

'Bet your socks on it.'

'My socks. Such turns of phrase, Miss Bloomfield.'

'Müller?'

'What now?'

37

'What the hell's this? Back there at Woonnalla, you kissed me and called me Carey. Was that because you thought I was going to get shot? Hey, we're dating. You can call me Carey now.'

'That was sarcasm, wasn't it? Let's go inside before the world comes to look,' he added, unlocking the door.

'Jesus!' she fumed as she followed him into the air-conditioned cool of the suite.

'Sit,' he said as he shut the door.

'I'm no goddammed pet animal, Müller.'

'Take a seat. Please.'

Reluctantly, she sat down in one of the deeply comfortable wicker armchairs.

'A cool drink?' he suggested.

'A cool talk would be better.'

He sank into another armchair. 'I'm all ears.'

'Hey. It's the other way round. You talk, I listen.'

'Alright. You've obviously got questions churning away. Ask, and I shall answer.'

She gave him a look of pure scepticism, but, despite herself, said, 'Müller, I know something's on your mind. It's not to do with your moonlighting killer-cop, ex-colleague Mainauer, or with Jamie Mackay's death, or even with the fact that you feel you led *The Semper*'s hit man to the Hargreaves ... It's something to do with Woonnalla itself. What did you see out there that's giving you such a hard time?'

'The truth?'

'Don't even try to bend it.'

'I honestly don't know. That's the point. It's ... it's a strange feeling; a kind of déjà vu. But I know that can't be. I've never been to Perth before – or Broome – never mind Woonnalla.'

'What are you saying?'

'That I'm confused.'

'*You*? Confused? Müller, that word's not in your vocabulary.'

He stared at her, a faraway look in his eyes. He said nothing.

'Are you here with me, Müller?' she asked. 'Or somewhere else entirely?'

'I'm here.'

'You could have fooled me.'

'A deal,' he said.

'This should be good.'

'When I really do know what's troubling me, I'll tell you.'

'*That's* the deal?'

'It's the best I can offer. At this moment, what's in my head is so outlandish, I'd have to be taking leave of my senses.'

She stared at him. 'Wow! You are serious.'

'I am. If I told you about the thoughts that are nagging at me, you'd be convinced that I'd lost what marbles I've still got, as you would say.'

'I never say that.' She was still staring at him. 'Well, whatever it is, it must be a doozy.'

'And more. Now can we leave it for the moment?'

'OK,' she agreed after a while. 'But I'm keeping you to your promise.'

39

'As you wish. Now let's go to dinner.'

'I've got a better idea. Let's order in, then go out to your verandah and watch the ocean while we eat.'

'I'll buy that.' He smiled at her. 'You do say that.'

'Sometimes,' she said.

At the same moment in time,
it was 13.30 in Berlin.

The documents room – which everyone but Kaltendorf called the Rogues' Gallery – was, without exception, the most secure place in the entire building. It contained, among the highly sensitive material stored there, vital information on *The Semper.* Only Müller, Pappenheim, and Kaltendorf had autonomous access, which was by code-protected, keypad entry.

Three of its vast walls were lined from floor to ceiling with wide, steel cabinets, each with its own keypad. A tall, wheeled ladder capable of withstanding a strain of two tons hung from a solid rail, and could be manoeuvred to each bank of cabinets in the room. The centrepiece was a wide and solidly built table with a white top, which doubled as a photographic light box.

The wall without cabinets was reserved for an extremely powerful computer and its ancillary equipment. Flanking the keyboard were a pair of unexpected items: a joystick and throttle that seemed uncannily like the

40

controls of an F-16 jet fighter. They belonged to the goth, who enjoyed flying one of the best combat flight simulators ever created for computer use.

Because of her astonishing capabilities with computers, and the invaluable contribution her skills had made to their investigations, Müller had given her a virtual carte blanche to fly, whenever she was called to the Rogues' Gallery. It was an offer she never refused. It was, inevitably, an offer that drove Kaltendorf wild, but it was also something the Great White could do little about, given what Müller and Pappenheim now knew about him.

Pappenheim was already waiting when the goth, in diaphanous white with blood-red fingernails, red eyelids and lips, made her entrance. On her feet were flat-soled, yin-and-yang-decorated, ballet-style shoes.

Pappenheim had wisely chosen to make no comment. The goth's manner of dress was now a legend in the building. No one – not even someone in drunken haze – would ever imagine she was a police officer. It was a subterfuge that served her well.

She was at the computer, having already installed her new program.

'How fast have you made this machine now, Miss Meyer?' Pappenheim asked with idle curiosity.

'It's about much more than just speed, sir,' the goth replied patiently, as if to a slow child. 'If I told you it's now got six gigs of RAM, or that I've optimized the BIOS, or that I'm using 1600 by 1200 resolution, would you know what I'm talking about?'

'If that's your polite way of telling me I'm computer illiterate, you've succeeded.'

'Not putting you down, sir. Just explaining there's more to it than speed. Although, for my money, you can never have too much speed.'

'Well, whatever you keep doing to it, it seems to thrive. I expect it will get up and walk one day.'

'Now who's making fun of whom?'

'Miss Meyer...'

'Sir?' She did not look round from the machine.

'Never mind,' Pappenheim said, giving up.

'We're nearly there,' she said, as if he had not spoken. 'I've one more thing to do, then we'll be ready. Well ... two things.'

'Which are?'

She reached for a phone by the computer. 'With your permission?'

'Be my guest.'

Pappenheim watched, bemused, as she dialled. Noting the length of the number, he said, 'Are you dialling abroad?'

'Washington.'

'*Wash* ... Miss Meyer...'

'Shhh! I've got an answer. You'll hear. On the speakers.'

'Hello?' the male American voice answered. 'This is George ... Hello! Who's this?'

The goth remained silent.

'*Hello!*' the voice came again, irritated now.

42

'Hello! Who the hell's this?' A brief pause, then, *'Asshole!'* A savage click ended the call.

The goth replaced the phone calmly. 'I've got enough, I think.'

'Miss Meyer...' Pappenheim began. 'Was ... was that...?'

'I've no idea,' she replied. 'Now I need your voice.'

'My voice? What for?'

'Please, sir. Just speak into the mic.' She reached back without looking round. A small, cordless microphone was in her hand.

Even more bemused, Pappenheim said, 'What do I say?'

'Anything. Imagine you're talking about the investigation.'

He gave the back of her head a stern look.

'No point glowering at my head,' she said, not turning round.

'You've got eyes there too?'

'The mic, sir, if you please. My arm's getting ready to drop off.'

Pappenheim took it from her.

'Thank you for saving my arm,' she said.

Pappenheim shook his head slowly, then began to speak.

'So when can I have this information?' he said into the microphone.

'That should do it,' the goth said, hand reaching back once more.

Pappenheim returned the microphone.

'Now listen,' the goth said as she took it.

Her fingers began to fly across the keyboard for what seemed like several minutes, but was in fact barely two. Then she hit 'enter'.

Hardly daring to believe his ears, Pappenheim heard a conversation in which he had not taken any part.

'Hello, Pappi. Got something for you.'

'Interesting?'

'You betcha.'

'Try me.'

'We got something over here on those people you're chasing. Came up on the radar unexpectedly.'

'I like unexpected surprises ... the good ones.'

'Oh, this one's good. Your boy's in Florida. Miami.'

'Florida? We never thought he'd go there.'

'*The Semper* have their tentacles reaching far. Remember Adams?'

'I certainly do.'

A sudden a burst of static followed.

'That should do it,' the goth said again, turning round.

Pappenheim was staring at her. 'How did you do that? That sounded just like me! And as for the Washington voice...'

She smiled at him. 'My magic program.'

'You can *fake* telephone conversations?'

'As you know, sir, people can doctor conversations by editing; but first, they've got to record them. That's child's play. *I* can script a conversation. They can't do that.'

'Edited conversations can be scanned, and taken apart. But *this*...'

'Don't worry. It would never hold up in

court. I've sampled the voices, that's all. Perfect samples, of course – as close as possible to the real thing.'

'Of course. I would expect nothing less than perfect from you, Miss Meyer.'

The red-lidded eyes surveyed him with ethereal superiority. 'Flattery ... but I forgive you.'

'I'm grateful.'

'Hmm,' she said. 'Without the right kind of equipment to hand, no one could tell the difference. That's the magic of my program. But a detailed voiceprint test would discover the fake modulations. Computers don't have vocal chords. Well, not yet. But for our purposes, it's perfect. Now listen to what it sounds like when I've played around with it.'

She turned back to the machine and hit a few keys. The 'conversation' began to replay. This time, it came in random bursts, fading in and out, and distorted by static.

'That's what anyone trying to intercept would hear,' she said, when it had finished. 'Some words will get through. Enough to make whoever it is think he's got something.'

'They'll hear Florida mentioned, and believe...'

'Exactly,' the goth said. 'And we both know the boss has not gone to Florida after the dirty colleague, don't we, sir?'

'Do you want an answer to that?'

'I don't need one.'

Pappenheim studied her with something approaching awe. 'And for your next trick?'

'A wormhole.'

Pappenheim looked at her as if she had just sprung from a box. 'A *wormhole*? What are you talking about?'

'Don't you watch space movies, or read science fiction?'

'The only science fiction I read is in newspaper reports of political speeches,' Pappenheim said. 'They're usually full of fantasy.'

'You're missing a lot.'

'I think I'll survive. Tell me about my very own wormhole.'

'You will be able to make *the* most secure call to the *Hauptkommissar* ... wherever he may be. *She* is with him, isn't she?' the goth suddenly added with venom.

Pappenheim sighed. 'Miss Meyer, Miss Meyer. Now tell me what to expect.'

'A perfectly clear conversation.'

'What I mean is ... how exactly does this "wormhole" work?'

'I've created a wormhole for your conversation—'

'I've got that far—'

'A tunnel, if you like, linking you directly with the boss. No other traffic. The two of you might as well be alone in the entire universe, while you're in there. No one will know; which means they can't eavesdrop. To them, your conversation will not exist—'

'As long as we're in this ... "wormhole"...'

'Exactly,' the goth said. 'But just in case there could be someone out there really smart enough – very unlikely – to somehow

46

find it and piggyback, I'll also run your fake conversation with Washington. I'll make it a little easy for them to find, to keep them busy; but not so easy that they'll get suspicious. And, of course, I'll be listening to *them*, but they won't know.'

'Miss Meyer,' Pappenheim began with feeling, 'you're lethal. I am so glad you're with us. The damage you could do doesn't bear thinking about, if you ever worked against us.'

'That's not going to happen. I love it here.'

'What a relief.'

'Now get ready to make your call. I just *know* she's with him,' Hedi Meyer could not resist adding again.

Broome, Western Australia

'My ears are burning,' Carey Bloomfield said. 'Someone's talking about me.'

Having finished their excellent room-service dinner, Müller gave her an amused look.

'You're not telling me you believe in such things.'

'Don't mock, Müller. What do you find so disturbing about Woonnalla? Can you explain it?'

'Point taken ... I'm suitably chastened.'

'There you go.'

After dinner on the verandah, they had decided to go inside to discuss the day's events, to avoid the possibility of being overheard. Müller had slid shut the large glass panels, and they now sat with their chairs close together – but not close enough to touch – facing the ocean. The night sky was so clear and bright, the shimmering surface of the water was a reflection of it.

'And speaking of talking,' Carey continued, 'have you told Pappi about what happened today?'

Müller gave a slight shake of the head. 'I wanted to gather my thoughts first. But if I know Pappi, he'll soon be making contact. So I think I'll just wait. More time to try and work out what's wrong with the Hargreaves. Something about them is definitely not right.'

'Well, they certainly took off, once Mackay had warned them you were on your way. I don't quite get that, either. I mean, why run? Their police friends would not have kindly given a hit man directions...'

'Assuming the police would have known he was a hit man. Mackay, despite his experience, was taken by surprise. I would bet on it.'

'I think the Hargreaves would have run, hit man or no hit man. They weren't taking any chances.'

Müller nodded. 'I agree.'

'So what now?'

'I'm going back to Woonnalla. I want to look the place over.'

'You mean go *inside* the house?'

'Among other things, yes.'

'As they're not there,' Carey Bloomfield said, 'I can't see that cop ... er...'

'Wishart.'

'I can't see him agreeing. He's been their friend for years. He even told us they are his son's godparents. I really can't see him agreeing. And we can't just break into the place. I don't think his enforced cooperation will stretch that far.'

'I'll ask him to accompany us. He can't complain about that.'

'But will he agree?'

'He has to. One of his officers, also a good friend, was killed at Woonnalla. The least he can do is try and find out why that happened. He has Mainauer's body; a dead hit man from Germany. He has seen the Dragunov. As a policeman, he can't ignore all that. As Wishart, he certainly won't. He'll come with us.'

'And the Hargreaves? They're not going to be sitting around waiting for a second visit, so they'll get their cop friend to stall you. He will have told them you still want to meet them.'

'Wishart is a good policeman. Whether the Hargreaves are friends or not, if he had the slightest belief that they were implicated in Mackay's death, he'd haul them in. You saw me plead their innocence. It made an impact, but he will still be full of curiosity. In his place, I would be curious to know more. He'll come,' Müller repeated.

'And when is this going to take place?'

'When it will achieve the greatest surprise, just in case they have returned. Tonight.'

She stared at him. 'Are you kidding me? Are you out of your mind? *Tonight?*'

'It's alright if you wish to remain behind...'

'Don't you give me that! While you were out on your walkabout, Müller, I did some light reading – in my case, horror reading. The hire people put plenty of outback survival books in the all-wheel. One is about snakes. You know me and snakes, Müller. In the States, we've got some mean rattlers and cotton-mouths, but they're *pussycats*. Out here, they've got all the snakes that escaped from the Garden of Eden. The top-ten Jurassic chart of the world's nastiest are right here in Australia.

'I checked out that snake that used Mainauer as a pin cushion while I watched. If I'd known I was standing so close to a speckled mulga, I'd have had a nervous breakdown. The speckled mulga is a bad-tempered son-of-a-bitch that likes to keep on biting. I know. I saw it. It's venom is so toxic, it doesn't even need to bite you. A few drops of the stuff on your skin is just as dangerous. Some snake. And there were two of them!'

Müller looked at her with mild amusement. 'As I said, you can remain behind.'

'I'll come, but I stay in the car. I'm not walking out there in the dark with those things out on patrol.'

'I hate to tell you, but snakes tend to coil themselves about the axles of the car. They enjoy the residual warmth.'

She stared at him. 'Are you telling me I could be sitting with a *snake* below me?'

'Under the car,' he corrected. 'I did not say

one will be there. I merely said snakes tended to do that. They have been known to climb into vehicles, campsite toilets—'

'You're enjoying this, Müller. But don't laugh too soon. I can't see Wishart thanking you for dragging him out tonight to go back to Woonnalla. He won't stretch co-operation that far.'

'I think—'

His mobile rang.

'That,' he continued, 'will be Pappi.'

'Saved by the bell, huh?' She began to get to her feet. 'I'd better leave...'

He waved her back down. 'You don't have to go. Hello, Pappi,' he continued to Pappenheim.

'And how is life down under?' Pappenheim asked with a brightness that alerted Müller.

'Full of excitement. You sound remarkably clear.'

'Thank the goth. She has worked some magic. We are intercept-proof.'

'A true genius.'

'And the rest. So ... you first? Or me first? On second thoughts, youth before age. That means you.'

'We got Mainauer. To be precise, Miss Bloomfield did – with a little help from a snake.'

'A snake? I thought she hated the things.'

'With a passion. But sometimes, you can get help from the unlikeliest of places...'

'Well, well, well,' Pappenheim said. 'The

51

super sniper taken. By a snake, and by someone with a phobia about them. Our col-
league-killing hit man certainly travelled far,
and fast. How did it happen?'

'I think you should sit down.'

'I'm almost sitting. I'm leaning against the
computer desk in the Rogues' Gallery.'

Somewhere within the Berlin environs,
at the same instant

'I've got something!' a man with headphones
exclaimed.

He was in a small room, full of state-of-the-
art eavesdropping equipment, in an anony-
mous, five-storey building. He was alone, but
was speaking into a throat mic.

'I'll patch you in,' he added, and made the
connection. 'Got it?'

'Yes,' came the response. 'Fragmented.'

'They're jamming, of course, but we'll still
get enough. They don't know what they're up
against.' The man grinned.

'Does that voice sound familiar to you?'

'It's Pappenheim.'

'I don't mean Pappenheim!' came the
impatient response. 'The man he's speaking
to. How could Pappenheim have direct access
to...'

'It's not him. It just sounds like him. They
seem to think Mainauer's in Miami.' The
eavesdropper gave a soft laugh.

'All the better.'

'Has he made contact since the last time?'

'Mainauer knows he can't risk making contact too often. He'll be in touch when the job's done ... *after* he has left the area. Meanwhile, keep on this conversation.'

'They'll have me with them all the way.'

The eavesdropper was smug in his certainty.

In the Rogues' Gallery, Pappenheim glanced at the goth as he continued speaking to Müller.

Spider headset on, her fingers were doing their magic dance over the keyboard. He knew she was adding new lines of dialogue to his 'conversation' with Washington, and would do so for as long as his real call to Müller lasted.

Then she stopped.

Pappenheim stared at her. 'Just a minute,' he said to Müller. 'Miss Meyer,' he continued to the goth. 'You've stopped! What's wrong?'

'Nothing,' she replied calmly without looking at him. Her attention was firmly on the large monitor. 'There's plenty of dialogue to get through. I'm well ahead of the conversation.'

'Oh. I see. And are we being intercepted?'

'Oh yes. They think that *we* think their man is in Miami. The person doing the intercept thinks he's so smart. He's leaving a beacon that a child in nappies could follow.'

'I can see you're having fun. I'll leave you to it. I'm back,' Pappenheim said to Müller. 'The goth has everything under control.'

'And that's where we are for now,' Müller said to Pappenheim, coming to the end of his recap of the day's events.

'You have been busy. Good that Petey Waldron did his stuff.'

'We could not have got this far without him. He smoothed our path, and pulled only God knows how many strings. The locals are very co-operative, if, perhaps in Wishart's case, now a little reluctantly, given what has happened.'

'I'll make sure it's smoothed out on our side, especially regarding the rifle. We'll be able to conclusively match the bullet that killed poor Johann,' Pappenheim said. The victim was the policeman who had been killed by Mainauer, a member of the same rapid-response team he had once commanded. 'Johann's wife will be pleased that bastard finally got his due. Should I tell her? Or do we sit on it for now?'

'Sit on it. *The Semper* probably don't know about Mainauer as yet. For her own protection, it may be best to leave her out of the loop for now.'

'I agree. Hold on for a moment,' Pappenheim said. 'Let me check something with the goth.'

'Miss Meyer,' Müller heard, 'have you picked up anything about Mainauer from our listeners?'

'They mentioned his name once. I got the

impression they haven't heard from him.'

'That is very good news,' Pappenheim said. 'Jens? Did you hear?'

'This call is so clear, I couldn't miss it. This gives us a very good advantage, if they don't know their man is down. The longer they stay in the dark, the better.'

'What about the Hargreaves running out like that?'

'In their place,' Müller said, 'I might have done the same. Reasonable precaution ... I may not be Wishart's favourite person at the moment,' Müller continued. 'Our arrival has upset his well-ordered life. An officer and close friend is dead, and he now has to look at other friends – people he's known for twenty years or more – with new eyes. Add to this a dead professional hit man with links to God knows what ... I've brought a mess into his life. I'm definitely not his favourite person.'

'Before you go overboard blaming yourself,' Pappenheim began firmly, 'why don't you look at it another way? Had you not gone down there, Mainauer would eventually have found the Hargreaves. They would most certainly be dead, as would Mackay, who might still have got in the way. Mainauer would have stayed in the area until he had found what he was looking for; which he would have, eventually.'

'If this is supposed to make me feel better—'

'It isn't. Those are the facts. Yes, you might

55

have towed Mainauer there, but he did not catch you out. He's the one who's dead. In the case of Mackay, it is never good when a colleague goes down, as we well know. But that was not your fault, Jens. You would be bawling out a junior colleague under similar circumstances—'

'Are you bawling me out?'

'I'm not warmed up yet. Give me time.'

Despite himself, Müller gave a tired smile. 'I'm not that crazy.'

'Besides, I don't have the strength, and I need a cigarette. So you're going back to the place?' Pappenheim added.

'Perhaps we can surprise them.'

'If they've returned.'

'There is that.'

There was a pause in their conversation.

'Why do I have the feeling there's still something you haven't mentioned?'

'Not worth mentioning.'

'You've just hit the curiosity button.'

'I have a sense of déjà vu,' Müller said at last. 'Stupid, but there it is.'

'Why stupid?'

'I've never been here before.'

'So?' Pappenheim seemed to pause for thought. 'Where do you get this feeling?'

'At the place.'

The pause was longer this time. 'What is there about it that brings this on?'

'The thought is so insane, I dare not contemplate it.'

'Which means you're not about to tell me.'

56

'Pappi, I don't even want to tell myself.'

'Then I won't push. To brighter things – then you'll be the one who needs to sit down. But first, how's the colonel?'

'Right here. Want a chat?'

'I'll say hi.'

Müller stood up, passed the mobile to Carey Bloomfield, then went out on to the verandah. He shut the glass doors behind him, placed his hands upon the verandah rail, and stared out to sea.

She watched him with curiosity for a brief moment, before saying into the phone, 'Hi, Pappi! How nice of you to think of me.'

'Always a pleasure.'

'I remember how you didn't trust me, once.'

'That was once. This is now. Nice work with Mainauer.'

'I could have done without the snakes ... but as it turned out, they probably saved my bacon. And Müller did the really dangerous part, setting himself up for target practice. I just crawled about trying to get behind Mainauer. That lowlife was very good at what he did. If he hadn't decided to stab that first snake, I'd never have spotted him, and he might have got me. He was very fast—'

'He had practice,' Pappenheim said grimly. 'One piece of pollution less. Is the man treating you well?'

'In his own way.'

Pappenheim gave a brief chuckle. 'I can read so much into this, I'm not going to pry.'

Then he lowered his voice. 'Is he near you?'

'He's out on the verandah, looking at the ocean. He can't hear if I don't shout. I'm kind of worried about him.'

'So am I. Look after him, Carey. Whatever's on his mind is seriously disturbing him. The last time he had that faraway tone in his voice was the time he found out about what really happened to his parents. He keeps talking about déjà vu. Perhaps something at Woonnalla has reminded him of them ... but I can't imagine what that could possibly be.'

'Even if you're right, Pappi, it would be crazy. Out here in the *outback*? Makes no sense at all.'

'Exactly. So it must be something else.'

'But what?' she asked.

'There, you've got me. It was Vladimir/Grogan, our mysterious Russian informant who could be American – or vice versa – who pinpointed the Hargreaves. Both you and Jens saw him face to face at the time of the Romeo killings—'

'I remember. The Hargreaves are called Jack and Maggie. I've heard Grogan's wife – if she *is* a real wife – call him Jack. Perhaps that's what nagging at Müller.'

'Possibly.' Pappenheim did not sound certain. 'But it doesn't make sense. Why would Grogan set up an elaborate paperchase to arrange a meet in the outback, then disappear just as you two arrive?'

'This is where I say, now you've got me.'

'More questions than answers.'

'Oh yeah.'

'Just keep an eye on Jens, will you?' Pappenheim said.

'Count on it.'

'Thanks, Carey. Now if you could pass him back, have I got some news for him.'

'Sounds interesting.'

'More like fishy.'

'Then I'd better get him.' She went out on to the verandah and returned the mobile to Müller. 'Time to change shift,' she said. 'Pappi wants another chat. I'll stay out here.'

Müller took the phone with a slight nod, and went back inside.

'Yes, Pappi.'

'Now you'll need to sit down for this one.'

'Doing so,' Müller said, regaining his seat.

'Does the word "wolfhound" ring any bells?' Pappenheim began.

'Wolfgang Melk. Interior Ministry.'

'Got it in one. He's paid us a visit.'

'*The* Melk? What was he doing? Slumming?'

'I got a call from a contact, warning about Greeks bearing gifts...'

'Too many readings of the Trojan War?'

'Timely warning,' Pappenheim said. 'Gifts there were aplenty. You, *Polizeihauptkommissar* Müller, are now a *Polizeirat*, if you want it. And I have been exalted to *Polizeihauptkommissar*. Ours for the taking. In fact, it's almost an offer we can't refuse.'

Müller was stunned. '*What?*'

'You might well say so.'

'Getting us out of the way?'

59

'Oh, he's so quick, it does hurt. Our thoughts are pinging together. It seems as if we have come to the notice of certain people. That's why we're being "rewarded", if you get my meaning...'

'I do get your meaning. Someone high up somewhere is feeling the heat, and wants us stopped. What else are they offering?'

'Would you believe a "new" unit, yours to command and pick your own team?'

'Answerable to whom?'

Pappenheim was eloquently silent.

'Melk,' Müller said in a hard voice.

'He did say we would come under the aegis of the Ministry; but it doesn't take a rocket scientist to read between the lines.'

'So Melk wants to hobble us. Why?'

'That should provide some interesting answers.'

'Dig into him.'

'Already being done, O Bright One. I take it you don't want that gold star, then?'

'He can—'

'Tut-tut-tut, no harsh words about that nice wolfhound.' Pappenheim said with a distinct chuckle. 'I can see it now. We'd be reduced to supplying Ready Group units for peacekeeping purposes on certain marches...'

'Then he'd have a hard time getting them from me,' Müller said. 'I do not follow orders blindly. Last time people did that, see where it got us a few decades ago. I would not order a single colleague to go out on to the streets to protect the kind of people who would destroy the country's democracy, and abuse its constitution for their own political ends.'

'Uh-oh. Your career as a *Polizeirat* will be very short-lived.'

'I should worry.'

'You should, if you want to pull the plug on *The Semper.*'

'We'll still do it. There are many ways of saying no to Melk, even if we were foolish enough—'

'Or sneakily cunning—'

'Or sneakily cunning to take his sweets.'

'I'm certain we can cook up a few ways to say no; but you do realize, of course, that he will have studied you in fine detail, and can engineer the kind of provocation that could trap you into sacking yourself ... if you see what I mean.'

'I do see. We'd better do some "fine detailing" ourselves.'

'Clean details? Or dirty?'

'Clean, dirty, and every other kind.'

'Them's fighting words that I like,' Pappenheim said with undisguised glee. Then he gave an exaggerated sigh. 'Shame. When I think of all those extra G-Blondes I could buy with the extra money a third silver star would bring ... And as for you, an extra light bulb for your Porsche—'

'Pappi,' Müller interrupted in warning.

'A man can dream. So I take it,' Pappenheim went on more seriously, 'we can tell him to stuff it?'

'Or words to that effect.'

'The thought of being answerable to Melk makes even the Great White a pleasure to have as a boss; and that's saying something. You do further realize we'll be making a nasty enemy.'

'He's already nasty, without our help. Know thine enemy.'

'Amen to that. As we are in a fighting mood and the man does not like to be refused, I'd better make strengthening the defences a priority. Just what we need – Melk and *The Semper* both coming at us.'

'They may not be so far apart.'

'Funny. That's the thought that's been doing gymnastics in my head.'

'Then listen to it, and plunder your network. See what we can find.'

'Consider it done.'

'Anything else?'

'For now, no. Hang on ... the goth's looking at me. She says to tell you to be careful. '

'Tell her I'm always careful, and thank her for the exceptional work she's doing.'

'I'll pass it on. And, Jens...'

'Yes?'

'Whatever's on your mind, don't let it beat you.'

'It won't.'

They ended the conversation together.

In Berlin, the eavesdropper was staring at his monitor.

A jumble of letters had suddenly appeared, filling the entire screen. Then they did a whirling dance before settling into two sentences – one in German, the other in English. Both had the same message:

HOPE YOU ENJOYED THE CONVERSATION

Then the screen went black. All the other monitors, a further five, then went black, in sequence. Then all the computers went down.

The man with the headphones stared at his dead equipment in horror.

'Shit!' he exclaimed. *'Shit!* It was a set-up! We've been hit!'

In frantic desperation, he tried to revive his machines, to no avail. In the end, he was forced to give up.

In the Rogues' Gallery, Pappenheim slowly put down the phone.

'So, Miss Meyer, anyone try to get to us?'

'There was that eavesdropper who thought he was so smart. He just found out he wasn't.'

'What did you do?'

'He just lost all his data, and his computers are dead. He'll not be doing any more eavesdropping until he gets some new stuff put together. And when he does, he'll think twice about trying to hit us again. But there was someone else...'

Pappenheim looked at her with sharp interest. 'Who?'

'I don't know. This one was smarter. He

popped his head over the wall to have a look, but decided it was too dangerous. It was a very fast look. Just a blip. But someone was definitely trying. Probably hoped I'd missed it.' A soft breath of derision came from her. 'Whoever it was would have to get up very early to get past me. This wasn't early enough.'

'No chance to pinpoint?'

She shook her head. 'Imagine a pencil torch. A quick flash, and he was back into hiding. But he was definitely interested.'

'Grogan, perhaps?'

She shook her head. 'Grogan has a specific signature. We have an interested party somewhere. I'll set up a snare. If he tries again – even if the computer is in sleep mode – the snare will be on sentry duty. If he does try, I'll have him. Even a blip won't save him.'

'You're awesome, Miss Meyer.'

'I know.'

Something about her posture made Pappenheim say, 'Yes?'

'I knew *she'd* be down there.'

Pappenheim gave her a fatherly pat on the shoulder. 'Hedi, Hedi...'

'Well...' she began.

'Here's something to excite your vitriol,' Pappenheim told her soothingly. 'Leave a message for Grogan. Wolfgang Melk.'

'Just that?'

'He won't need more. He shouldn't. See what he throws our way.' Pappenheim gave a slight cough, as if embarrassed. 'I need a cigarette, or two. I'll be back in half an hour. If we get no reply within that time, we'll leave it for now. Fly if you want to.'

'Those things will kill you,' she said.

'So what's new?'

Berlin, intercept room

The eavesdropper was close to ripping his hair off his scalp. All his attempts to revive his equipment had failed, and he was forced to accept that he had been hit by a ferocious virus. He had not yet reported what had happened to the person he had previously been speaking to.

'I think,' he muttered, 'I should start considering a long trip to somewhere very, very far away.'

Then his nemesis rang.

He stared at the phone. 'Shit.'

It rang a further three times before he picked it up. 'Yes.'

'Well?'

The eavesdropper remained silent.

'What's wrong?' the caller barked.

'It was a set-up.'

'What do you mean, precisely?'

'They knew we were listening. They sent us a virus. Everything is down.'

'We are not operational?'

'We are dead in the water.'

There was an ominous silence. 'You were supposed to be the best. You were paid well because of it.' Then there was a sharp click.

The conversation was over.

'And *I*,' the eavesdropper said to himself, 'am dead in the water, if I don't get out of here fast. I did not like the use of the past tense at all.'

He left almost immediately and made his way down, using the stairs all the way. He had no intention of using any of the lifts. He reached the ground floor without incident, and quickly made his way to the underground garage.

He breathed a sigh of relief as he reached his car.

He was in the act of opening it when a voice behind him said, 'Going somewhere?'

He whirled round to see three solid-looking men with unsmiling faces looking back at him.

Three

Broome, Western Australia

As soon as he had finished the call with Pappenheim, Müller picked up the hotel phone and called the police station.

'Sergeant Duggan,' a deep voice answered.

'This is Müller, Sergeant. We met earlier...'

'Ah, yes, Mr Müller,' Duggan said. 'How can I help?'

Müller had a feeling that some warmth had gone out of Duggan's voice between his first response to the call, and learning who was calling.

'Inspector Wishart back yet?'

'I'm afraid not, sir. I'll be going off soon, but Senior Constable Murray will be taking over the shift. I'll let him know you wish to speak with the Inspector.'

'Thank you, Sergeant.'

'No worries, sir. Goodnight.'

'Goodnight, Sergeant Duggan.' Müller hung up. 'Well he didn't sound too happy to hear from me.'

Müller went out on to the verandah to join Carey Bloomfield.

'Pappi had some interesting news,' he began.

'Do I hear it out here? Or inside?'

'Inside would be better ... We've been offered promotion,' he continued when they were back in the room.

'Hey, that's great! They finally show their apprecia ... tion.' Her voice faded when she saw his expression. 'Not great?'

He shook his head. 'Not great.'

He told her about Wolfgang Melk.

'The bribe,' she said, when he had finished.

'It looks very much like it.'

'And he made it personally. You must be getting too close. You're beginning to cause some pain.'

'Well, he did imply that we were getting noticed – although he tried to pretend it was in a positive way.'

'The Brits have a term for this kind of pay-off. "Kicking you upstairs"...'

Müller nodded. 'I'm familiar with it.'

'Of course you are. That Brit education again.'

'For my sins,' Müller said with a fleeting smile.

'I guess you said no to the bribe.'

'Pappi virtually did so. But, yes, he spoke for me too.'

'But Melk won't give up.'

'I'd be very surprised if he did.'

'A *Semper* man?'

'I reserve judgement ... for now. But it would not surprise me.'

'Jesus,' she said. 'How far are these people reaching?'

'As far as it takes. Remember your own Toby Adams.'

'How can I forget,' she said with some bitterness. 'Toby was my mentor. I trusted him with my life—'

'With which you very nearly paid.'

She nodded slowly. 'Toby being in *The Semper* was a shock. Yet they still had him killed.'

'To frame you – and it came close to working. That is why if Melk turns out to be one of them, I will not be surprised.'

'So what are you going to do?'

'It's already being done.'

In Berlin, Pappenheim had enjoyed his half hour of smoking nirvana.

'I was just about to call you,' the goth greeted him as he returned to the Rogues' Gallery.

'We've got a response from Grogan?' he said as he approached her.

'See for yourself.'

He peered at what she had onscreen. 'A list of ... dates ... twenty in all ... different years ... That's it?'

'That's it.'

'Dates for me to check,' Pappenheim remarked with certainty. 'Can you do me a printout?'

For reply, she handed him a sheet of paper. The dates were on it.

'Miss Meyer...' he began as he took it.

'A million euros will do.'

'Don't be ridiculous. I'd keep that for myself.' He grinned at her. 'Thank you, genius. Fly as long as you wish, until Hermann Spyros starts screaming at me down the phone. Then I'll scream at you down the phone. Failing that, leave when you want to. The door, as usual, will reset itself when you leave.'

She smiled beatifically at him and had launched her flying game before he was out of the room.

Back in his office, Pappenheim was on the phone to one of his contacts. 'I have a date for you.'

'Promises, promises,' the female voice said. 'But, as I'm already married, what do you really want?'

'I want to know what someone was doing on a date I shall give you. I have many more – twenty in all. But here's one for starters. It's in 2000.' Pappenheim gave her the full date. He had chosen it at random.

'And who's the lucky person?'

'Wolfgang Melk.'

He could almost feel her sudden silence. It was as if she had stopped breathing.

'What are you getting me into, Pappi?' she said at last. 'You know where I am. This is very close to home. And dangerous.'

'If it's going to get you into bad trouble...'

'All trouble is bad.'

'Don't I know it. Look, forget I said anything. I'll try another way.'

'You've tickled my interest, you rogue, as you knew this would. I've swallowed the bait.'

70

'I do mean what I've just said about not getting you into trouble.'

'I know you do, otherwise I'd have hung up on you by now. Give me an hour.'

'The hour is yours.'

They hung up together.

Pappenheim lit a cigarette, leaned back in his chair, and blew four smoke rings at the ceiling. They were so close together, they almost seemed to be one.

'I don't like people who think I'm stupid enough to be bribed with a fake promotion. Brings out the mean streak in me.'

In Broome, Müller did not have to wait for Wishart in the end. Wishart came to him.

He first picked up his Beretta, then went to the door of his suite in answer to the sharp knock.

Carey Bloomfield got her own weapon, which she carried with her at all times, out of a small canvas bag. She waited, out of sight.

Müller held his gun behind his back. 'Who is it?'

'Graeme Wishart,' came the answer.

Still keeping the gun, Müller opened the door. A tired-looking Wishart stared back at him.

'May I come in?' Wishart asked, removing his bush hat and wiping his forehead with the back of his hand.

'Of course,' Müller said. He stood back for Wishart to enter. 'Please take a seat.'

'Mark Duggan left a message from you,'

Wishart explained, as he gratefully sat down. He glanced around. 'The colonel not with you?'

'The colonel is,' Carey Bloomfield said, coming out of the bedroom. Her gun was back in the bag.

Müller brought the Beretta out from behind his back. 'Can't be too careful,' he said. 'Someone could have been using you as an unwilling shield.'

Wishart looked at each in turn. 'Do you two always operate like this?'

'In circumstances like these, yes,' Müller told him.

Wishart seemed to be studying Müller intently. 'Well, I'm here.'

'A drink first?' Müller suggested.

'If you've got something that looks like a cold beer.'

'The minibar is well stocked.'

Müller got him the beer, then remained standing. Carey Bloomfield took the other armchair.

'I'll come straight to the point,' Müller began to Wishart. 'I'd like to look at the Hargreaves' house.'

Wishart paused in the act of putting the bottle to his lips. 'When?'

'Tonight. Surprise them – if they have returned.'

Wishart took a drink. 'And if they haven't?'

'I still want to look.'

Wishart took another drink. 'Not tonight. For a start, I'm done. I've had a long day, and just got back from a very long drive – ten hours on the road. I have an officer killed, and people I've known as friends for a good twenty years were recently the subject of a hit attempt. I don't know why anyone would want to kill them, and I'm not allowed find out. The high-ups tell me this is to be done your way, not mine. In short, the incident is not to be the subject of a public investigation.'

'With good reason,' Müller said. 'We don't want another hit man finding out where they are. Bad enough I brought this one with me.'

'You intrigue me, Mr Müller. You want the Hargreaves—'

'Correction. I don't *want* them. I need to have a word with them. That's all.'

'For which you've come halfway round the world...'

'Yes.'

Wishart said nothing, and finished the beer slowly.

'Another?' Müller offered.

'No thanks.' Wishart gave a brief smile that was more of a wry grimace. 'More driving to do. Home to get to. Your visit to Woonnalla will have to wait.'

'The colonel and I can go alone...'

Wishart's eyes looked hard at Müller. 'Mr Müller, I may be under instructions to do things your way, but this is still my beat. You don't go back to Woonnalla without me. If you can wait a few hours, get some sleep – *I* need some – and we can leave as early as you

73

would like in the morning.'

'The dawn raid?'

'If that's what you would like.'

Müller decided not to push it. 'Fine. Can you meet us here at six? It's not exactly dawn, but as you've said, you need to catch up on your sleep.'

'Six will be fine.'

Müller nodded. 'Very well.'

Wishart got to his feet. 'I thank you for the beer, Mr Müller. I'll see you at six.' He put on his hat as he went out.

'You backed down, Müller,' Carey Bloomfield said as Müller shut the door.

'Strategic withdrawal,' he corrected. 'Pushing him further would have been counterproductive. He would not have budged, and we would have had an acrimonious stand-off. Instructions or not, he could still have made life difficult by being as obstructive as possible. A policeman has many ways to do this.' Müller gave a fleeting smile. 'I should know. This way, he is still onside, if reluctantly.'

'Can't say I'm sorry we're not going tonight. All those snakes crawling around out there in the dark. Ughh! Notice anything ... special about him?' she added.

'That he wished I had never disturbed his peace? Oh yes.'

'I mean something else.'

'You tell me.'

'He was looking at you very strangely.'

'I agree his eyes were not very friendly—'

74

'Not that, either. He was looking at you as if trying to match you with something he has in his mind.'

'Probably hoping I look like some criminal he's been hunting.'

'I'm not joking, Müller. Something about you is bugging him.'

'That's not a surprise.'

'Damn it, Müller! Listen up!'

'What do you want me to say? I've no idea what you're talking about. Do you?'

'That's just it,' she said after a while. 'I don't.'

'Then let's leave it. If it is important, it will surface at some time.'

In Berlin, the hour was up, and Pappenheim got his return call.

'Where did you get this?' the contact asked immediately.

'The principles I apply regarding you, apply to everyone else,' Pappenheim countered.

'That's good to know,' she admitted grudgingly. 'Well, whoever it is, he or she has access to some very sensitive material.'

'You've got something?'

'Pure gold,' came the reply. 'I'd hate to think what your other dates point to. You've been given a powerful weapon. In naval terms, a killing broadside.'

Pappenheim took the eternal cigarette out of his mouth. 'You're joking.' He put the cigarette back in quickly, as if afraid it would get cold.

'Not about this. What you've got hold of is a career destroyer.'

Pappenheim felt his heart lift. 'I love the sound of music in the afternoon.'

'Pappi?'

'Yes.'

'Remind me never to upset you.'

'You'll never upset me.'

'That almost feels like the tip of a pointing sword, touching my throat.'

'Come on. You know me. Cuddly—'

'With sharp bear claws.'

'Enough with the compliments. What do you have on the subject in question?'

'Illegal arms deal to a Middle Eastern country ... with a fat payoff.'

'I *love* it! When can I have some details?'

'If you have a *very* secure transmission route, I can have it copied to you.'

'I have one of the most secure. I'll have it set up.'

'OK. If this is ever traced, I'm finished.'

'I've never spoken to you in my life. You know that.'

The contact chuckled. 'As I've said, you make a bad enemy. Those other dates...'

'Yes?'

'If you possibly can, don't pass them my way.'

'I'll do my best.'

'Pappi...'

'I'll do my very best.'

'I'll have to accept that, I suppose.'

The emptiness of a secure call abruptly

ending greeted Pappenheim's ear.

He put down the phone. 'Well, well, well, Wolfgang. Been lining our pockets, have we?' He picked up the printout and ticked off the relevant date. 'What other treasures await?' he added softly, studying the remaining nineteen.

He picked up his second phone and called the Rogues' Gallery. The goth was still there. He asked her to prepare for a secure incoming transmission, and gave her the details.

That done, he lit a fresh cigarette, humming to himself as he blew several smoke rings at the ceiling.

In a matter of minutes, the goth was on the phone to him. 'It's here,' she said. 'I don't think I want to know about it.'

Pappenheim got to his feet and killed the cigarette in seemingly the same movement.

'On my way,' he said.

He moved with surprising speed to the door.

'How much is there?' he asked the goth as he entered the Rogues' Gallery.

'At least ten pages,' she answered without turning round, 'plus photographs. I've printed it all out, then saved the original document, encrypted, on the server.'

'Good work,' he said, taking the printouts from the tray.

He went over to the table and spread everything out upon it. The goth swivelled her chair to watch, but did not get up.

The ten pages were damning. They were

77

full of the details of Melk's dealings: meetings, dates of such meetings, the people he met and at which locations, the amount paid to him, and even the account number at the bank into which the money had been paid.

'One can only imagine where all this came from,' he remarked softly.

There were five photographs, each numbered. Four of them showed Melk with Middle Eastern clients. Their numbers corresponded to itemized information on the last of the ten pages. The fifth also showed him with a Middle Eastern client, in the client's country. But there was another person in that photograph that made Pappenheim catch his breath.

'My God,' he whispered.

He checked the photograph with the itemized information. There was no mistake.

'Well, well, well...' he continued, almost breathing the words. 'General A. D. Armin Sternbach, no less, with "our colleague" at the Ministry in the process of lining his pockets. Hot stuff. Very hot stuff.'

Pappenheim studied the sheets of paper, and the photographs, closely.

'I have you, Wolfgang Melk,' he said to the photograph of Melk and Sternbach. *'The Semper* are not the kind of playmates a man at the Ministry should have. You never saw this, or heard this, Miss Meyer,' he added to the goth.

'See what, sir? Hear what?'

'Nice to see you forgot your contact lenses.'

'I don't need contact lenses, and I also

78

forgot the hearing aid I don't need.'

'Knew you would. Can you set up another wormhole connection with Jens Müller? I should let him know about this.'

'No problem. Ready in one minute.'

In Broome, Carey Bloomfield was on Müller's verandah when Müller received the call from Pappenheim.

'You'll need to sit down for this one as well,' Pappenheim said as soon as Müller answered.

Müller glanced out and saw that Carey had turned to look at him. He indicated that she should come back in.

She entered, closing the glass doors behind her, an expression of open curiosity upon her face.

'I'm sitting,' Müller said to Pappenheim as Carey leaned against a wall.

'Done a little probing of our friend Melk,' Pappenheim said.

'And?'

'A lot of sludge rising to the surface. Our Russian/American/Russian sent over some dates – twenty in all. I had a contact check just one, so far. We hit pay dirt, as they say in those old movies.'

'How much?'

'Not fool's gold.'

'Tell me.'

Müller went absolutely still as Pappenheim told him.

'Pay dirt indeed,' Müller said grimly when

79

Pappenheim had finished. 'Now we know.'

'We certainly do. But we've got a weapon. A naval broadside, career killing, my contact called it.'

'It certainly is that. Not to be squandered.'

'Definitely not.'

'Those other dates should turn out to be interesting too.'

'I can hardly wait,' Pappenheim said, barely containing his glee. 'I thought I'd save them for later.'

'Good idea. This first one should be enough to start with. Don't use it until I get back.'

'And when will that be?'

'Three days at most ... unless things develop unexpectedly. Then you can use it as you see fit.'

'I can wait. The longer the wait, the riper the fruit for the picking.'

'Alright, Pappi. I'll do my best to close things down here as soon as I can, one way or the other.'

'I thought you'd be wanting to enjoy the beauts of Oz for a while longer.'

'I'd like to do that, having come all this way; but as you've just shown, some people need attending to first. But I'll certainly come back here.'

'What it is to be a sinner.'

'Are you talking about me, or you?'

'Both of us,' Pappenheim said with a cackle. 'Any new developments?'

'I won't be going to the house tonight. The local head colleague turned up and said no go. So we do it tomorrow.'

'You *agreed* to be put off?'

'Call it strategic necessity.'

'Ah. A cover for many things.'

'Yes.'

'Then I'd better let you get your sleep. It must be nearly twenty-three hundred down your way.'

'That's early.'

'Then enjoy the evening – what's left of it.'

'We'll have a few beers, and watch the ocean.'

'Very Oz,' Pappenheim said with a laugh as they ended the call.

'How much of that did you get?' Müller asked Carey Bloomfield as he put the mobile away.

'Not enough to string much together. But I can tell you got some meat.'

'That we did. Melk is dirty. Very.'

'That was fast work.'

'Pappi has a web of contacts. If you believe in such things, in his last life, he must have been a spider. Remember retired General Sternbach?'

'*The Semper* bastard who shipped one of his goons to get me, right in my home town?'

'That's the bastard. Pappi's got a photograph of Melk with him, in the Middle East, doing an illegal weapons sale.'

'Oooh wow! That's a nail. So Melk *is Semper.*'

'Even if not, he's too close to them for comfort.'

81

'It explains the sudden offer of promotion.'

'The "kick upstairs" – as if we had not already suspected. I feel better, knowing the true face of my enemy.'

'You're not short of those, that's for sure. You're dealing with a virus, Müller. And the infection seems to be spreading faster than you can deal with it.'

'Perhaps. Perhaps not. Let's have some cold beers on the verandah, and watch the ocean.'

They got the beers, and made themselves comfortable on the verandah.

'Müller?'

'Mmm?'

'Do you remember that plane we saw on the way to Woonnalla, earlier today?'

'The Hargreaves' plane, heading off after Mackay had warned them.'

'Notice anything special about it?'

'It was a small plane. Twin booms—'

'A Cessna 337,' she said. 'I know that type of plane very well. Our people used the military version as forward air controllers in Vietnam. It is very manoeuvrable. Some of the civil versions can fly very high – up to thirty thousand feet in some cases, if you spend the money. That design is seventies into eighties. The one we saw was close enough to tell it is very well looked after. It could be new.'

'What are you trying to say?'

'Why would eco people like the Hargreaves have a machine that is in such perfect condition?'

'Planes have to be.'

She made a scoffing noise. 'The space between what they should be, and what some of them actually are, is so big—'

'I've got the idea.'

'It just seems to me that the Hargreaves having that plane in such good order is more than just excellent airworthiness.'

'Fast getaway?'

'It sure works. We've seen it in action.'

'Meaning, the Hargreaves are always poised to flee,' Müller said.

She nodded. 'All those years of living quietly in the middle of nowhere, yet come the moment, they move like greased lightning.'

'Well prepared to move at a moment's notice. Reflexes not dulled by the years of living at an easy pace. That takes discipline.'

'Strange for eco people,' she said. 'Wouldn't you say?'

'We'll have a closer look tomorrow. See what we can find. Meanwhile...'

'Müller?'

'And what is it this time?'

'When you've closed things here, why not stay a day or two extra and take a camel ride along the beach?'

'Do you mean those touristy, Cable Beach things?'

'Lighten up, Müller. *Anyone* who does not belong to Broome is a tourist, and that includes Aussies.'

'Let's negotiate over an ice-cold...'

In Berlin, Pappenheim replaced the phone.

'Want to continue flying?' he said to the goth.

'I think I should get back to my department before *Kommissar* Spyros begins to think you've kidnapped me. Unless you still need me...'

'No. You've done plenty for now, and excellently as usual. I'll let you know when.'

'Then I'll shut down the computer, unless you want to work...'

'Computers don't get on with me. You can shut down.'

'OK.' She did so, then stood up. 'Just call me when.'

He nodded. 'I will. Count on it.'

As she left, Pappenheim went back to studying the information he had received.

'I've got you nailed, Melk,' he said to the photograph.

Woonnalla Station. 2315, local

Maggie Hargreaves came out of the main bedroom to join her husband in the kitchen. Her eyes were red-rimmed. She was clutching something small to her chest, as if never wanting to let it go.

'All done?' he asked.

She nodded. 'I've taken it down.'

He sighed. 'Sorry you had to, but there was no choice. All we need is in the plane,' he went on, 'and anything that could betray us is well hidden. The Lyserts can look after the place until we get back. I've already warned them we'll be away for a little while. They know what to do.'

'Will we ever return here?'

'Sooner or later, he must return to Berlin. He can't stay out here forever. He's a Berlin policeman, not a tourist on a world trip.'

'What about that sniper? If they can send one, they can send others.'

'This one had luck, by accident. You've heard what Graeme had to say. Müller believes the sniper trailed him. But that won't happen again. He and the colonel killed the man they sent. The hit man would not have had time to report. So our sanctuary is safe — for now.'

'How can you call him "Müller"?'

'I must, my dear. I must. It's the only way.' Hargreaves fished into a pocket and brought out Müller's card. 'See what he left. I found it under a pot on the terrace.'

Still clutching whatever it was she held, she took the card with a free hand to study it. Tears spilled down her cheeks as she looked at it.

She handed it back. 'You must return it to exactly the same place, or he'll know we came back here.'

'Of course,' he said. 'I just wanted you to see it.'

She nodded, wiping at her tears. 'Thank you.'

'I'll put it back now. Then we should leave.'

Again, she nodded. 'I'll wait in the plane. You can close things down.'

As he went to return the card to its place beneath the flower pot, she looked at the thing she had been holding close. It was a small, framed photograph.

It was of Müller, as a boy of twelve.

In Broome, on the verandah of his hotel suite, Müller and Carey Bloomfield were enjoying their iced beers and watching the ocean, while Jack and Maggie Hargreaves took off in their plane for a destination known only to themselves.

The next morning, a refreshed Wishart, bush hat on, was as good as his word. He knocked on Müller's door, promptly at six.

Looking none the worse for wear after their ocean-gazing nightcap, Müller and Carey Bloomfield were ready to go.

Wishart looked at Müller with opaque eyes, then glanced at Carey Bloomfield. 'Good morning, Colonel. Mr Müller. If you're ready.'

'Good morning, Mr Wishart,' said Carey Bloomfield.

'Good morning,' Müller answered. 'We're ready. Our four-wheel-drive is re-equipped. Everything necessary, with a safety margin.'

Wishart gave them a slight nod. 'Can never be too careful out here. Let's be going.' He turned and headed back to where he had parked.

They set off for Woonnalla, Müller driving, Wishart leading in his police vehicle.

As Broome Road joined the Great Northern Highway, Carey Bloomfield said, looking ahead to Wishart's vehicle, 'Do you trust him?'

'As a policeman? Or as a friend of the Hargreaves?'

'Both.'

'As a policeman, he'll be professional and co-operate; but only just, because of what happened to Mackay. As a friend of the Hargreaves ... I won't commit on that.'

'Which means you don't trust him.'

'I would not put it in such harsh terms. Let us say I'm keeping my options open.'

'You don't trust him.'

'I don't trust him.'

She stared at him. 'Why didn't you just admit that at the beginning? Sometimes, Müller, getting an admission out of you is like pulling teeth.'

'A few minutes on the road, and we're having our first row.'

'We're *not* having a row, Müller.'

He smiled to himself, and kept pace with Wishart.

They made good time. Just under two hours later, they turned off the sealed high-way and on to the un-signposted, red unsealed road that led to – and ended at – Woonnalla, twenty or so kilometres further.

'Turning on to this road again has remind-ed me of something,' Carey Bloomfield said as they trailed into the boiling red wake left by Wishart's vehicle. 'Constable Mackay.'

'What about him?'

'He was staring at you too. Just like Wishart.'

'I must have a criminal face.'

'Joke all you want, Müller. Something's weird about all this.'

The now familiar road, with its border of stunted clumps of bush, and a straight that was at least three kilometres long, tempted Wishart into pushing up more speed than might have been usual on such a surface. The dust billowed in a high, plumed tail that surged upwards before spreading downwards and outwards like a floating, living red carpet.

Sometime later, Carey Bloomfield said, 'Although I've seen it before, it's still a wow of a knockout.'

The vegetation on either side of the road had now undergone its equally familiar metamorphosis, the road itself entering the wide, shallow, cultivated valley that had so unexpectedly greeted them before, with its neat segments forming their patchwork of vivid colour; the small trees that were dotted within the patchwork; and the astonishingly beautiful low, white house in the middle of the tableau.

The road came to its natural end in the sealed section that went right up to the house. As before, distance had deceived, the house being far bigger than it had seemed at first sight, and surrounded by the beauty of its vast, flourishing garden.

'An oasis,' Carey Bloomfield said. 'I know I said that the first time we came here, but what the hell.' She looked at the tower with the vaned wheel at the top. It was turning. 'The water pump's working. Looks like someone's home.'

But Müller had glanced at the telltale strip that looked like a road in the wrong place. 'No plane.'

'Maybe they've parked it under cover.'

'Maybe I'll win the lottery.'

'Why would you want to win a lottery, Müller? You've probably got more cash than one of those really big wins.'

'I don't play,' he said.

'I should hope so. Leave some for us poor folks. Ah ... heads up. The friendly policeman's getting out of his car.'

They had drawn up to the house, and had stopped a little way from Wishart's vehicle. A short distance behind the main house, the big outhouse they remembered from their previous visit, within its border of low trees, seemed somehow different.

Then Müller realized what it was. The last time, there had been some machinery in front of the outhouse, and the big attached garage had been open, with two lorries parked inside.

The machinery was gone, and the garage was closed.

'Someone has definitely been back here,' he said to her.

'What do you mean?'

'The outhouse. The machinery that was here when we first came is now gone. And the garage with the trucks is closed. Time to get out,' he went on. 'Our co-operative policeman's on his way.'

They got out of the Explorer and, as before – even this early in the day – it was very warm by comparison with the air-conditioned atmosphere of the vehicle. They took the opportunity to put on their own bush hats.

This close, they could see that the patchwork that had caught them by surprise the day before – especially when they realised that they had been looking at vast tracts of ecologically grown vegetables, fruit, and flowers – had recently been watered.

'Looks like you could be lucky,' Wishart began as he reached them. 'Someone's here.'

'But no plane,' Müller said.

'No plane. But that doesn't mean both Jack and Maggie are gone. One of the Lyserts is a pilot. He flies the plane sometimes.'

'I see. Who are the Lyserts?'

'Peter and Paul. Twins. One has light hair, the other dark. Easiest way to tell them apart. Pete's the pilot. He's the one with the dark hair. They've been with the Hargreaves since their early teens. Jack said Pete had the aptitude for flying, so he taught him. Took to it like a duck to water, Pete did.'

'I see,' Müller repeated. 'Shouldn't someone have come out to meet us by now?'

'They'll have seen my vehicle with yours. Someone will be out soon enough. Pete and Paul are of The People.'

'The "People"?' Carey Bloomfield asked.

'The world generally calls them Aborigines,' Wishart explained. He did not quite manage to keep the contempt out of his voice.

There was an awkward silence, and no one said anything.

This was broken by the appearance of the dark-haired Lysert, Pete. Tall and slim with it, Pete Lysert, with his neck-length crop of loose curls showing richly beneath his bush hat, could have easily been mistaken for someone from the southern shores of Europe.

'He's a looker,' Carey Bloomfield commented.

Wishart gave her a quick stare. 'Was that condescending, Colonel?'

She was astonished by his reaction. 'No, Mr Wishart,' she said in a hard voice. 'I stated a fact.'

'My mistake.'

'Yes, it was.'

'Why don't we all agree to forget it before he gets here?' Müller suggested.

'Forgotten,' Wishart said quickly.

'Same here,' Carey Bloomfield said.

'And just in time,' Müller said in a low voice.

Lysert was just coming into earshot. He grinned hugely at Wishart. 'Graeme! How're ya, mate?'

'Same as always, Pete. Struggling to keep up.'

'Yeah. Sure.' Lysert was cheerfully sceptical as they shook hands.

'Pete,' Wishart continued, 'Miss Bloomfield from Washington, and Mr Müller from Berlin.

'Miss Bloomfield. Mr Muller.'

As they shook hands, Lysert appeared to stare at Müller for a moment too long. It was the barest of pauses, but it was there; and it had nothing to do with Müller's ponytail, nor his earring.

'They'd like to look over the place, Pete,' Wishart said. 'Jack and Maggie in?'

'Sorry, mate. They've gone off on one of their trips. They like doing that, as you know.'

'After all these years, I do know. OK if I show them around?'

'Is it official business? Miss Bloomfield being from the States, Mr Müller from Germany...'

'It is, Pete. Sorry.'

Lysert paused uncertainly. 'Reckon it'll be OK, mate, as you're here with them. I'll get some keys.'

'Thanks, Pete. They may want to look around outside as well.'

'No worries. I'll get those keys.'

'Thanks, mate.'

As Lysert hurried away, Carey Bloomfield looked the house over. 'Even seeing this a second time,' she said, 'is like the first. Beautiful.' She glanced at Müller. 'What do you think?'

Müller was staring intently at the building, and did not reply. He did not see Wishart studying him closely. Then Wishart looked away, sensing that Carey Bloomfield had glanced at him.

'What did you say?' Müller asked her.

'Wasn't important. And here come the keys.'

Lysert was returning.

'Right,' he said as he reached them. 'Who does the honours?' He was looking at Müller as he said this.

Müller turned to Carey Bloomfield. 'Ladies first, I would think.'

'I'm it, huh?'

'You're it.' Müller had already looked away, and was staring out across the shallow valley.

Wishart looked at Lysert, whose eyes kept glancing at Müller, as if unable to break a habit.

'Pete, a word with you later?'

'Sure, mate. Call when you're done.'

'Right. And thanks.'

'No worries.'

'Where's the brother?' Müller asked as Lysert returned to whatever he'd been doing.

'Out in the valley somewhere, if I know him,' Wishart answered. 'When Jack and Maggie are away, those two practically run the place. They're like sons to Jack and Maggie.'

Müller nodded, still looking at the house,

mind seemingly elsewhere.

'Coming, Müller?' Carey Bloomfield urged.

'What? Oh, yes.'

Followed by an increasingly curious Wishart, they went up to the front door.

Carey Bloomfield unlocked it, and opened it wide.

They entered a cool, white, and spacious interior. The terracotta floor had been perfectly chosen. Several areas were segregated by low walls with columns reaching to the high ceiling. Huge windows were dressed with white Roman blinds that let in floods of natural light. The carpeted floor of the dining area was a cool, neutral colour. The table and chairs were identifiably classic antiques.

'Gawd,' Carey Bloomfield exclaimed softly. 'This looks even more beautiful close up than when I peeked in yesterday. Not something you expect to see way out here in the middle of nowhere. Not the stereotypical eco people, eh, Müller? I wouldn't be surprised to find Armani suits in the ... Müller? You OK?'

There was a paleness to Müller's expression that startled her. He also appeared to be sniffing.

'Müller? What the hell? Are you *sniffing*?'

He did not reply. Instead, he turned to Wishart. 'Do you know where the master bedroom is?'

'My family and I have been here often enough during the last twenty years,' Wishart replied. 'I'll show you. I don't have to remind you to treat the place with respect.'

'No,' Müller said. 'You don't.'

They reached the door to the master bed-room.

Müller looked at them. 'I'd like to go in alone. I know what I'm looking for.'

Both Wishart and Carey Bloomfield stared at him.

'Müller...' she began.

He raised a hand briefly. 'Please. I know what I'm doing. Humour me.' He looked at Wishart. 'Mr Wishart, do you have any objections?'

Wishart's eyes did most of the talking. 'No objections.'

'I'll leave the door open.'

Leaving Carey Bloomfield and Wishart to give each other surreptitious glances, Müller entered the huge bedroom. He walked in a few feet, paused, and sniffed. Whatever was in the scent he caught, it sent a visible tremor though his body.

Outside, Carey Bloomfield was standing in a position that gave her a clear view of him. She caught the tremor. This made her frown without realizing it.

'What the hell?' she whispered to herself.

She glanced to her left to see that Wishart was staring at her.

'What?' she asked.

He made no reply, turning instead to look towards the bedroom.

Müller had gone further in, and was now out of both their view. He moved slowly towards the neatly made bed. He stopped, looked at it closely for long moments, noting the way the bedclothes had been arranged.

The walls were adorned with paintings, mainly landscapes of Australia, but their positioning seemed familiar. He felt that somehow, the paintings seemed to jar. It was not that they did not belong; the colours in each fitted the general décor of the room. Yet he felt certain something was not quite right.

He sat down on the edge of the bed, on the left side, and did not move for a full minute. He fought the conflicting emotions within him, trying to understand why the house was affecting him so strongly. He could find no logical reason.

Absently, he reached to his left, in a habit of childhood. The hand moved, until it came to a particular tuck in the top sheet. It was an envelope tuck, with a pocket into which he used to put his hand as a child, pretending it was trapped.

He pulled the hand away, breathing harshly, heart thumping. Most people tucked a top sheet, or a blanket, in a straight fold. Most people. He knew of only one person who made a special envelope tuck on one side of the bed, so that a child could pretend his hand was trapped.

Body shaking, Müller stood up, and went to the other side of the bed to check. It was a straight tuck.

'Oh, God,' he whispered. 'I'm losing it. This

is not possible. How could someone on the far side of the world...'

He stopped, and went back to the left side of the bed. Just to the left of the solid, polished headboard was the small square of a picture, within easy reach of someone lying in bed. Like the others in the room, it was a landscape study, but Müller felt that somehow it did not belong there.

With a slightly shaking hand, he lifted it, to look at the faint paleness beneath. It did not match.

'A slightly bigger picture was hanging there before,' he said to himself.

He had the uncanny feeling he knew what that picture was, but could find no rational explanation for that thought. He touched the bed. Despite the obvious freshness of the bedclothes, there was a faint scent that propelled his memories back in time. He felt a sudden heat behind his eyes, and remained in the bedroom until he was certain he had everything back under control.

Nothing was making sense.

He left the room, to confront the openly curious stares of Carey Bloomfield and Wishart. He gave them no explanations.

'The terrace,' he said.

They followed him through to the elegantly stylish kitchen, and out on to the terrace. He checked where he had left his card. It was still there. He looked at it closely. He felt certain it had been moved. A digit on the telephone number was further in than when he had placed the card there. Deliberate? Or inadvertent?

If deliberate, was it a message? To tell him ... what?

He did not touch the card.

Four

Wishart had left Müller and Carey Bloomfield on the terrace, and had gone to find Pete Lysert. He found him tinkering with one of the lorries, inside the now opened garage.

'Ho, Pete,' he called.

Lysert stopped, put down the tool he'd been using and came out, wiping his hands on a barely soiled rag.

'That truck's already gleaming,' Wishart said. 'What is there to do on it?'

'Always something to do on anything mechanical, mate,' Lysert said, grinning. 'That way, you keep the big breakdowns away.'

'Must be a pilot thing.'

'Well, up there, a big breakdown clips your wings fast.'

'And down here in the wrong place in the outback, the same thing can give you a slow death.'

'Too right, mate. Well, Graeme?' Lysert went on. 'What d'you reckon?'

'About?'

'Him. Müller.'

'I was about to ask you the same thing.'

'If I didn't know better...'

Wishart nodded. 'Me too. It's...'

99

'Yeah.'

'But it doesn't make any sense,' Wishart said.

'Since when does life make sense? Did it make sense for Captain Cook to find this land?'

'It's too early in the day for one of your philosophical remarks, Pete.'

Lysert gave another of his easy grins. 'It's never too early. So what are you going to do?'

'About Müller? What can I do? He's got powerful backing. Whatever he's investigating, Jack and Maggie are involved. He needs to talk with them, but he's worried about putting them in danger as well. It's a crock, and I wish I didn't have to deal with it. A Berlin copper who speaks like a Pom, international hit men, CIA agents—'

'*She's* CIA?'

'She's supposed to be a colonel...'

'Bit young, isn't she?'

'Exactly. She's not what she says she is, I reckon. By the way, mate, she thinks you're a looker. I think you've got an ugly mug, meself.'

Lysert's smile betrayed evidence of years-long badinage between them. 'She's got a sexy walk, I'll say that. Feet turned in a little. Love that in woman ... She may have said that about me,' he went on, 'but Müller's the one making her heart do handsprings. She's trying to make him jealous.'

'You spotted all that in the short time

you've met them?'

'How long have you been married, mate? Still don't know about women? They're smarter, cleverer, more cunning than we could ever be. They've always been smart, clever and cunning ever since the time they sent us out to hunt dinosaurs...'

'Thank you, Pete,' Wishart began with mild sarcasm. 'I needed that. Now can we get back to Jack and Maggie? Seems to me they had this getaway thing planned a long time ago. All nice and smooth. Some things I remember seeing are missing from the house. They didn't all go on the plane. It would never fly...'

For the first time, Lysert's easy smile vanished. 'Graeme, you share the blood, but if it's a choice between Jack and Maggie, and you ... you lose, mate. They're like parents to us.'

'Christ, Pete. I'm not asking you to betray anything. They're my friends, remember? My boy, Jack, is their godson. I just want to bloody understand what the hell's going on.'

There was a long silence as Lysert appeared to be arguing within himself.

'Look,' he said at last, 'I'll tell you just this ... Some years ago, they told us that perhaps one day some people might come looking for them. They told us about it because they wanted us to be safe. They said that if it ever happened, we should get away from Woonnalla, and stay away, until they told us it was OK to come back.

101

'Paulie and I didn't want to do that. We wanted to stay, to help them out. They said no. We would help them best by staying away. Then they went through the escape routine with us. Made us practice and practice until we could do it in our sleep. I'm not sure they were talking about Müller; more about the kind of man who killed Jamie Mackay.'

Wishart nodded. 'Yeah. I think they meant that killer. His type of people. As for Müller...'

'Yeah. Something, isn't it? You stalled him, didn't you?'

Wishart gave Lysert a neutral stare. 'What do you mean?'

'You put Müller off till Jack and Maggie were well away. So you're keeping your little secret from him.'

'It was the least I could do for them.'

Lysert nodded. 'And appreciated, I'm sure. How was he in the house?'

'Hard to explain. He was ... strange. Like he'd been in there before. But, of course, we know he couldn't have been.'

'Why not? Perhaps...'

'No, Pete. No more of the philosophy.'

'Stranger things have happened. You know the dreamtime stories...'

'I'm a copper, Pete. Sometimes, I have to look at things more ... rationally, for want of a better word. And talking of words, there are some we're dancing around.'

Lysert's eyes fixed themselves upon Wishart. 'You mean he could be related?'

102

'Perhaps. But we know that can't be possible, don't we?'

'Do we?'

On the terrace, Carey Bloomfield was looking anxiously at Müller, who had been quiet for some time.

'Hey,' she said. 'Are you talking today?'

'What? Oh, just running some things through my mind.'

'Well, that thought had occurred to me, believe or not. You OK?' she added, uncertainty creasing her forehead.

'There is love in this house,' he said. 'I can sense it. The Hargreaves truly love each other. It reminds me...' He stopped to look at her. 'You're frowning,' he told her. 'You'll make those creases permanent.'

'So you keep telling me. Don't duck and weave, Müller. What happened to you in there? And what are you reminded of? And don't try to evade. I saw you go very pale, just before you went out of view. And what was that sniffing about?'

'Which question do you want answered?'

'All of them. But I'll settle for just one.'

'What happened in there was that I was reminded of something.'

'That's *it?*'

'That's a new question, but I'll answer: that's it.'

'Jesus...'

'And don't fume. You'll be stamping your foot next.'

103

'Urrggh. *Müller!*'

'I wonder if they've got a secret room somewhere here,' he went on, ignoring her reaction. 'A cellar, perhaps. No point asking Wishart, or the Lyserts. I suspect they would not tell.'

'Enjoying your monologue?'

'Thinking aloud, it's called.'

'Müller! Sometimes ... sometimes...'

'We should leave.'

'*What?*'

'No point remaining.'

'Don't you want to look this place over?'

'No point,' he repeated. 'I needed to speak with the Hargreaves. They're gone and, I'm certain, won't be back as long as I am in the area. They'll be waiting to hear either from the Lyserts, or even Wishart. They've already been back, to pick up some things, and to make changes in the house—'

'How do you know all this?'

Müller pointed to the flower pot. 'See that?'

'A flower pot. Is ... that a business card under there?'

'It is.'

'Yours?'

'Mine. I left it—'

'When you jumped out of the Explorer yesterday, to come back here.'

'Yes.'

'You said nothing to me.'

'No. I wanted to try something.'

'And it worked?'

'It worked. The card has been moved, then

104

replaced.'

'That could have been one of the Lyserts.'

'I am very certain it was not.'

'If the Hargreaves were here last night, it means...'

'Wishart knew, and stalled us. It gave them enough time to return, make their arrangements, then take off again. He said he'd been on the road for several hours. I think he met them somewhere. After what happened, he would have wanted to check with them. He made contact, they told him where they were, and he went to them.'

She nodded. 'I'll buy that.'

'So trying to get information from anyone here will be a waste of time. I need the Hargreaves. Without them, I won't get much further at the moment. But I'm a little wiser than when we first came, and that helps. I now know that they are important enough for *The Semper* to want them dead.

'Even when *The Semper* eventually find out their man is down, they won't know that I've found the Hargreaves. That little secret is a weapon for use against them. I will also ensure that the location of Woonnalla remains a secret. There are, of course, two items of almost equal importance.'

'Which are?'

'Mainauer's Dragunov. Someone got it into the country. Mainauer – who would have used an overtly legal passport under another name – would not have risked being caught trying to smuggle it in. This means that some-

105

where on this huge island there is a *Semper* cell. Either that, or it was a sub-contracted job; which is no better. Sub-contractors who are skilled enough to smuggle weapons like a Dragunov SVDS can also sniff around very competently. Then there's the 4WD he used. It did not come from Broome. Someone drove it there, after the box for the rifle had been fitted...'

'Like the one on Rügen.'

'Exactly like the one on Rügen. I'll have to make quite certain that neither Wishart, nor the Lyserts, talk about what happened here.'

Müller began to look about him.

'What?' she asked.

'Something to write with. Terraces like this, and kitchens, tend to have pens or pencils lying around...'

'I think I saw one in the kitchen,' Carey Bloomfield said, and hurried to find it. 'Found it,' she announced, returning with a ballpoint. 'I can never understand people who do this.'

'Do what?'

'Leave pens with the top off. Now what?' she said, staring at his expression. 'You've got that weird look again.'

'Er ... it's nothing,' he said, coming back from wherever his memories had taken him.

'Sure,' she said, not believing it.

He took the pen, withdrew the card from under the pot, then wrote a short message on the back, while she looked on curiously.

106

If you do use this, DO NOT announce yourself.

He did not sign it. He put the card back the way it had been left, then lay the pen across it.

'That should get their attention,' he remarked. 'Now let's find Wishart and Lysert.'

'Back through the house?'

'No. Let's go through the garden.'

'Don't snakes come into gardens in Australia?'

'Yes ... in places like this. Houses too. Sometimes.'

'Thanks for nothing.'

'But don't worry. I don't think this happens so often here. You haven't seen one since we got here, have you?'

'I saw *two* poisonous monsters yesterday. I'll very happy if that's my quota for the next hundred years. And...' She stopped and turned round. 'Müller, what are you doing?'

Müller was peering at a small blue seashell that he had missed before, and would not have noticed it now had he not paused to write. It was in a second pot with a flourishing plant. The shell was almost hidden by the plant.

'It will help it to grow.' He spoke so quietly that Carey Bloomfield did not hear.

'Did you just pick something out of there?' she asked.

'No. I thought I saw something. Besides, there could be a snake lurking...'

'Not funny, Müller.'

107

They were just getting to the front of the house when Wishart and Lysert appeared.

'Just coming to find you,' Wishart said.

'Saved you a walk.'

Wishart, not sure how to take that, gave Müller a wary glance but chose not to say anything.

Lysert looked on neutrally, but his eyes were lively.

'We're finished here,' Müller said.

Both Wishart and Lysert looked surprised.

'Yes,' Müller went on. 'I know I said I wanted to look around some more; but I feel I've seen all I need to for now. After all, it's the Hargreaves I really want to see.'

Müller paused, his manner clearly indicating he was about to tell them something important.

'Mr Wishart, Mr Lysert ... if you really do care about the Hargreaves, I must insist that you do not talk, *ever*, about what happened here yesterday. Mr Wishart, that goes for any of your officers who have been involved in the recovery of the bodies of both Jamie Mackay and the sniper.

'The people after the Hargreaves are so dangerous that you can consider yourself potentially responsible for their deaths as well as your own – and your families – should you talk about this to *anyone*. If I am frightening you, good. Attempts have already been made on my life, Miss Bloomfield's, and the teen-aged daughter of my immediate superior. My colleague, partner and second-in-command, was shot right outside the police building in Berlin. He survived because he had chosen, on a whim, to wear his armoured vest that evening. It was at very close range, with a heavy calibre weapon, and the force of the blow knocked him out.

'The wife of an American colonel was kidnapped, raped, and then murdered for good measure. They brutalized his young son, then they tried to have the colonel killed. Another of my colleagues was blown up, and at least two were shot dead by dirty policemen who belonged to this group of people. The sniper who came here was also a dirty colleague. They repay any failure by their own people by killing them. Should we ever be fortunate enough to take one alive, you can be certain that keeping him or her that way will be a full-time job. The same goes for anyone with information to hurt them.

'Now, you may both be thinking that had I not turned up, none of this would have happened here. Up to a point, you are correct. You may even find yourselves at some point thinking that if the Hargreaves had not been here, none of this would have happened either – at least, not in your part of the world. Again, you might be correct, but again, only up to a point. The Hargreaves are important because they have knowledge that could help sink these people. You could say, Mr Wishart, using the language of our profession, that what I am doing is a kind of witness protection.

'Mr Lysert, everything I have just said goes for your brother as well. Please make certain he understands this. Someone supplied the vehicle,' Müller continued, mainly to Wishart, 'and the box to hide the gun, to the sniper. This could mean that whoever they are – one person, or more – might still be around. If they pick up the merest hint that something happened at Woonnalla, there will be more visits from people like the man who was here yesterday. By some time today, they should have worked out that their man is not coming back. They will try to determine his location when they last heard from him, then work from there. This means, I would suggest, that Broome is the most likely area. It does not matter whether he made contact from Broome or not. That is where he picked up his vehicle, which, to them, makes it his last known location; and a starting point from which to begin their search for him ... and the Hargreaves.'

Müller stopped. They stared back at him, shocked.

'Sweet Jesus,' Wishart said at last.

'The Hargreaves have done a lot for me, and for my brother,' Lysert said in a quiet voice. 'I'll not be ratting on them.'

'Then we understand each other,' Müller said. 'Do we, Mr Wishart?'

Wishart nodded slowly. 'We do, Mr Müller.' He paused, seeming to want to say more.

'I know you gave them the breathing space

to get away,' Müller told him. 'No matter. I am more interested in their safety.'

Wishart looked embarrassed.

'Do not feel embarrassed, Mr Wishart,' Müller continued. 'They are your friends. I do understand. Like you, I will sometimes go out on a limb to help—'

'What he's trying to say,' Carey Bloomfield interrupted, 'is that he can be an insubordinate SOB at times.'

Wishart looked at Müller anew. There was almost a glimmer of respect. '*You?*'

'Despite that ponytail and earring, he comes across all correct and German, doesn't he?' Carey Bloomfield jumped in again. 'Don't you believe it.'

'Miss Bloomfield exaggerates.'

'Miss Bloomfield does not,' she insisted.

Wishart looked at each of them, as if unsure what to say next.

'You've ... er ... told me about the people on your side who were lost...' he began uncertainly to Müller. 'Apart from that fella yesterday, how many of them have you ... er ... got?'

'We've had some successes,' Müller replied.

'What he means with that classic British understatement,' Carey Bloomfield said, 'is that they've been hurt. And some.'

'He does speak English a bit like a Pom,' Wishart agreed.

'Oxford,' she explained, 'plus British relatives.'

'He's *half* Pom?'

'Don't look so shocked. No. He's all German, but there are British relatives in the family, by marriage ... plus that Oxford education.'

'I like being talked about in the third person,' Müller said.

For the first time since they'd met him, Wishart actually smiled with some humour. 'Mr Müller...'

'Jens,' Müller said.

'And I'm Graeme, as you know.'

'She's Carey,' Carey Bloomfield said with a straight face. 'He still insists on calling me Miss Bloomfield from time to time.'

'The German? Or the Brit?'

'Who knows?' she said.

Lysert's easy grin was back. 'And I'm—'

'Pete,' Müller said. He smiled at Lysert.

'So, Jens,' Lysert said. 'You reckon we're OK for now from these blokes?'

'Just stay as you've always been, and *don't* talk. I'll keep Woonnalla's secret. See that you do. Graeme, keep watch for people who don't belong in your area; or are asking the wrong questions about the Hargreaves.'

'Woonnalla produce is well known,' Lysert said.

'Yes. And it was well known before yesterday's nightmare. That hasn't changed. The kind of people I'm talking about will not be interested in your produce, only in who produces it – if they ever find out. Graeme, do not underestimate these people. Watch out for anyone trailing you, especially if you're coming here. Continue to do this long after we've left Australia. Being a policeman will not protect you. Remember what happened to Jamie Mackay.'

'I'll remember for the rest of my life,' Wishart said, expression grim. 'I'll call my team to warn them that they must say nothing about this.'

'Insist upon it,' Müller said. 'And do it in such a way that if by chance anyone wanders on to your frequency, they won't know what you're talking about.'

Wishart nodded. 'I'll handle it.'

'Graeme,' Müller went on thoughtfully, causing Wishart to look at him with a question in his eyes. 'The sniper picked his vehicle up in Broome ... but that does not necessarily mean he intended to remain within the general area...'

'Lose the vehicle,' Wishart said, immediately picking up on what Müller was suggesting.

'Lose the vehicle. Steer his—'

'Mates way off.'

'Exactly,' Müller said. 'The outback is a vast place...'

'And vehicles and people can get lost, and not found for—'

'Years?' Lysert put in. 'We've got deep gorges, croc pools, salt lakes, channel country, flash floods ... A man can fall into a gorge, get eaten by a croc, die of thirst on a salt pan, drown where there used to be dry ground ... Now, you take what happened back in 2002 with the Big Wet—'

'The Big Wet?' Carey Bloomfield said.

'Yeah. More water than we knew what to do with. The road between Broome and Derby was under a lake. Some even said it was a big inland sea between Broome and Derby. People had their boats out to water-ski...'

'Come on. You're giving us a tourist story...'

'She's straight,' Lysert insisted. 'Biggest Wet ever. The Fitzroy River was thirty kilometres wide in places.'

'It's true,' Wishart confirmed. 'Sometimes you look at this land and it seems as if water is something from another world. Then you get the Wet.'

'So many things can go wrong,' Lysert continued, warming to his theme. 'Snakebite is only a small part of it. A fella not knowing his way around could get into trouble without even trying, couldn't he, Graeme?' he finished enthusiastically.

'He could, mate,' Wishart replied, looking at Müller. 'Will you handle any awkward "bureaucratic problems" that might turn up?'

'I'll back up whatever you do. Say those were my instructions.'

'Don't your bosses scare you?'

'No. But the people who sent the sniper do. I know what they are capable of. Next to them, my so-called bosses are children in a playpen.'

Wishart gave Carey Bloomfield a quick glance. 'I see what you mean,' he told her in a dry voice.

'I don't believe anyone's going to lose sleep

114

over what happens to the sniper's vehicle,' Müller added.

'Or his body?'

'Or his body. Although he was shot in the thigh, actual cause of death was the snake-bite. This will confuse his masters even more.'

'Foolish man,' Wishart said. 'He annoyed a snake.'

'He certainly did,' Carey Bloomfield said with feeling.

Lysert noted her expression. 'You have a thing about snakes?'

'They don't agree with me.'

'She was bitten as a child,' Müller explained, 'and that was almost the end of her.'

Lysert looked interested. 'What snake?'

'A big Florida cottonmouth,' Carey Bloomfield answered. She gave a tiny shudder.

'Florida cottonmouth,' Lysert repeated.

'A kind of water moccasin,' she said. 'The black one, with the white inside the mouth.'

'Ah yes. A serious snake. Respect. But nothing like a big mulga.'

She shuddered again. 'Tell me about it.'

'She's alive today,' Müller said, 'because of her brother. Although just a little older, he kept his nerve, went into the creek where the snake had bitten her to haul her out, and gave her the required emergency treatment. His quick thinking saved her life.'

'A precious brother,' Lysert commented, full of appreciation.

'He was.'

'Was?' Wishart repeated.

'The people who killed Jamie Mackay killed him too,' Müller answered, 'not so long ago.'

Silenced by this unexpected news, Wishart stared at Carey Bloomfield. 'I'm very sorry,' he said at last. 'Very sorry.' He looked at Müller. 'What kind of ... creatures are they, these people you're hunting?'

'You've just heard about some of their activities. You've got what happened to Jamie Mackay. These ... criminals are playing for very high stakes. I know from bitter experience just what they are capable of. They will let nothing, and no one, stand in their way.'

'He hasn't told you the nice part about these nice people,' Carey Bloomfield said. 'They blew up his parents in their plane.'

Wishart gaped, looking at once shocked and confused. 'They *killed* your parents?'

Müller's mouth tightened. He gave a single, tiny nod. 'I was twelve at the time. They have a very long-term strategy.'

A heavy silence descended. Lysert stared at Müller as if transfixed.

'There isn't much a man can say to something like that...' Wishart began. 'I mean...' Then he stopped, words failing.

'There is nothing anyone can say,' Müller told him. 'I have long learned to live with it.'

'Well,' Wishart began after a pause, 'someone playing it by the book could say that, strictly speaking, that vehicle is evidence at a crime scene; but if "losing" it will help keep these people away from here, from Broome,

116

from anywhere near my beat, consider it done.'

'Strictly speaking,' Müller said, 'given the circumstances, the vehicle is my evidence, which I am redeploying to further help me with my investigations.'

Wishart gave a sudden, hesitant grin. 'If that isn't a Pom mouthful, I don't know what is. The vehicle will be "redeployed".'

'I thank you. "Losing" it should do more than merely keeping them out of your hair temporarily. We want them permanently away from here so however you do it, this *must* give them a completely wrong location, as far away from here as possible. But it must be done very quickly, and without its being observed.'

Wishart nodded. 'No worries.' He gave Müller a slip of paper. 'Radio frequency of my vehicle, should you need it while you're still here.'

'Thank you,' Müller said, taking it. 'When either of you get the chance,' he continued to them both, 'please tell Jack and Maggie to use the card, whenever they feel they need to. I shall be very glad to hear from them.'

'Card?' Wishart asked. 'What card?'

'They'll know,' Müller told him.

'You did not tell them that the people you were talking about are *The Semper*,' Carey Bloomfield said.

'I've frightened them enough for one day. Grogan sent us here,' Müller went on, 'be-

117

cause he obviously knows – or believes – that the Hargreaves have very important knowledge about *The Semper*. *The Semper*, somehow, may well know that too. Perhaps. They just don't know where the Hargreaves are. I've got to make certain they never find out. Mainauer got far too close for comfort.'

They were on the Great Northern Highway, heading back towards Broome. After contacting his colleagues, Wishart had remained at Woonnalla, wanting a talk with the other Lysert twin.

'And do you think they'll be alert enough to watch out for any *Semper* who might be around?'

'I hope to God they will be. They have no real idea of what they're up against, despite what I've told them. How could they? Even after all this time, I'm still not certain of the extent of what we're up against.'

'The outback is their territory,' she said, 'not *The Semper*'s. That should help.' She said this more in hope than anything else.

'For Wishart, the Lyserts, and the Hargreaves, against people like that, every little counts.'

They drove on in silence for a kilometre or so.

'You're not going to tell me, are you?' she said.

'Tell you what?'

'About what really happened to you back there at the house.'

'Nothing to tell.'

118

'Aah, yes. I just saw a pig do a barrel roll, a double loop ... Have you any idea how difficult it is for a pig to fly straight up?'

'That,' he said, 'must be sarcasm. I think I just recognized it. I felt a nip on my nose.'

Another silence fell.

But she did not give up. 'Did you notice that kitchen in there, Müller? Not as amazingly stylish as yours back in Berlin, but it runs it a close second. There's a vague similarity of taste. Now, what are the odds, do you think, of finding something like that, way out here in the outback?'

'Australia is not on another planet where the Jurassic period is just beginning. Would it surprise you to know that people, even those living in the outback, actually do have access to brochures of modern kitchens?'

'Ouch. That one did bite me on the nose.'

'Call it a draw.'

'For now,' she said ominously.

The new silence lasted a whole ten kilometres.

'Müller?'

He knew that when her voice took a rising turn at the end of a syllable, she wanted something.

'Let me guess...'

'Don't guess,' she said. She glanced at her watch. It was only just past 09.10. 'As we're done earlier than expected, the whole day's ahead of us. I thought we could do that Cable Beach thing. We can't leave Broome without doing that, at least.'

'We should leave Broome quickly,' he said. 'The longer we remain, the more likely it is that any *Semper* people who may be around will assume there's something here to interest them. I can only hope that Wishart's colleagues take his instructions to heart and make no unguarded comments to their friends, or families, about Jamie Mackay and Mainauer.'

'So it's a no, then.'

'I did not say that.'

Back at Woonnalla, Pete Lysert was slowly shaking his head as he tried to absorb what Müller had said.

'Took the wind out of my sails, I can tell you,' he said to Wishart. 'His parents dead, killed by those bastards, all those years ago. No wonder he wants their guts. I would. Kind of spoils our theory, though.'

'Why?' Wishart asked. 'He could still be related. Stranger things have happened. Still plenty of questions that need answers.'

'Yeah. But not our problem.'

'No,' Wishart agreed. 'Thank God.'

Lysert gave a quick, reflective smile. 'She's a beaut, though, that colonel. Isn't she? Sexy walk. Feet turned in a bit. I love that in a woman. And her beauty's all God-given; not some walking skeleton thanks to a plastic surgeon, and a starvation diet that makes her look like a picture from Africa. She's the real thing.'

Wishart stared at him. '*You*, were checking her out?'

'No, mate. I was checking her *and* our Berlin copper. Every time she moved, his eyes would do a quick little dance, so quick you'd miss it if you didn't look for it.'

'Well *I* missed it.'

Lysert grinned. 'He's got the hots alright.'

'Well, mister philosopher, psychoanalyst pilot and anything else, she may be a beaut, but she's a beaut with a gun, and knows how to use it. She shot the sniper – a pro hit man and a dangerous bastard – despite being scared out of her brains with those mulgas around. That took guts.'

Lysert suddenly began to sing, doing a passable imitation of Bob Marley: 'She shot the sniper, but she didn't shoot the con-stable...'

'Pete!' Wishart looked horrified. 'For God's sake, mate! That's Jamie you're singing about.'

Lysert was unrepentant. 'Yeah. The Jamie you knew? Or the Jamie I knew?'

'What do you mean?'

'Jamie had a weird sense of humour. Remember that time a bunch of us were out by Cape Leveque having a night on the beach? Jamie was out of his skull. Then suddenly, he gets very serious. "Fellas," he says. "If I ever get it out there, I want no long faces. Get some amber, go to the beach, and fill up till you chuck. I'll join you."'

'I remember,' Wishart said quietly. 'Jamie could chuck with the best.'

'Reckon he knew something was going to

happen to him soon?'

'I don't even want to think about that. Let's go find Paulie.'

'Yeah. And let's have those beers on the beach for Jamie. Reckon he'll come to join us, like he said?'

'Give us all heart attacks, mate, if he did.'

'Yeah.'

As they moved off, Wishart began to sing: 'She shot the sniper...'

Lysert joined in.

In their own way, they were trying to come to terms with what had happened to Jamie Mackay.

Müller and Carey Bloomfield were now quite some distance from the turn-off to Woonnalla.

She glanced at the car radio. 'Don't you miss your Porsche, Müller, with its fancy sound system? Or the all-road Cayenne? It would be good out here.'

'What are you really trying to say?' he asked.

'You've got all those interesting CDs...'

'If it's music you want, turn on the radio.'

'Let's see what we've got.' She turned it on, noting the station frequency display. 'It's set to six-seven-five on AM. Wonder what that is?'

'...*and that's the local Broome weather...*' a male voice was saying.

'We've got the local radio station,' she said. 'How far are we?'

'A little over an hour to go,' he replied, 'at this speed.'

They were driving at an easy pace – a steady 100kph on the sealed road.

'No rush.'

'*Last year*,' the radio host went on, '*we had a state-wide discussion over road train accidents. Some of you may remember the accident where a rear trailer lay right across both lanes of a narrow road, blocking it completely, and right on a bend. Cars coming from one direction could not see it, until too late. Luckily, in that instance no one was hurt or killed. Unfortunately, this is not always the case.*

'*So for those of you on unfamiliar roads, watch out for road trains. Be extra careful if you want to overtake. Err on the side of caution. Pull over when you see one coming. Overtake only if you can see clearly, far ahead – a kilometre should be the minimum. A road train tows a high cloud of dust, and has a powerful slipstream. And remember, the driver is towing a vehicle that is a good fifty-four metres long. He can't see you behind him...*'

'Or doesn't on purpose, I'll bet,' Carey Bloomfield muttered. 'But it's good advice,' she went on, looking at the radio to search for another channel.

' *...and for you out-of-country visitors to the outback*,' the radio host continued, '*enjoy the beautiful landscape; but treat it with respect for the environment, and for your own safety. Watch out for the wildlife, or stock. They cross the road when they feel like it, and won't wait for you to* *pass. There are plenty of road kills to prove it. Apart from death or severe injury to the animal, your vehicle can be seriously damaged, causing you to be stranded. And remember, even Aussies get lost, and sometimes die out there. Don't become another statistic...'*

'Thanks for the cheering news,' Carey Bloomfield remarked, 'even though it's sensible advice.' She felt Müller beginning to slow down.

She glanced at him. 'Hey, you don't have to slow down because of me. I was only...'

'I'm not slowing down because of you.'

'Then what...?'

'Stay down! Stay right down.'

'What the...?' But she did as he had advised. 'Müller, what's happening?'

'I'm not sure. Can you reach your gun?'

'My *gun?*'

'Can you reach it?'

'Yes, but—'

'Get it. And stay *down.*'

'You going to tell me what's going on? Or do I stay down here breathing the car mat...?'

'There's a road train up ahead.'

'A *crash?* That's spooky.'

'Not a crash as such. But it's right across the road ... It looks like a tanker of sorts. Three trailers.'

'*Blocking* it?'

'Blocking it. It seems to have jack-knifed. One trailer is diagonally across the road. We've seen just six vehicles since we've been on this section, going the other way, so traffic

124

at this time of the morning seems scarce today...'

'This is spooky. Right after that radio guy...'

'It could have been there for some time. It only came into view after the bend. We're still some distance from it.'

'Think he's radioed for help?'

'If he's genuine, I would expect so. If not, by the time whoever is out there sees into our Explorer properly, they'll see just the one person.'

'You think it's an *ambush*?'

'I won't know until we get there.'

'I'd worked that out, Müller.'

'I'm open to anything. Just be ready.'

'Shit,' she said. 'Why would any *Semper* trooper try this? They don't know where we are...'

'They're not supposed to, but you never know.'

'Could be the people who equipped Mainauer's car. They might be looking for it...'

'Perhaps. Perhaps not. Unless this is a genuine accident, it can only be a deliberate roadblock.'

'Maybe nothing to do with *The Semper*. Perhaps some enterprising guy trying his luck. You know, checking out the tourist trade. If so,' she added, 'he's got a surprise coming.' She checked that her automatic was ready for instant use.

Müller was glancing from side to side.

'What are you doing?' she demanded.

'Looking for tracks that lead on to this road.

125

If this is an ambush, there could be a back-up vehicle somewhere that might try to come round behind us.'

'Müller, if that's the case, how do they explain the truck to passing traffic? Somebody will warn the cops.'

'There's not much traffic at the moment. The six cars we saw were probably the entire morning's traffic so far, and perhaps for longer. Another one might not come for hours. If one did come, all whoever's up ahead would need to do is say he's got it under control. No need to raise an alarm. By the time anyone did report it, it will be long gone. This is not a city. This is the outback, with more square kilometres than many entire countries put together; and with a population density to match. A hundred-kilometre separation can sometimes mean a close neighbour.

'We're nearly there,' Müller went on. 'So far, no other vehicle. We've passed seven tracks; three on the left, four on the right. Still no other vehicle that I can see. There's a slight rise beyond the road train. Hard to tell if anything's hiding beyond it. Get ready.' His voice had sharpened. 'A man has just come out from somewhere behind the cab, and is waving us down. He's dressed as if he really is a truck driver. Moment of truth. When I stop, *stay* down. I won't stop too close to the road train.'

'How will I know if...?'

'You will.'

126

Müller bought the 4WD to a halt.

'What about *your* gun?' Carey Bloomfield hissed at him.

'I'll leave it on the seat as I get out. I won't move away from the car. Just to the front. I'm leaving the door slightly open.' He climbed out. 'Can I help?' she heard him call to the unseen man,

'G'day, mate,' she heard from some distance away. 'Am I glad to see you, mate. You a Pommie?'

'No. German.'

'Too many "mates",' she said to herself. 'And he doesn't sound Australian. And maybe they say "Pommie" out here; but whenever I've heard it, it's always "Pom".' She held her gun ready.

'Your English sounds just like a Pommie, mate.' The unseen man laughed at his own joke. 'We get lots of Germans out this way, but none sound like you.'

'And his laugh is not real,' Carey Bloomfield whispered.

'I get told that,' Müller said in easy, friendly tones. 'Often. So, how can I help?'

'Hydraulic loss. Suddenly, she was all over the place. As if that was not bad enough, my radio's crook. Can I use yours to call my next stop? They'll arrange some help.'

'Perhaps they say "crook" a lot too,' Carey Bloomfield said to herself. 'But it sounds all wrong.'

'Of course,' Müller said. 'Come over.' He moved back, and made a show of checking inside the car. 'He's coming over,' he said to Carey Bloomfield urgently. 'So far, he seems alone. Perhaps it's genuine.'

'The way he speaks sounds wrong.'

'You too? I thought so as well. Whatever it is, they must move quickly, in case more traffic turns up. Let's see how this goes...' He straightened, and went back to his original position at the front, a smile of helpful friendliness upon his face.

That was when he saw the other two men fan out from behind the supposedly stricken road train. They were in khaki shirts and trousers, and had guns.

'What's this?' he said in a deliberately sharp, startled voice that warned Carey Bloomfield. 'Guns? Is this a robbery?'

'Nothing for you to worry about if you're just a harmless German tourist.' The man's voice had changed considerably.

'I *am* a harmless German tourist. Who are you?'

'Federal Police. Sorry about the subterfuge with the road train.' The man was almost conversational. 'We're looking for a German, as it happens. On his own. Dangerous. Armed. A killer. We believe he is in the country on a contract.'

Müller remained calm. He even gave a short laugh. 'Well you're looking at the wrong German. I'm no contract killer.'

'A harmless tourist, as you've said.'

'Yes.'

'Then you have nothing to worry about.'

128

'No more "mate",' Carey Bloomfield said, barely whispering. '"Federal Police"? Hah.'

'Can I see some ID?' Müller asked pleasantly. 'Can't be too careful. Long, empty road. You could be anyone.'

'So could you,' the man countered. 'Tell you what – you show me your ID, and I'll show you mine.'

'My stuff's in the car. I didn't expect this.'

'Of course you didn't. Stay where you are. We'll do this together. I'm coming forward. My ... colleagues will stay back to ensure nothing goes wrong. OK?'

Müller nodded. 'Fine.'

Inside the 4WD, Carey Bloomfield got her cue, and was ready.

The man approached Müller with rapid strides, while his pals remained where they were, watchful, and seemingly ready for anything.

But they were not ready for what happened next.

The man who claimed to be Federal Police had reached Müller, but was not yet close enough to spot Carey Bloomfield.

'Let's do the ID exchange,' the man said.

'Fine,' Müller repeated, and backed towards the driver's door.

'Nothing foolish,' the man warned.

'Nothing foolish.'

'I think I'll open the door,' the man said. 'Just in case.'

'Fine,' Müller said for a third time.

The man came past Müller, yanked the

door open, and stared into the snout of Carey Bloomfield's Beretta. His eyes widened in total surprise.

'Hi,' she said. 'You've got a problem. As you can see, there's another gun on the driver's seat. It's his. If you're thinking of making the slightest of wrong moves, forget it. You don't have a chance. I'll shoot. If your friends make the slightest of wrong moves, you won't have a chance. I'll shoot. Over to you.'

The man glared at her, but remained perfectly still.

Müller moved round so that the man was now between the other two men by the road train, and himself. He reached into the car, picked up his gun, but kept it out of sight of the other men.

'Who are you again?' Müller asked mildly. 'Federal Police, is it? Do you believe him?' he asked Carey Bloomfield.

'Nope.'

'Oddly enough, neither do I.'

'Hey!' came a call from one of the other men. 'Finish it off, and let's get out of here before some nosy tourist comes along.'

The shouter sounded genuine Australian.

'Definitely not Federal Police,' Müller said. 'Impatient, too. What are you going to do?' he asked the man. 'Tell you what – call them over. Say you've found something.'

'I would,' Carey Bloomfield said, emphasizing the point with a slight movement of the Beretta.

The man gave her another glare, but he had

no choice. 'Come over here! I think you should see this.'

'We haven't the time...'

'Get the hell over here!'

They came, but warily. Something elemental within them made them over-cautious. As they drew closer, their expressions changed first to uncertainty, then to the realization that something had gone wrong.

What they did next was quite unexpected. They shot the man. They did so together. The man opened his mouth in sudden pain and astonishment as the bullets struck home. He was already dying as Müller dropped to the road, bringing up his own gun. The men had to adjust their aim, and this gave Müller precious time.

He fired at the nearest of the two.

By this time, Carey Bloomfield was out of the 4WD via the passenger side, and, like Müller, had dropped to the road. The man Müller had fired at was toppling. The other, suddenly finding his attention divided, suffered an infinitesimal hesitation as he tried to decide on his choice of target. It cost him.

Carey Bloomfield fired three rapid shots. She did not fire to wound.

The sudden spark of violence was over within less than a minute. All three men were dead.

'I guess that takes care of Cable Beach,' she said, getting to her feet.

Five

The Great Northern Highway, Western Australia

'Are they all dead?' Carey Bloomfield asked of Müller, who was checking.

'Very,' he replied as he straightened.

'Shit.'

Müller looked towards the road train. 'We should move the bodies over there, and I should move that monster off the road.'

'Shit,' she repeated. 'I've got to carry those things?'

'I could drag them. Not far to go. But that might leave blood smears.'

'I'll help,' she said without much enthusiasm. 'And how can you move that other thing? The monster truck. Can you drive it?'

'How difficult can that be? I'm taking it no more than a few metres.'

'You've got to straighten it first. That should be fun. I guess we'd better get those stiffs out of the way. It's hot enough already. Won't be long before they start to stink. The flies will love this.'

'They are all body shots. If we move quickly, there won't be much blood on the road yet ... if at all. Don't get any on you. Ready?'

'No. But let's do it.'

Taking each body by the feet and shoulders, they moved them into a clump of scrub bordering the highway, near the road train. They worked quickly, and it took less time than they expected.

'You're stronger than you look,' Müller said to her.

'Such nice things he says to a girl. Any blood on the road?'

'Just a few small patches. I doubt they will be noticed. And even if they are, people will think it's another unfortunate animal that got hit. The ground in the scrub will probably be soaked with it soon.'

'And all the crawly things will come looking. Ugh. I need to wipe my hands with a travel wipe.'

'You'd better get back to the car. I'll try moving the monster. Someone is bound to come along soon. The road's been empty long enough, even for this place.'

She went back to the 4WD, while Müller went to the road train, climbed up into the cab, and made a gruesome discovery.

The body of the real driver.

He stared at it. The man had been shot, then dumped into the bunk compartment of the cab.

'Now we know,' Müller said.

He got behind the wheel.

In the 4WD, Carey Bloomfield cleaned her hands with the travel wipe. She had considered washing them, but though there was plenty of water in the on-board supply, she chose not to waste it. Finished, she went to the passenger seat to watch Müller's efforts with the road train.

At first, there was much jerking and the hiss of brakes as he wrestled with the behemoth. Then, suddenly, it began to move smoothly. The trailers straightened out, and soon he was parking it off the road in a neat line on the edge of the highway.

'Not bad, Müller,' she said, watching with approval. 'You could almost put a carpenter's rule along it, it's so straight.'

She watched him climb out, shut the door of the cab, then cross the road to come back towards her, a strange purpose to his stride.

She frowned. 'Now what?' She followed his progress with her eyes.

'The real driver is dead,' he told her immediately in a hard voice. 'Shot. So much for the "Federal Police" trick. They must have hijacked the truck a long way from here. There's no other vehicle around.'

She fell into a thoughtful silence for some moments. 'So *The Semper* have got people in the area.'

'I'm hoping we've just got the last three,' Müller said as he got back in behind the wheel.

'What was that banging sound I heard?' she asked.

'What banging sound?'

'A sort of low ringing. Like a deep bell.'

134

'Oh, that. When I was trying to come to grips with the monster, it jolted a bit. The sound you heard came from the trailers. The fuel containers are empty. The whole contraption was lighter than normal. Made it easier for me.'

'You didn't do badly, Müller. I'm impressed. Now what's for the encore?'

'Becoming Graeme Wishart's least favourite person again. I'm going to call the frequency he'll probably wish he never gave me.'

'That will make his day.'

'Tell me about it, as you would say.'

'Yes. I do say that.'

Müller kept a straight face as he turned on the in-built HF radio, and tuned it to Wishart's frequency.

'Someone is bound to log that call,' she suggested.

'Most likely. So I'll keep it innocuous. Wishart will understand.'

Müller got the frequency and made his call.

Wishart came back immediately. 'Trouble? Over.'

'Yes. Over.'

'Where are you?'

'About an hour and a half or so from Broome.'

'I'm not far behind you. Can you wait?'

'Yes.'

'I won't be long. Out.'

'Out. He won't like what he finds,' Müller continued, as he signed off. 'But who said life was easy?'

135

'Not me.'

'Nor I.'

'According to the package we've got with this car,' she said, 'we can use the HF to make calls to any phone...'

'Ye-es...'

'Don't you want to call Pappi? See what he's got?'

'No.' Müller paused. 'Calling Pappi on this would be like taking out a flashing sign saying "Here I am". More to the point, why are you twitchy?'

She was staring at the road train, two fine perpendicular lines of a thoughtful frown faintly creasing her forehead, just above the bridge of her nose.

She did not reply.

'I got the impression,' Müller continued, 'that Wishart was not far away. We should not have too long a wait.'

'I'm worried about how come those guys knew we were coming along this route.'

'They did not. They were fishing. After their man failed to return, they made Broome their starting point, and spread their net outwards, hoping for a clue to where he had gone. For all we know, they may have already tried that "Federal Police" game on other roads. No one's going to call the police to say they'd been stopped by the police. They would have used different vehicles each time. I don't *know* this is what they have done, but it does seem a likely scenario. But people talk. Sooner or later, casual conversation will have the rumours flying around, about the federal police stopping people in this area.'

'*If* that's what they have done.'

'If,' he agreed. 'That driver just happened to be in the wrong place, at the wrong time. They probably got him either at a roadhouse when he had stopped for a break; or flagged him down with their police routine. Either way, it was very bad news for him.'

'And for his family, if he had one.'

'Yes.'

'Bastards,' Carey Bloomfield said with quiet savagery.

'*The Semper* are most certainly not saints.'

Another silence descended as they waited for Wishart to arrive.

Müller stared along the road towards where he had parked the road train. A slight heat shimmer gave the road surface an intermittent mirroring. He stared into the distance, mind travelling back to when he was twelve and had received the news of his parents' crash. He felt again the strange numbness that had gripped his entire body. He remembered how his body had vibrated uncontrollably, when a tearful Aunt Isolde had broken the awful news. His shaking had been so violent that when she had embraced him to give him comfort, rather than absorbing the shaking, her own body had been assailed by it. Then he had become so still, she had thought he had fainted. He had, she told him years later, been as rigid as a statue; but had been so remarkably controlled it had worried and frightened her.

A *pfftt* sound dragged him away from his memories.

Curious, he looked to his left, in the direction of the sound. Carey Bloomfield had grabbed at the calf of her left leg, studied it without enthusiasm, and had made the sound.

'What are you doing?' he asked.

She jumped as if caught stealing sweets.

'Müller!' she said crossly. 'Don't sneak!'

'How can I "sneak"? I am sitting right next to you.'

After a long second she said, with marked reluctance, 'My legs are too big.'

He gave this some serious thought. The shorts she wore showed them in all their glory. Her legs were the most perfect he had ever seen; curves in all the right places, full, straight, nicely rounded, not wretchedly skinny, begging to be stroked. The indentations behind her knees were centres of eroticism, as were the soft movements of muscles beneath the skin when she walked.

To Müller, the way she walked was a thing of wonder.

'Your legs,' he said, 'are not big. May I say something?' he added.

'And if I say no?'

'I won't.'

She wanted to say no, but a surge of contrariness won. 'Say it.'

'You are a lieutenant-colonel in the US Air Force. In the time that I have known you, you have shown more balls – if you'll pardon the expression – than some men I could mention—'

'Are you saying I'm *manly?*'

This was a dangerous question that needed a carefully thought-out answer, he told himself.

'Miss Bloomfield, do belt up and let me finish. You are not some vacant-brained, emaciated bimboid who needs a couple of centuries in front of a mirror to become sufficiently pleased with herself, before displaying what she believes is her perfect presence to the world. You are a supremely confident woman, in all the best possible ways. Don't spoil it. Now I'll belt up.'

'Allow me to be neurotic about my body,' she said, after spending several minutes considering what he had just told her. 'It's a woman thing.'

'It's a foolish thing.'

She was saved from having to make a comment as Müller, who had been glancing in his side mirror at infrequent intervals, now spotted a tiny speck rounding the distant bend.

'Wishart must have been quite close,' he said, 'and has been doing some speeding. He's in the mirror. It's roughly only twenty minutes since we spoke.'

She opened her door slightly to look back. The heat had increased perceptibly during the short time they had been waiting. It launched itself into the cool of the air-conditioned Explorer.

'He is burning the rubber,' she agreed, shutting the door again. 'He'll have seen the road train and be wondering what happened.'

'Nothing he could be thinking is going to prepare him for this.'

'Now we can stop worrying about curious traffic. They'll see the police car and keep right on going, glad it isn't them.'

'Police do have that effect.'

'Are you trying not to smile when you say that, Müller?'

'Would I?'

'Yes. You would. And we haven't finished that little talk.'

'I thought we had.'

The arrival of Wishart's car at that moment stifled her response. She watched as Wishart pulled across the road to park opposite, facing the wrong way, but well into the side of the road – almost into the bushes – so as not to obstruct any traffic that might happen along. He parked a few metres from the road train. The lights of the patrol vehicle began to flash, giving warning for long distances in both directions.

'Saved by the bell again, Müller,' she said. 'This time it's called Wishart.'

'I'm not sure the word "saved" will be on his mind when he hears what I've got to say.' Müller began to climb out as he saw Wishart leave the police 4WD. 'Coming?'

'I'll sit here for a while and watch the fun.'

'As you wish.'

He shut the door and walked towards

Wishart. They met about ten metres away from the Explorer.

'You made good time,' Müller greeted him.

'I'd finished making the arrangements with the Lyserts, so headed back. Paulie's going to drive the sniper's vehicle, with the body, to an area not far from our border with the Northern Territory. That's some good distance from Woonnalla. Hundreds of kilometres. They're doing it tonight. If anybody knows the bush, they do. A relative the Lyserts trust will follow in another vehicle to drive Paulie back to Woonnalla.' Wishart glanced towards the road train. 'That the trouble?'

'Part of it.'

'Part? And the other?' Wishart had a wary look in his eyes.

Müller did not waste time preparing him. 'Four bodies.'

Wishart's eyes nearly popped. *'Four...'* He stopped. 'Four *bodies?*'

He suddenly began to look like a man with the weight of the world upon his shoulders and, though he did not say it out loud, the *why me* was implicit in his eyes.

'Who's responsible?' he asked, seeming to fear the answer.

'We are ... for two of them.'

Wishart darted a glance at the passenger seat of the 4WD, where Carey Bloomfield was sitting.

'She shot one, and you the other?'

Müller nodded. 'Yes. They are responsible for the other two bodies. One of their own,

141

and the driver of the road train.'

Wishart sighed. 'Tell me.'

Müller gave him a detailed account of what had occurred. Wishart said nothing whatsoever while Müller spoke – not even to ask a single question – as they walked to where Müller and Carey Bloomfield had put the bodies.

Wishart looked at each of the corpses expressionlessly. The flies were having a field day.

'Jeez,' Wishart uttered softly when Müller had finished.

He said nothing more as they went round to the cab of the road train. He climbed in to look at the body of the driver, then got out quickly.

'You parked it well,' he said to Müller. 'We won't be able to hide this one,' he added.

'No need. In fact, publicize it.'

Wishart stared at him. 'What? But I thought...'

'If those three are the cell I suggested earlier, the people who sent them should know they've been caught ... but not, of course, by Miss Bloomfield and me.'

'Three criminals,' Wishart began, almost to himself, 'hijack a road train for reasons as yet unknown. They kill the driver, are surprised by a police patrol. On being approached, they open fire. The police return fire. Men killed. Body of driver discovered. That kind of thing?'

'Very close.'

'They shot their own man,' Wishart continued in wonder. 'Why?'

'Perhaps they hated him and took their chance to get rid of him. But I suspect the real reason was efficiency. They knew something had gone wrong. They did not want to risk the possibility that he might talk. They would have killed us as well, had they been given the chance.'

'No witnesses.'

'Exactly. That's how these people work. Their own members are equally expedient in certain circumstances.'

Wishart's mouth turned down. 'Honour among thieves.' He glanced back at Carey Bloomfield, who continued to remain in the Explorer. 'How was she, when you carried the bodies?'

'She did not like the idea, but she coped.'

'Strange. The way she can use a gun ... you'd have thought...'

'Not necessarily. She has an aversion ... again, because of her brother. She went against orders to rescue him after he had been kidnapped in a Middle Eastern country, by the same people who are after the Hargreaves. She found him, but he had been tortured. Torture is horrific enough, but in that case, it had been particularly sick. He was near death.' Müller paused. 'He'd been peeled alive—'

'*Jeezus!*' Wishart seemed ready to vomit.

'The brother begged her to kill him. He was virtually a corpse. One can only imagine his

143

suffering, and what it's done to her. She keeps that image hidden very deep, somewhere within her consciousness.'

'Poor kid,' Wishart said with genuine sympathy.

'She went hunting, and followed his tracks to Germany. It took her some time, but she ran him to ground. That was how we first met, although I had no idea of her reasons at the time. The same man tried to kill me, and my aunt. But we got him.'

Wishart again took a quick look at the Explorer. 'She actually killed him?'

'Yes. We both did. We fired at the same time.'

'Remind me not to get on her wrong side.'

There was a smile in Müller's voice as he said, 'She can be determined when the mood takes her.'

'This man who tried to kill you ... under orders?'

'Most definitely.'

Wishart stared at him. 'What did you do to these people?'

'I'm the son of the parents they killed. That's enough of a reason. The irony of it is that I had no idea then, even as a policeman, that my parents had not died in an accident as I had believed all those years. I was still none the wiser after we shot the skin-peeler. In trying to eliminate me because I might have known something – perhaps information my parents had left for me – they got my interest. Otherwise, I might have still been

144

living in blissful ignorance.'

'I was about to say it's lucky, because that brought them into the open ... but that's not what I would call luck.'

'No,' Müller said in a voice that carried too many bad memories. 'It isn't.'

Wishart looked at the road train. 'And now, some of these bastards are operating in my territory.'

'No longer – at least for those in the bushes.'

'Too right. Time I called up the cavalry,' Wishart continued. 'Got to get this all cleaned up. You two should not be here when they arrive. Less to explain. They'll come by plane and chopper. An hour by road from Broome is no distance by air. Hang a right at the main junction, and go via Derby for long enough, then turn back, so that you seem to be coming from there to Broome,' Wishart advised. 'Just in case anyone's interested in your movements. Got enough for the extra mileage?'

Müller nodded. 'Plenty, plus spare.'

'Good. You'd be surprised how many people get into situations where they run out of juice, or water. Normally sensible people too, some of them.'

'I would not be surprised,' Müller said. 'Graeme,' he continued, 'we'll be on our way, and...'

'Do you plan to come down under again?'

'I'd like to spend at least six months having a look around, if I can find the time. I should think it really needs about two years, or more.'

'It takes a lifetime,' Wishart said, 'to know this country properly. Perhaps not even then.'

Müller nodded. 'I agree.'

'Well, whenever you decide to come back, do it as a tourist, not as a copper. Please.' Wishart grinned as he said that, and held out a hand. 'Watch yourself, mate,' he said as they shook hands. 'Are we likely to meet again before you leave for Germany?'

'That depends on two things: the Hargreaves, and the time I have available to wait for them. As things look, I may well have to go back without seeing them, and can only hope they will make contact. Thank you for the support.'

A smile lurked about Wishart's lips. 'I'm "co-operating".' Then, impulsively, he gave Müller a friendly pat on the shoulder.

They began walking back towards the Explorer. As they got there, Carey Bloomfield opened her door and climbed out.

'Been busy, I see,' Wishart said to her.

'They didn't leave us much choice.'

Wishart nodded, and again held out his hand. 'It's been a pleasure knowing you. But I would have preferred different circumstances.'

'So would I,' she said as they shook hands.

'Jens says he plans to come back for a longish stay.'

She gave Müller an unfathomable look. 'Oh ... does he?'

'I hope you'll be with him.'

'Is that an invitation?'

146

'It is – but as a "touring" visitor. Please. I've already told him that.'

'Then I'll be down. No worries.'

'No worries,' Wishart confirmed with a ghost of a smile. 'Now, the two of you, make yourselves scarce before the crowd arrives.'

As they drove off, Carey Bloomfield looked back to see Wishart standing by his vehicle, giving them a parting wave.

'He looks so lonely in all this,' she remarked as she looked forwards again. 'Yet at the same time he seems part of it. Does that make any sense?'

Müller gave a slight nod. 'It does.'

She waited for some time before posing the question that had been on her mind. They had turned right, and on to the road north-wards, for Derby.

'That trip you plan...' she began in a voice so without guile that it was like sugar-coated poison.

'Yes?'

'Without me?'

'With you.'

She digested that. 'You just saved your bacon, mister.'

'I'm relieved to hear it.'

'I'll join you on one condition.'

'Which is?'

'We do Cable Beach.'

'We do Cable Beach,' he agreed.

'Don't grit your teeth so hard, Müller. You'll kill your fillings.'

'I don't have fillings.'

147

She stared at him. 'You've got to be kidding me.'

'I kid you not.'

'God,' she said. 'People can hate people for less ... Hey, listen to this...'

They had left the local radio station on, but at a low volume. She turned it up.

'...*the Great Northern Highway*,' the announcer was saying. '*Some breaking news. Sometime this morning, police foiled a hijack attempt. Three men tried to hijack a road train, but were surprised by police officers on routine patrol. The men discharged firearms at the officers when confronted. Fire was returned. Thankfully, no officers were hit, but the would-be hijackers were shot dead.*

'*Sadly, they had already murdered the driver of the road train, in their failed attempt. His identity is being withheld until his family have been notified. The identities of the would-be hijackers are also being withheld while further investigation into this incident continues. Reasons for the hijack attempt are so far unclear. More on this as we get it. Now we return you to...*'

She lowered the volume. 'Graeme has fed them a neat story.'

'Yes. I thought so myself. He's handled it well. And it is basically true...'

'Except that we were the "police officers".'

'I am one.'

'And I am. Kind of.'

'So it is a basically true story. When *The Semper* eventually get to know of this,' Müller went on, 'and Mainauer's body, and his car,

148

are eventually found hundreds of kilometres away from where he started, they'll have second thoughts about the Hargreaves being in this area.'

'Let's hope so.'

Several minutes passed in silence as they continued towards Derby.

'Müller?'

'Yes?'

'If you ever want to talk to me about something that's ... bothering you, I'm here to listen. Just so you know.'

He touched her shoulder briefly. 'Thank you. I'll remember that.'

He did not look at her, not wanting her to see the sadness of the years which at that moment, he knew, had come into his eyes.

A short while later, he began to slow down. 'I think I should call Pappi.'

He pulled off the road and stopped the car. Since leaving Wishart and turning on to the Derby road, the first car they had seen was coming towards them. A couple with two children in a Land Rover went past. All four occupants waved at them. Carey Bloomfield waved back.

'Will it be secure enough, calling from here instead of waiting for him to call you?'

Müller's mobile phone had its own autonomous secure capabilities. Though not as fully effective when calling an unsecure phone, it was still able to partially block intercepts.

'It will be a very short call.' Müller turned the engine off and got out the mobile. 'He won't thank me for this. It's ten past four in the morning where he is.'

'You have a habit of calling people at all the wrong hours, Müller. I remember a call to Annandale. Let me see … it was roughly the same kind of time…'

'Did I do that?' Müller did not sound repentant.

'You did do that.'

'Bad habit,' he said, and called Pappenheim.

Pappenheim answered so quickly, it was doubtful that he had been asleep.

'I'll make it short,' Müller began. 'Are the colleagues still in the south?'

'They are.'

'Tell them their holidays have been extended.'

'Will do. I'm assuming we'll talk later.'

'We shall.'

'I'll call you.'

'Yes,' Müller said. 'Now get some sleep.'

'I'm talking to you in my sleep.'

Müller gave a fleeting smile as they ended the call together.

'Very cryptic, Müller,' Carey Bloomfield said. 'What does it mean?

'I've asked Pappi to extend the stay of two colleagues from the Ready Group, who are down at Aunt Isolde's. They've already been there for a few days, and are well armed. They are highly professional. I trust them to do the job, if need be.'

'Bodyguards?'

Müller nodded. 'Keeping ahead of *The Semper*. They will not be pleased when they get the news about what has happened down here. They might have another try at Aunt Isolde, just to get at me. I would not put it past them.'

He restarted the Explorer and moved back on to the road, keeping to an unhurried pace. They left the radio on, in case there was more news about the hijack.

Half an hour after the call to Pappenheim, Carey Bloomfield said, 'Listen. Something's coming in.' She raised the volume.

But it was not about the hijack.

'This is a special request,' the radio voice was saying. *'Maeve is from Ireland, and has been on a three-month stay at Lombadina, doing some wonderful work out there. She's returning to Ireland today, and her many friends are going to miss her. Now, let me tell you something about this song...'*

'Should I turn it back down?' Carey Bloomfield suggested.

'No, leave it. I'm intrigued by this little story. Unless you...'

'No, no. I'm OK with it. I'm kind of curious too.'

'...so when I was a kid,' the announcer's reminiscence continued, *'my mum played it to me. She loved that song – still does – and so do I. In fact, I grew to love it so much, I play it to my boy of five. It's the kind of song that's a heart-breaker; unbearably sad, yet at the same time absolutely great. It is a song that transcends*

151

generations – as any great song should. It grabs you by the throat, and does not let go. You play a song like this to someone you truly love.

'Maeve, your friends must have great love for you. I hope you won't mind sharing this song with me, because I'm just going to mellow out, and enjoy it. I know those who are driving you to Broome airport have got the radio turned on. Have a good journey home, and come back soon. Now I've blabbed long enough to make you chuck, so here's the song. James Taylor's ... "Fire and Rain". Enjoy.'

Müller suddenly swerved to the side of the road, stopped, and slowly put his head on the wheel as the eviscerating song began.

Carey Bloomfield was alarmed. 'Müller! You OK?'

He swallowed hard. 'I'm ... I'm fine.' He did not look at her. He took a deep intake of breath. 'Look, would you mind driving?'

Even more alarmed, she said, 'Of course not.'

She got out of her seat quickly as Müller climbed out.

He shut the door, went round to the other side of the Explorer, squatted down on his heels, and leaned against its warm side, head down. There was not even a breeze, and the road at that moment was free of traffic. It was as if it was the end of time, and they were all alone in the wilderness. The ribbon of sealed road was like a path that came from nowhere, to lead nowhere.

She looked down at him. 'Jesus, Müller.

You're white as a sheet. You're scaring me! What's wrong?'

'Nothing for you to worry about.' He did not look up. 'It's ... it's the song. My father really liked it. He played it often. I grew to like it, but without really understanding its meaning at the time. On the night before my parents made their last flight, he played it to me. I remember thinking how sad he looked. He must have known then that they might not be coming back. After the crash, I never played that song again. Now here, in the outback, at this time, there it is...'

She began to reach into the Explorer. 'I'll turn it off—'

'No. Leave it. Let it run through. I owe them that.'

He remained in the same head-down, squatting position, leaning against the 4WD, as the song continued.

Leaving the door open, she slowly lowered herself close to him and, after a moment's hesitation, stroked his back gently.

Then she rested her forehead against his shoulder.

The haunting words and music of 'Fire and Rain' flowed over them in the heat of the outback. For that instant it seemed that time belonged to them.

Carey Bloomfield had been driving for about an hour. The time had passed in almost complete silence and, in the passenger seat, Müller was preoccupied with his thoughts.

She did not intrude upon them.

About ten minutes later, a small clearing in the red earth that bordered the road came into view.

'We've gone far enough towards Derby,' Müller said. 'Stop there, turn round, and we'll head back to Broome.'

'OK.'

There was no traffic in either direction. She stopped, reversed into the clearing, then turned back the way they had come.

They had continued to leave the radio on, again with the volume turned down, but nothing more had been said about what had occurred on the Great Northern.

Then a new voice – female this time – came on.

'*We have some more on that hijack attempt...*'

Müller reached forward to increase the volume.

'*According to police reports,*' the voice on the radio continued, '*it would seem that this incident is rather more than it at first appeared to be. The hijack attempt may have been a mistake – a plan gone wrong, perhaps. Not that this helps the unfortunate driver of the road train, or his family. Two of the criminals were Australian, both suspected by the Federal Police of being implicated in illegal arms sales – including explosives – to certain Asian countries, though there has never been sufficient hard proof to obtain solid convictions. Well, they won't need it now.*

'*The last member of the trio was not an Australian citizen. His nationality is currently being*

154

withheld. Delicate diplomatic issues, perhaps. However, the police have released an intriguing fact: it would seem that the non-Australian was shot dead by his own comrades. Quarrel among thieves? This, of course, brings into question the mysterious killing of Senior Constable Mackay, a much-liked officer. The police have not released details of any possible suspect. Is there a link between the hijack and Jamie Mackay's death? Only time will tell, as they say. This has all the makings of a major national – and perhaps even international – story. Stay tuned. We'll keep you updated.

'And now to more pleasant matters. Those of you who were listening earlier may have heard Jim Raeburn's message to Maeve, who is returning to Ireland today. Well, Maeve kindly rang to thank Jim for the nice things he said. Jim's off for the moment, Maeve, but we'll pass it on. I am certain he will appreciate the sentiment. Just to let you know, Maeve, I love that song too. A real choker, isn't it? You have a good journey, and we all hope to see you again. What a lovely person...'

Müller turned down the volume. 'That should set some cats among the pigeons.'

'What guesses on the nationality of the non-Australian?'

'*The Semper* have been using international contacts for years. Remember where your own brother was taken. This man could have come from anywhere in Europe, or—'

'The States.'

He nodded. 'Or the States.'

★   ★   ★

155

At roughly the same moment in time, other things were happening elsewhere that would eventually impinge upon Müller and Bloomfield.

On the outskirts of Berlin, the phone rang in retired General Sternbach's bedroom. The vast mansion, though modernized, was furnished and decorated in a way that betrayed its heritage. A medieval baron would have felt at home.

The general picked up the phone at the second ring, and glanced at his bedside clock. It was 05.40.

'It has gone very wrong down there,' the caller said without preamble.

'How?'

'Three down. It's all over their national news. Hardly low profile. We don't need such exposure. Still no news from the other?'

'No.'

'It does not look good. Those three went out of control. A citizen was killed. And we have a man missing. This will generate unwelcome interest. I need not remind you that we must avoid this at all costs.'

'No. You need not remind me.'

There was an icy pause. 'I am not apportioning blame.' The unspoken 'yet' hung in the air.

'I'm happy to hear it.'

'Then there is Müller...'

'The carrot has been offered,' the general reminded his caller.

'And if refused?'

'There is still the stick,' the general said in a cold voice.

The call was ended without pleasantries.

The general calmly went back to his interrupted sleep.

At a place that was not in Germany, someone asked a question.

'How much did you get?'

'Very little. His phone has autonomous defences. I'll play what we've got.'

The speaker played back the recent recording. Only random words from Müller and Pappenheim's entire conversation had been picked up.

'Can we do anything with this?'

'If you want my honest opinion ... no. These words are too random. We have no suggestion of a chronological pattern.'

'Can you string together a recognizable sentence with what you've got?'

'A snowball on a hot day would turn into an icicle first.'

'Then do better than the snowball, damn it.'

Müller and Carey Bloomfield found Wishart's patrol vehicle waiting, parked by their hotel. Wishart himself was nowhere to be seen.

'That was a short goodbye,' Müller said as he climbed out. Then he saw Wishart approaching as Carey Bloomfield got out from behind the wheel.

'Thought you'd seen the last of me?' Wishart greeted them as he came up.

'I always expect the unexpected,' Müller told him, expression watchful.

'We heard the radio,' Carey Bloomfield said. 'That was good stuff.'

Wishart looked pleased, but a slight frown creased his forehead. 'Yeah. It wasn't bad. The Federal boys have got involved now, of course. I'll soon be edged out ... but I have some news I thought you'd want to hear. Your hotel room?'

Müller nodded. 'Let's go.'

In Müller's suite, Wishart got straight to the point. 'You've heard about the two Aussies. Well-known villains who managed to remain – in strict legal terms – "clean". They were like Teflon; nothing stuck. The nastiest of the two was Eddie Adelmann – two "n"s—'

'He's from *Germany*?' Müller interrupted.

'If you want to stretch it to 1830,' came the dry return. 'The first Adelmann came to Oz in that year, and started as a digger. Removed one 'n' to change the surname to Adelman – perhaps to make it more "English". He made a fortune, and lost it – twice. His son got tired of going from rags to riches and back, and decided to take what he could not make. The son became a bushranger. Successful, too. Then he got caught, and was lucky not to be hanged. He hadn't killed anyone during his time as an outlaw. Prison changed him. He kept to the straight and narrow, and actually made it rich – legally. By the time Eddie came along, there was a good family business running.

'Then Eddie changed everything. The business branched out into "consultancy", which covers many sins. Eddie was making *real* money, *big* money. Suddenly, he became very interested in his German roots. He put the "n" back and reverted to Adelmann. The Federal crew got wind of illegal arms dealing, slush money and the rest, went sniffing, and came up with nothing. Rumours floated around that Eddie was not shy of even doing some killing himself. But, as I've said, nothing stuck. The Federals have lost at least two good agents trying to find something concrete to pin on those two. One of the officers went down in Bali. So they will shed no tears that those two are dead...'

'Do they know we were the ones who shot them?' Carey Bloomfield asked.

Wishart gave them each a speculative look. 'The interesting thing was that they were not interested in knowing. No officer around here uses your kind of gun,' he continued, 'but they were not interested in the bullets found in those two. Whoever's watching your back, Jens, is doing a good job. Your names never came up. The bullets in the third man proved he was shot by his own mates. And here it gets even more interesting.' He looked at Carey Bloomfield. 'The third man is American. Despite the fake Federal ID, and no further identification on him, it did not take long to match him with a photograph. Even out here,' he added drily, 'we do have the Net, and access to some useful databases.'

'So who was he?' she asked, curiosity rising.

'Well, that's just it,' Wishart answered. 'All we were allowed to know was that he was American. Then the door closed.'

She stared at him. *'What?'*

'Not even the Federals were allowed further access.'

'Müller?' she began, still looking at Wishart in astonishment. 'What do you think?'

'You already know what I think,' he replied.

'I'll not ask what he means,' Wishart said to Carey Bloomfield.

'Don't ask,' she said.

Wishart gave a world-weary sigh. 'I had that feeling.'

'How many Federal officers have come?' Müller asked Wishart.

'Two.'

'They were quick getting here. Were they already in the area?'

Wishart shook his head. 'Not in Broome, but – and here's the joker – they were already chasing those fellas, regarding the illegal arms business. As it turns out, they were down in Carnarvon on the trail of our pals. They'd picked up some info that they were headed this way. It was old info, but you can't have everything. The bastards were already here, even before you were in Australia. They and their American mate were here to fix things for our sniper.'

Müller nodded. 'I'm sure of it.'

160

'So while you and Carey were sending them where they belong, the Federals were in the air, on their way to Broome, but not expecting luck in finding them.'

'A fishing expedition.'

'Too right. But see what they caught in the end. As I said, they're almost jumping for joy. And to tell you the truth, knowing that these bastards – with their big houses and fast boats paid for with their dirty business deals – arranged for the gun that killed Jamie Mackay, I'm not sorry you offed them. Unfortunately,' Wishart added with a wry smile, 'I'm going to be knee-deep in more of my Federal colleagues before long.'

'What will you do now, about the sniper's body and his vehicle?'

Wishart grinned. 'Long gone.'

'You're kidding,' Carey Bloomfield said.

'Paul Lysert was not far behind me when you left the road train. He made very good time to Broome. So, while you were on your detour to Derby, he picked up the body and vehicle, and was away before the Federal crew got here. A relative came for his own 4WD. I hope you keep your word, Jens, about watching my back, or I'll be so deep in it, I'll wish I was a croc's breakfast.'

'I never break my word.'

Wishart's smile was now sheepish. 'Didn't think it was something you went in for.' He heaved himself off one of the armchairs he'd been sitting in. 'When do you plan to leave?'

'Earliest practical flight tomorrow. The

161

Hargreaves won't return as long as we're here. I am certain of that; and things are happening in Berlin that require my attention.'

Wishart held out a hand. 'Well ... a second goodbye.' They shook hands. 'Enjoy what's left of the day. Have a little walkabout. Go down to the beach and watch the ocean, take in the sunset, and forget all this stuff for a little while.'

'It's good advice,' Müller agreed.

Wishart made no move to go. 'If you plan a dinner away from here,' he said, 'there's a nice place where they serve fresh seafood. Close to the police station, in fact. And no, I'm not moonlighting as a publicity agent,' he finished in a dry voice.

'If you want excellent food at reasonable prices, go where the locals go, and forget the tourist traps, is that what you mean?'

'You know the trick,' Wishart said. 'I've had people tell me they hate Broome – too much commercialism, too many drunks at the bad end of town. As a copper, I know all about the drunks. But I think these people were looking for Hawaii, or the Seychelles, and ended up in the wrong place. I know people who hate London, New York, Paris, or the south of France...' Wishart had a reflective smile on. 'I, for example, love the top of Norway...'

'You've done the Aussie pilgrimage to Europe?' Müller said.

'Oh yeah. I was not immune.' He grinned. 'I love those fjords they have up there. So cool. I reckon because I'm from down under, the top end of the world fascinates me. Sometimes, we find what we're looking for.' The reflective look was back. 'You take Jack and Maggie Hargreaves ... when they first came to Woonnalla, it was not just a place God forgot. It looked like He'd given it a good kicking, and buried it as well. Well, you've seen what they've done with it. Turned it into Eden. Interesting people, Jack and Maggie. They've got their special place too. When the mood takes them, they fly out to Cape Leveque, just to sit on the beach and stare at the ocean.' Wishart paused, then turned to Carey Bloomfield. 'Carey, you make sure this fella brings you back.'

'Count on it,' she said as they shook hands warmly.

Wishart gave Müller a knowing look. 'I think I'd listen, if I were you.'

'I'm duly warned,' Müller said with a straight face.

'You'll just be missing our festival – the Shinju Matsuri and the festival markets. People from all over Oz and beyond come. Even the coppers have fun. Sometimes.' Wishart gave a quick grin, and jammed his bush hat back on.

'Perhaps another time,' Müller said.

'Yeah, well...' Wishart cleared his throat. 'Get into some Broome-time. You two watch yourselves.'

'You take your own advice as well, Graeme,' Carey Bloomfield said, a fond look in her eyes. 'You'd better be around next time we're here.'

'I'll be,' he promised. 'I must. I'd hate you to be mad at me.'

'You remember that.'

Müller went over to open the door for him. Wishart seemed reluctant to leave.

'Get out of here, Wishart,' Carey Bloomfield said with unexpected gentleness.

'Yeah.' With a quick nod at Müller, Wishart went out.

'Two things are pinging at me,' Carey Bloomfield said as Müller shut the door behind Wishart. 'I get the feeling that he's getting to like us a little.'

'Under the circumstances, I consider that a bonus. And the second?'

'That little talk about liking or hating some place was a cover for real information.'

'The Hargreaves and Cape Leveque?'

She nodded. 'No reason for him to tell us, unless he wanted us – *you*, Müller – to know where to look. I'd say he just gave you a present. His way of telling you he trusts you with the information.'

Müller went into another of his long, thoughtful moments, looking out beyond the verandah, and towards the ocean.

'The problem is,' he said at last, 'they won't return before I go back to Berlin. Not this time.'

'But?'

Müller looked back at her. 'An unannounced return to Broome, then to Cape Leveque,

164

might bear fruit. That was his real message.'

'Will you do this sooner? Or later?'

'Sooner, rather than later.'

'Do I get to come?' she asked.

'Do you want to?'

'You try and stop me.' There was a warning look in Carey Bloomfield's eye as she said this. 'Well, Müller?' she went on. 'What *do* we do with the rest of the day? It's just after three.'

'We'll do as the man suggested – do a walkabout, or a drive about, around Broome. Enjoy the time, for tomorrow—'

'We leave, as the man said.'

'He said something else, but I do understand. We can check the beach – but *no* camel ride...'

'No camel ride. I've got your word on that for another time – which you'd better keep, mister.'

'I would not dare break it.'

'Smart.'

Six

In his suite in Broome, Müller had a local map opened out on the floor.

'How about Gantheaume Point?' he suggested to Carey Bloomfield. 'Then we head back, find that place Graeme Wishart recommended, have dinner, gorge ourselves on seafood, and watch the sunset.'

'Sounds OK to me.'

Müller refolded the map, leaving the section with Gantheaume Point open, ready for quick perusal. The map had a panel full of information about the general Broome area.

'It's only six kilometres away. Let's see what that part of the world is like, then we return for that long, relaxed dinner. Doing Wishart's "Broome-time".'

'You've got a customer.'

'Keep your gun with you. Better to have it and not need it. And unlikely as it may be...'

'Needing it but not having it would be shit.'

'Graphically put, but essentially correct.'

'Müller?'

'Yes?'

'"Graphically put, but essentially correct"?'

He looked at her, vaguely expectant.

'Oh, forget it,' she said.

166

* * *

In the place that was not Berlin, a man spoke.

'So, what have you got of that call between Müller and Pappenheim?'

'I've put each line in the order in which it was spoken,' came the reply. 'Bear in mind that many of the words are missing. This is a first example, which may be well off the mark. It's...'

'Let's hear it.'

'Very well.' There was the barest suggestion of resignation in the voice as the second man tapped on his computer keyboard. 'Take a look at the monitor. A green dash represents a clean word. Yellow, a corrupted one. Red, one that is missing completely and could not be grabbed.'

'...*short*,' came Müller's voice, '...*still ... south*?'

The man at the computer paused the recording. 'Four words missing before "short". Three before "still", and two before "south". Then Pappenheim answers with just two words, but they're missing, as you can see. We can assume he answered the question either with a negative, or a positive ... or that he didn't know. Then we have this next.'

The recording continued.

'... *them ... holidays ... extended*.'

The man paused the recording again. 'He says "them", so ... people on holiday? If so, they're somewhere in the south, on extended holidays. But where south? There's a whole planet to choose from. I'll run the next

167

section without stopping. Easy to tell who's speaking in each case.'

He ran the continuation.

'...*do ... assming ... later.*'

'*... ...*'

'*I'll ... you.*'

'*Yes ... get some...*'

'*I'm ... you ... my...*'

'That's it,' the man at the computer said. 'As you've heard, where the words are missing, there's an alternating pattern of total silence, and heavy distortion – "assming" is distorted, but has to be "assuming". So we've got "... *do ... assuming ... later*". Do what, assuming later? If that's what it means, which I doubt.'

'Can't you fill in the blanks and see what turns up?'

'You mean like this?' The man tapped at the keyboard.

'*Yes, I'll get some food tomorrow*' appeared on the screen.

'Are you trying to be funny?'

'In present company? Not a chance. Just trying to show you how we could be here for God knows how long, trying to create sentences that would match exactly what was said. By the time we did that – if at all – Müller will have moved on, and will be getting closer.'

'Have more faith.'

'Faith does not pay the rent.'

'Another attempt to be funny?'

'I don't flog dead horses. Look. We could

feed this into any computer, as powerful as you could wish for. It would give us choices in the hundreds of thousands – millions ... who knows – and still not come up with the right conversation...'

'It might get close enough.'

'Alright. Will you take the responsibility for sending in, as fact, a report based on a computer probability?'

'No.'

'As I thought. This recording is useless for our purposes; but feel free to use it, if you'd like. I'll try to see what more I can get out of this take; but I'm not going to say it's a factual representation. If you want my advice – which you're free to reject – I would suggest waiting for the next call between those two that we manage to tap into. That might yield something we can add to what we've just got.'

A stony silence greeted this.

'Life's a bitch,' the one at the computer said.

'You'll never guess what I'd like to do at this moment.'

'Surprise me,' Carey Bloomfield encouraged.

Müller gave her a strange look. 'I have a yen to play the Hammond.'

She took a long pause, as she pointedly glanced out at the passing scenery. 'This red earth is something ... The Hammond,' she went on. 'You have a "yen". For one of the two you've got back home in Wilmersdorf? Or are we going Hammond-hunting later in the Broome nightclubs, to see if we can find one?'

Deliberately ignoring her pointed glance, and the coated bite of her words, he said, 'One of the two. The B3. The original, beautiful monster.'

'Hold on, there's a weird light in your eyes. I'll admit I like the sound, but it's still just an instrument, Müller.' She was looking at him as though searching for evidence of some kind of terminal affliction.

'It's much more than that.' He warmed to this theme. 'I have a yen to play "Walk on the Wild Side". The Jimmy Smith version.'

She was still looking at him, but her eyes had widened slightly. 'Now that *is* a surprise. My dad is crazy about that recording. You really do worry me at times, Müller. You like music my *dad* likes?'

'I have an eclectic taste in music. It is inevitable that others will like some of the music I like.'

'I just knew that answer was coming.'

'You do not like Jimmy Smith's playing?'

'Surprise, Müller. I do. Because of my dad.'

'So even you like his taste in music.'

'Aah ... shaddup.'

Müller smiled to himself.

A few moments of silence passed. 'Müller?'

'Mmm?'

They were heading south along the Broome Peninsula, on the unsealed road to Gantheaume Point, with Müller at the wheel. The road seemed more of a challenge than the one that led to Woonnalla; most likely because of more usage. They bumped along, the ubiquitous red dust boiling in their wake. Even so, Müller thought the red swathe cutting through the landscape was in itself a spectacular portrait.

'God,' Carey Bloomfield said, momentarily shelving the question she had been about to ask. 'Will you look at that?'

'That' was a hardy cyclist with backpack, on a be-panniered bicycle, heading the other way. There were a lot of stickers on the bike, marking the places he had been to.

Müller gave him as wide a berth as possible as they passed.

The cyclist, head down against the whirling dust, lifted a hand briefly in thanks.

'I'd hate to think how much dust he eats on that bike,' Carey Bloomfield said, glancing round to follow the determined cyclist's progress. 'Poor guy. Wonder where he's headed.'

'Probably just back to Broome.'

'Yeah ... But did you see those stickers? The bike was covered in them. He's been to lots of places on that thing. Better him than me,' she added. 'That thing Jimmy Smith does...' She paused, as if unsure of how to phrase what she was about to ask. She glanced round again to look at the cyclist who was now an increasingly small, struggling figure as the distance increased.

'What thing?'

'When I was a kid,' she began in explanation, 'my dad used to hide in his study – like

every dad everywhere, with a study or without – to escape all those little jobs my mom –
like every mom everywhere – used to find for
him to do.'

'Was he successful?'

She gave a huge grin, remembering. '*Very*
rarely.'

'It's pandemic. My mother could always
invent things for my father to do, whenever he
was ... home...' Müller's voice trailed off.

'Hey, Müller,' she began quickly. 'I didn't
mean to...'

'No, no. I'm fine. Continue with your
conversion to Jimmy Smith.'

'OK.' She gave him an uncertain glance.
'One day, I peeked into the study. He has this
great, old armchair that's like a family heir-
loom, from his side of the family. His grand-
parents had to leave the Germany of the
thirties for reasons the world knows about,
and it was one of the few things they managed to bring with them. Dad inherited it. He
always had his little zizzes in it. That day, I
found him eyes closed, headphones on. The
stereo in the study was on, but I thought he'd
fallen asleep.

'I went up to him on tiptoe, and lifted one
of the headphones so slowly, he never moved.
I wanted to hear what he'd been listening to.
Then his right eye suddenly opened. It made
me jump, and I gave a little yelp. Without
saying a word, he removed the headphones,
and put them on my head. That's how I got to
hear Jimmy Smith for the first time. Dad was

listening to "Walk on the Wild Side".'

She paused once more and, out of habit, gave a backwards glance, then peered into her side mirror. She gave a slight frown. They were on a long straight, and there was no traffic ahead. She picked up the map, and briefly studied its local information.

'Shouldn't there be more traffic on here? Gantheaume Point is supposed to be one of *the* sights, according to this. We should be seeing at least a tour coach, or a local bus.'

'The buses will certainly not be running every ten minutes. We're probably in a lull. Perhaps the traffic has already arrived and is parked all over the place down there. Or the rush hour is trailing somewhere behind. Or ... it's anyone's guess. You get this, even in big cities, as I'm certain you know. Or is there something else on your mind?'

Jimmy Smith had temporarily left the conversation.

'A bike,' she said. 'This time, a motorbike.'

'Ah. You mean the Harley. I've been watching his plume ever since the bicycle turned into a speck. They've been trailing us since then...'

'"They"?'

'I saw him swerve to avoid something. There are two of them on there. Probably a couple. Some people like making bike trips around Australia – even on bicycles, as we have just seen.'

'Crazy.'

'To us, perhaps, but not to them. I, for

173

example, would one day like to do the trip in the Cayenne and take some months about it, stopping at locations that take my fancy for several days, just to enjoy the area. I knew someone who did so on the pillion of a motorbike. Not a Harley. It took her and her then boyfriend three months...'

'Her "then" boyfriend?'

'They were going to get married after the journey. It was meant to be their great romantic adventure of self-discovery. The relationship did not survive it. Nothing like close proximity under such conditions to test how well you'd like to spend the rest of your life together.'

'So she dumped him.'

'I think it would be more correct to say she ran, and never looked back.'

'That must have been some trip.'

'From what I heard, it had its moments.'

'That bad, huh?'

'Worse.'

An almost watchful silence fell after this.

Then she glanced back again. The motorbike seemed to be keeping perfect station.

'He's not getting any closer. I guess the name Hargreaves is not on *The Semper*'s radar, which explains why they keep following you.'

'The people on that bike may simply be going to Gantheaume Point – just as we are – and are keeping out of our dust cloud. It is a public road. Tourists, or locals, going to look at the ocean...'

'You believe that?'

'I'm keeping an open mind.'

'I know you, Müller. If you've been watching them...'

'I'm keeping an open mind,' he repeated.

'And I'm going to keep my gun ready, just in case you're wrong.'

'Oh,' he said. 'I'm not wrong.'

'About what? That they're tourists?'

'About keeping an open mind.'

She gave him a look of mild exasperation. 'Sometimes, Müller, I think you do this just to try me.'

'Why would I do that?'

'Because you're Müller, Müller!'

He resisted the smile he felt coming as he glanced at his side mirror. 'How is our trail doing? I can't see him.'

Carey Bloomfield peered into her own mirror. 'Same here. They must have found a track somewhere off the road, and gone on to the beach. Perhaps that's where they were really headed.'

'Looking for a private spot?'

'Could be.'

'We'll see,' he said. 'And what was that question about Jimmy Smith?' he added.

She gave the mirror another check before saying, 'When Dad put the 'phones on my head, a weird sound was coming from the Hammond ... well, at the time, to a kid, it sounded weird; but my child's curiosity was hooked. I wondered how he could make that sound and so I asked my dad about it.

"That," he said, "is the sound of the master at work, my cherub."'

'He called you his *cherub*?'

'Hey. Parents are supposed to love their kids.'

'They certainly are.'

The way he said that made her dart him a curious glance. But his eyes were concentrating on the road, his expression giving nothing away.

'The sound was like a fast bubbling on one note,' she said, 'sometimes flicking to another note. It stuck in my mind. I've always wondered how he did that.'

'Ah...' Müller said, taking frequent glances in the rear-view mirror. The motorcycle had still not returned. 'The famous Jimmy Smith signature.'

'You know how he does it?'

'I know how *I* do it,' Müller replied. 'Without knowing precisely how he did it, I experimented. Eventually, I ended up using attack, vibrato, echo, and choral Leslie. It's not Jimmy Smith, but I like what I've got.'

'And that bubbling sound?'

'The finger dance. First and second fingers sideways on the selected key – to make them fit if you're using just the one note – then you dance.' He briefly demonstrated on the top of the dashboard, fingers drumming. 'The Hammond keys have an exceptional rebound, so when you hit the selected one precisely, you get the rapid repeat. If you also use the effects I mentioned, then you can get quite a sound. If you want to use more notes, you do a rapid flick to hit the selected key or keys, briefly.

'It takes a little practice, but you get there in the end. Your father is quite right. Jimmy Smith *is* the supreme master. Since then, others have got amazing sounds from the Hammond, but many will tell you that he is responsible for bringing it out of the parlours, churches, and chapels, and into the hugely varied world of bands and styles. Some might disagree, but for me, he's *the* icon.' Müller again glanced in the mirror. 'Our biker friends really do seem to have gone.'

'No worries, then.'

Müller was not so certain. He would be very happy if the people on the Harley turned out to be nothing more than a couple hunting out a secluded spot. Yet it was just possible that there could still be more of *The Semper* cell around.

'Not much of a rush hour today,' Carey Bloomfield was saying.

The road ahead was still clear, and no other vehicle was keeping station behind. Then came a surprise.

'Well, what do you know...' she began.

A sealed section of road had come into view. Soon the ride got better on the firm surface. The section had a look of newness about it; as if it had only recently been sealed. Small clusters of chipping pockmarked the red earth at the sides, where they had been sprayed by passing wheels. There was still no other vehicle on the long straight ahead of the Explorer.

Then the smooth ride ended.

'I knew it!' Carey Bloomfield said as they found themselves once more on the dirt road.

The sealed section was clearly intended to serve the race course.

But they were soon branching off to the right, towards the Point itself. The road looped back towards Roebuck Bay, along the opposite shore of the peninsula, heading for Broome.

A space-frame lighthouse, with a small building within a fenced compound, had long come into view. Beyond the compound were two low buildings with pitched roofs, the larger having pitch-roofed windows in what would have passed as an attic, but was really a second storey. A little further on were what looked like the remains of another building.

'Minimalist lighthouse,' Carey Bloomfield commented as they parked. 'Doesn't seem to be much of a crowd,' she continued. There was no tour coach, and the few people were some distance away. 'Looks like we've got the place to ourselves ... almost.' She looked at the red earth and the striated rock formations. 'This is like somewhere from another planet. Cloudless blue sky, red earth, green ocean...'

'Turquoise.'

'Stop being so damned precise, Müller. To me it's green.'

She put on her bush hat and, taking her gun

bag, climbed out into the thirty-plus degree heat of the day. A weak sea breeze fanned gently.

Müller got out, a tolerant look upon his face. He put on his own hat, locked the Explorer, and followed. He carried a camera bag, slung across his chest from his left shoulder, but there was no camera inside. Instead, his Beretta nestled there.

They walked towards the ocean across a surreal landscape that seemed to belong to Mars. The red earth, strewn with ochre-coloured shrapnel from the element-sculpted rocks, enhanced the feeling of being in an ancient world.

'Doesn't this remind you of those early pictures of Mars?' she asked.

'Well...' Müller began.

'Come on. Doesn't it? Spooky, huh?' They came to an edge and looked out upon the blue-green of the Indian Ocean. The tide was on its way out. 'But God, it is beautiful.' She glanced about her. 'Heads up,' she said, not pausing in her movement. 'We've got company.'

Müller did not look round. 'How far?'

'Near the lighthouse buildings,' she answered as her gaze returned to the water. 'It's our biker friends. Well, they're wearing the Harley biker uniform: beat-up jeans, cowboy boots, black t-shirts with the Harley logo, sleeveless denim jackets. They're so obvious, it hurts. They've got bush hats on, but they're carrying helmets. Guess they weren't looking for that private spot on the beach after all. The guy's got a camera.'

'This is a very photogenic place.'

'I know you, Müller. What are you thinking?'

'Can you find a way down? The tide's far out enough.'

'You want to see if one of them follows?'

'It would certainly tell us something.'

'Hey, that's OK. I like playing judas goat.'

'You handled a big mulga. You can handle this.'

She gave a shudder as she remembered. 'I didn't "handle" that serpent. It left me alone, and I left it alone to do its job on Mainauer.' She peered around, looking for a way down to the shore. 'I think I see a route. Time to play bait.'

He went with her to where she had spotted a track down. 'No need to tell you to be careful.'

'No need, but good to hear. And you watch it, Müller, if they're *Semper*.'

'We'll know soon enough.'

She put on a show of being uncertain about the track, smiling with nervous determination for the benefit of any onlooker. She gave an apparently casual glance about her.

'He just took a picture,' she said in a low voice.

'Of the scenery?'

'If we're the scenery, yes.'

'Then let us see what they're really up to.'

'I won't be long,' she said loudly enough to

be heard well beyond where they were.

He gave a brief wave as she began to make her way down, then turned to look out to sea.

'A million miles away,' he said quietly.

Carey Bloomfield had safely negotiated her way down to the shore. Despite the heat, the sand still bore the vestiges of dampness. She turned left and, after a short while, found a perpendicular gouge between two outcrops.

The sand there was dry. She backed into the opening until she was hidden from the view of anyone approaching either from the right or the left. She was so well hidden that someone walking by would go right past without noticing.

She settled down to wait.

About five minutes after Carey Bloomfield had gone, Müller unclipped the lid of the camera bag, lifted it slightly and peered in, as if trying to decide on what gear to use. He turned slowly in a manner that clearly indicated he was looking for a motif that would please him enough to be worth a shot.

His scanning eventually brought the bikers into sight.

But there were no bikers. There was the one biker with the camera. The woman had gone.

Carey Bloomfield had her gun out.

She thought she could hear cautious footsteps and remained absolutely still, waiting until she could hear more clearly. But the

181

faint noise had stopped. There was only the murmur of the sea, faint voices on the breeze from further up the beach to the north, but nothing close.

She wondered whether there were snakes here, and tried not to think of one dropping down on her from above.

Then she heard the footsteps again. There was now no mistake. Whoever it was, exercised caution. The steps came closer, halted, then started again. This went on for what seemed like long minutes, but was in fact seconds.

Then the person came into view, went straight past her hiding place, and stopped just beyond the second outcrop. It was the female biker.

'Where are you, bitch?' she heard the woman say in a voice so low, it was almost a whisper.

Carey Bloomfield moved out of cover swiftly and was close enough to put her gun against the woman's back before the other knew what was happening.

'Right here, *bitch*,' she answered with supreme calm. 'What you're feeling against your spine is not my finger. I really would not move.'

The woman – a redhead of average height but strong physique – remained perfectly still.

Carey Bloomfield lifted the denim jacket and saw the pistol inside the jeans.

'You'd do yourself some serious damage if that thing goes off while you're wearing it. I'll keep it safe for you.'

She took the gun.

'You're out of your depth, girlie,' the biker said to Carey Bloomfield. The accent sounded British, laced with Oz. Perhaps she had been living in Australia for a while.

'Well, *girlie*, we'll just have to see, won't we? I've got a pal up top who would like to have a word, as he would probably say.'

'He's out of his depth too.'

'Why don't you tell him to his face? Let's see what he'll say to that. No need to tell you not to do anything stupid, is there?'

'I like my spine the way it is.'

'Smart,' Carey Bloomfield said.

The two helmets were on the ground near where the man with the camera was standing.

Müller had made his apparently pre-occupied way close enough for them to converse easily, if they wished.

The man seemed to want to talk. 'G'day,' he greeted. 'Tough trying to decide what to photograph, eh?'

'Hello,' Müller said, openly friendly. 'Yes, it is. So much to choose from.'

'Yeah. I know the problem. Great, great view.' The biker held out a hand. 'I'm Gino.'

Müller shook the hand. 'Jens,' he said.

'Jens? Swedish, is it? Reason I ask, I come from Queensland. We had a Scandinavian premier once. An Aussie, but of Scandinavian descent. You take me – my family are Italian.' The loquacious biker grinned. He had a dark, droopy moustache that seemed to go into a dance as he did so. 'With a name like Gino, what else?'

'Of course,' Müller said, nodding like an enthusiastic novice invited to join a private club. 'I am German.'

'Ah,' Gino said, as if he had just received world-shattering news. 'German. Lots of old German families in Oz. We're a right old united nations down here, in God's own.'

'I've seen it, if Broome is anything to go by.'

'Yeah. Great town. Sharon and me – that's my lady – she's out hunting shells down on the shore. Sharon and me have been doing the grand Aussie tour, working to pay our way. We've been on the road two years.'

'That's something,' Müller said. 'Isn't it a bit dangerous, though, doing this on a bike?'

'Ah well ... there are times when you've got to look out. But Sharon and me can look after ourselves.'

Müller nodded in friendly understanding. 'I had a couple of friends who tried that some years ago. They did it the quick way – three months – but after the trip, they went their separate ways.'

'Didn't go well?'

'It went very badly. She could not stand being in the same room with him after that.'

'Shame. You've got to pick the right partner for something like that. You take Sharon. She couldn't be more perfect for me. We met in the old country. My family originally come from Sardinia. I had gone to the top to visit relatives. Where they live is not far from a nature reserve. Plenty of little bays where the tourists don't go. I went to one of my favourites for a little time to meself, when I saw this red-haired goddess, lying there all, all alone...' He paused for effect. 'With nothing on.' Gino grinned again. 'Gino, I thought, this is your lucky day. A sheila like that, with the balls to be out on her own in her birthday suit, is someone you've got to know. Well, it *was* my lucky day. We've been together ever since. She's a tough lady ... strong. Legs of steel, if you get me.'

'I think I get the drift,' Müller said, playing it to the hilt and allowing an expression of mild embarrassment to show.

Gino's moustache did another dance. Teeth flashed beneath it as the grin switched on for a third time. 'Just how I like a woman.'

The garrulous man who called himself Gino was also tough looking. Heavily muscled, his droopy moustache somehow fitted his persona. The head beneath the bush hat seemed either bald, or had been deliberately shaved for the same effect. His eyes, of a cloudy obsidian darkness, were those of a predator.

'Then it was definitely your lucky day,' Müller remarked, continuing to play his part in the charade.

The moustache moved again, heralding yet another grin. 'Yeah.' Then suddenly Gino's over-ready grin vanished. His expression had suddenly transformed itself into something utterly dangerous. 'What the hell...?' He was staring past Müller.

Müller did not turn to look, but kept his eyes firmly upon Gino.

The dark pools of Gino's eyes snapped back to Müller. 'What's your game, mate? Robbery?'

'Try again, Gino. What's yours?'

But instead of replying, Gino's left hand was darting behind his back.

Müller had been waiting for it. His own hand dived into the camera bag, and came out with the Beretta.

Gino froze.

'Not a camera,' Müller told him, 'as you can see.'

Gino brought his hand slowly back, empty. The eyes glared with a murderous hatred.

'Don't even think of trying to jump at me,' Müller told him. 'You would never make it, and your goddess would be without her consort.'

'Hey, Müller!' came Carey Bloomfield's voice. 'See what I caught.'

'That would be Sharon, the red-haired goddess, I presume.'

'Hey! How did you know?'

'A very talkative Gino.' Müller shifted position slightly, so that he could see Carey Bloomfield approaching with an impotently furious Sharon, while keeping his eye on Gino. 'Turn round, Gino.'

Gino took his time about it, but complied.

Müller reached quickly forward to pull out

186

the gun Gino had been trying for. Müller was surprised to note the type. It was a Heckler and Koch, a German police-issue pistol.

'You've come a long way,' he said to the gun. He wondered if it had once belonged to Mainauer. He said nothing about that to Gino. Instead he asked, 'Whose was this before you got it? And did you kill him first?'

'Go to hell,' Gino growled.

'What a nice man,' Carey Bloomfield said as she arrived with Sharon. 'Now what?' she said to Müller.

'Wishart,' Müller replied.

'Oh, he'll love you.'

'Can't be helped. Alright Sharon and Gino,' he went on to the bikers, 'pick up your helmets, then we'll take a little walk to our car.'

Both he and Carey Bloomfield stood back slightly, putting themselves out of reach of a sudden lunge by either of the two.

'And I'll take that camera, Gino,' Müller added.

'You steal cameras as well?' Gino sneered.

'Every little helps. Hand it over.'

Gino glared at him, but did so.

They went towards the Explorer, both Gino and Sharon still looking as if they wanted to attempt something. They were never given the chance.

Müller called Wishart's frequency.

'You haven't found more trouble,' Wishart began pleadingly.

'It found us.'

187

Wishart's sigh was palpable. 'What kind ... No, don't bother telling me. Where are you?'

'Gantheaume Point.'

'At least you're close. Be right with you.'

'And bring two pairs of handcuffs.'

'Things are looking brighter already. You've left them alive. Wishart out.'

'That dry Aussie humour,' Müller said as he ended the transmission. He returned to where Carey Bloomfield was keeping a watchful eye on their captives. 'He's on his way,' he said to her. To Gino, he added, 'I don't suppose you'll tell me where you got that police weapon from?'

'Go to hell!'

'Thought not.'

'Great vocabulary,' Carey Bloomfield said.

'I've already told your soft girlie,' Sharon said, looking at Carey Bloomfield with the air of a feline about to pounce, 'that you're way out of your depth.'

'She thinks I'm a "soft girlie", Müller,' Carey Bloomfield said.

'There were people who were once perfectly convinced that the earth was flat. I shouldn't let it worry you.'

'I'm not worried.'

'A very bad idea to call her "girlie",' Müller said to Sharon. 'She hates that.'

'Ooh. I'm shivering.'

'You should be,' Müller said.

Something in his voice made the redhead blink, but she made no further comment.

Gino was looking at Müller with the smirk

188

of someone who believed he still held all the cards.

'Keep an eye on our smiling boy,' Müller said to Carey Bloomfield. 'I want a word with Sharon.'

'I'm not talking to you!' Sharon snapped.

'We'll see. Come on.'

Sharon looked at Gino, then at Carey Bloomfield.

'You should go,' Carey advised.

'I don't need any advice from you!' Then Sharon bared her teeth as if to take a bite of something – or someone. 'What's he going to do? Shoot me?'

'It's been known to happen.'

The redhead stubbornly looked as if she did not believe it, but there was doubt in the pale green of her eyes. 'Since when does a Berlin cop shoot people in cold blood?'

'They used to ... once.'

'A few decades ago,' Müller added for good measure. 'Different times now, of course...' He let his words fade.

'Well that takes care of the travelling couple,' Carey Bloomfield remarked drily. 'How did you know he was a Berlin cop? We did not tell you.'

Sharon stared at her, but said nothing.

'If you please, Sharon,' Müller urged firmly.

After a further moment's stubborn refusal to move, she surrendered with ill grace.

They walked until Müller felt they were far enough out of earshot, unless they shouted. 'This will do,' he said. 'Stop.' He glanced

189

out to sea as she did so. 'Beautiful, isn't it?'

'Did you bring me here to make small talk?' she snapped. 'You're not my type. The girlie is more your style...'

'I'm trying to save your life,' he interrupted, his voice so soft, it carried all the impact of a yell.

That brought her up short. For a fleeting moment, the unexpectedness of his remark tore through her armour.

Then she gave a derisive snort. 'And who's going to take it? The girlie?'

'She could do it. I've seen her take down people a lot more dangerous than you could ever be. Don't underestimate the "girlie". That has proved fatal for more than one individual. But I am not talking about her. I am talking about the people who employ you. Perhaps I should speak in the past tense. They hate failure, and today, you have failed.'

Müller stopped, and again glanced out to sea. 'It really is beautiful. A million miles away...'

'What?'

'Something ... someone ... once said to me.'

'Well I don't know what the hell you're talking about.'

'About the million miles? Or about your employers?'

'My "employers", as you put it, are the people we work for during our trip. You know – places we stop at for a few days...'

'Yes. Of course. That's why you carry guns...'

'It can be dangerous in the outback. Snakes...'

'And why you know I'm a Berlin police-man, and Gino tries to take secret pictures of us. Keep this up, and I'll arrange to have you turned loose to face the wrath of your employers...'

'I've told you...'

'One of the people the "girlie" killed work-ed for your employers too. She was a highly skilled assassin. The "girlie" got her in bad light too. Her name was Mary Ann. *One* of her names, I should say. She had many aliases, but you might have heard of this one.'

Over by the Explorer, Gino was looking in the direction of Müller and Sharon.

'What the hell is he up to?'

'He never does what is expected,' Carey Bloomfield said. She gave Gino a thoughtful look. He seemed fidgety. 'Not jealous, are you?'

'Don't be stupid!'

Sharon had clearly heard of Mary Ann.

She suddenly paled, and glanced in Carey Bloomfield's direction. 'She...?'

'She. Now that that has settled the "girlie" question, more to the point, what are you going to do?'

'Do? Nothing. I don't know what "em-ployers" you're...'

'You can play this game until the inspector gets here. It will not change your likely fate, unless you do something about it. Gino says he found you naked on a beach in Sardinia,' Müller added, suddenly changing tack.

It took her completely off guard. 'He said *what?*'

'So you don't have legs of steel. According to Gino, you have the kind of strong legs he likes. I leave the rest to your imagination.'

A sudden colour had flushed her cheeks, but it was not from embarrassment. It was fury.

'I'll...'

'Do nothing,' Müller told her sharply. 'I was already sceptical of his story, which I suspected he was using in an attempt to take me off guard.' Müller gave her a rundown of what Gino had said.

'He could have used a different story,' she snarled when Müller had finished. 'We are *not* a couple. We just teamed up for this a few days ago...' She stopped, suddenly realizing what she had said. She glared at him. 'You bastard!'

'I've been called worse.'

The sound of an approaching vehicle made him glance in its direction. It was Wishart's.

'And here's the inspector,' he said to her. 'If you change your mind, tell him. He'll make certain I get to know. Your life is now in your hands. Literally. Let's go and meet the inspector, shall we?'

They started walking back to where the vehicles were parked, Sharon wearing an expression of controlled rage.

★ ★ ★

The first thing Wishart did was put the cuffs on both Sharon and Gino.

'Would you mind watching them a bit longer?' Müller asked Carey Bloomfield.

'Come to Gantheaume Point,' she said. 'Play guard dog to two fake bikers. I love it.'

Müller gave her a ghost of a smile. 'Thanks.'

As Müller and Wishart walked away, Gino said to her, 'He just gives the orders, and you obey?'

'Quit while you're ahead, Gino.'

That shut him up.

Müller and Wishart stopped by a rock formation that looked like a sculpted saddle.

'Do you think,' Wishart began, as they looked out to sea, 'you'll be able to spend the next hours before your flight like an ordinary tourist? It will help my grey hairs...'

'You have no grey hairs.'

'I can feel them coming.'

'I'll do my best to delay their arrival.'

'I wish that made me feel better,' Wishart said, rueful eyes glancing at Müller. 'So what's the story with those two?'

Müller told him. When he came to the part about Sardinia, Wishart gave a chuckle, and glanced back at Sharon.

'Well, she does have the build of a beach guard,' Wishart commented, 'but in a good way. Gino seems to have allowed his libido to do his thinking.'

'And his wishful thinking,' Müller said,

193

'which was my good fortune. I've sown a few seeds of discord. Secure them well in your vehicle. She might want to kill him.'

'I wouldn't lose any sleep if she did.'

'After your Federal colleagues have had some time with them,' Müller said, 'it might not be a bad idea to release them.'

Wishart stared at him. 'What?'

'Oh, I'm certain they are not whom they say they are, and there is no doubt that plenty about them will interest your colleagues. But the people they work for are not kind to failure. They will feel vulnerable on the loose. I've suggested to Sharon that she gets in touch. If she decides to, she will tell you...'

'And I'll pass it on to you.'

Müller nodded. 'You never know. Reality might bite her hard enough to make self preservation give her the motivation she needs.'

'You're a devious bastard, Jens,' Wishart said. He was smiling.

'Gino called me that. He left out the devious. They've got their bike somewhere around here,' Müller went on. 'It's a Harley, or a good replica. There might be some interesting things on it. I'll keep the camera. It's a very advanced model. They'll have something like a palmtop for uploading information. I doubt if they would risk using an internet café, and leave traces of their traffic on someone else's server. You keep their guns, but I'll take the details of the HK. I want to know where it was issued, and to whom. One other

194

thing – can you manage to have a conversation with one of your colleagues – one that Gino and Sharon can overhear?'

'What kind of conversation?'

'One that suggests we could not find what we were looking for, because we came to the wrong place.'

'That can be arranged.'

'Thanks, Graeme.' Müller turned again to look at the ocean. 'A million miles away.'

Wishart gave him a sideways look. 'What was that?'

'Just a saying.'

After a while Wishart said, 'It's five thirteen. About half an hour to sundown.' He glanced upwards. The sky was already promising a fiery display. 'Watch the sunset. Enjoy the show, then go back to Broome and have a nice, relaxed dinner. And please, don't bring me any more flowers.'

'No more flowers.'

'Is that a promise?'

'Life does not make promises.'

'Philosophy. I hate philosophy.'

Seven

Gantheaume Point. 1741, local

Müller and Carey Bloomfield had taken Wishart's advice, and had stayed to watch the sunset. The dazzling upper sliver of the sun was just above the horizon, encased within a searing-yellow corona. A red-gold fire smeared itself across the sky, fading seamlessly above their heads until it reached far behind them, into the darker regions of the approaching night.

Several people had arrived after Wishart had gone, clearly for the sunset. The cameras were out in force. None of the recent arrivals were close enough to encroach, most having decided to stay around the lighthouse and its neighbouring buildings. Müller and Carey Bloomfield thus had a perfect vantage point, virtually to themselves.

Out to sea, a sleek cabin cruiser was slowly crossing from right to left, from the direction of Broome. Its design gave the strong impression that it had been specifically built for high speed. At the moment, it was moving so slowly it was almost stationary.

Perhaps, Müller thought, it was going to

196

round the point and head into Roebuck Bay.

An optical illusion made it appear to be entering the corona, giving the vivid impression that it was catching fire.

From where they stood, the furnace-like blaze of the setting sun played upon the high gloss of the cruiser's hull and superstructure, giving it a fierce glow that was itself powerful enough to reflect upon the surface of the water. It was, Müller thought, an impressive display.

'Now this,' he said, 'deserves a picture.'

'You've got smiling Gino's camera in that bag.'

'Evidence. I want to keep Gino's snapshots.'

'Oh, come on, Müller. One shot. Maybe two. These things have enormous storage space. Come on! It will be gone in two minutes.'

'Alright. On one condition.'

'Anything! Just *hurry*.'

'Stand just over there.' He pointed to a striated pillar of red.

'Me? No way, José. I'm not getting into any picture.'

'Alright.' He made no move to get the camera out. 'Two minutes to sundown,' he reminded her.

'I hate myself in pictures.'

'So do many people. Time waits for no—'

'*OK* already.'

She went to the pillar and placed a hand upon it. 'Don't take all day, Müller. People are watching, and I feel stupid.'

He took out the camera and raised it to his eye. 'No one's watching. They're all trying to get their sunset shot of a lifetime. Say "cheese".'

'You wish.'

At the moment he took the shot, several things happened, one of which was the buzz of a hunting, twilight insect going past his right ear. The buzz was loud, and he decided it must have been one of those huge dragon-flies that seemed to inhabit Gantheaume Point.

The small section of the rock pillar Carey Bloomfield had been using as a prop gave way. She stumbled untidily, and screamed at the same time. It was a cry of real pain.

And fear.

Müller ran towards her. 'Are you...?'

'I've been *bitten*!' she cried. 'Oh God! I've been bitten by one of those goddamned snakes! Damn it, damn it, *damn it*!' She gasped with the pain of it. 'My left shoulder! It's going numb! Oh Jesus, Müller! One of the ten deadliest snakes—'

'Don't move!' he commanded. 'Worst thing you can do,' he went on, forcing himself to remain calm, 'is excite yourself.' A cold fear had gripped him.

They were not out in some isolated place, he told himself. Help was close at hand. Were there snakes in this area? And what kind? How deadly?

'Let me have a look,' he continued, maintaining his outward calm.

198

'Oh Jesus, Müller ... This is scaring me...'

'Don't be scared. Just let me have a look. We're only minutes away from expert help.' There was still plenty of light for him to see clearly. He felt a wave of relief. There were no puncture marks whatsoever. 'The good news is you were not bitten by any snake that leaves that kind of mark.'

'And ... and the bad news?'

'It looks as if you've been shot...'

That explained the night insect that had gone past his ear.

'Shot? Are you kidding me? Where from?'

'I don't know.' There had been no accompanying report. A silencer, perhaps? 'But you were very lucky. It's just a bad graze. Not even that bad, really...'

'Well, thank you!'

'Hardly any blood now,' Müller went on, ignoring the remark in his relief. 'Probably a little more as the shock wears off. If that piece of rock hadn't broken—'

'And I hadn't fallen...'

Müller said nothing. They both knew she could have been shot dead.

'Jesus, Müller. Who?'

Müller looked out to sea. The cruiser was heading so fast for open water that it was practically standing on its stern. It seemed to be heading directly for the last pinpoint of the disappearing sun and the last red-gold afterglow smear of its passing. The snarl of the cruiser's powerful engines came very clearly upon the fast approaching night.

199

Probably a guess, Müller thought. The shot might not have come from the cruiser at all. But it had been almost dead in the water, had been directly opposite, and now, within seconds after the shot, it was racing out to sea. Coincidence? Perhaps. Perhaps not.

He said nothing to her about the cruiser.

'It's anyone's guess,' he replied. 'Are you ready to get up?'

She nodded. The light was strong enough to enable him to see her kill the grimace of pain as she moved.

'Did people look?'

'One or two. They were far enough away to think you just fell.'

She took his hand as she levered herself to her feet. 'Could have been one of them...'

'Possibly. But I have my doubts. Let's get you to the car and the first-aid kit.' He peered at her wound. 'Very, very lucky. It won't even leave a scar. Hardly any blood. Less than I expected. Let's clean it up.'

'Well you got your picture – and nearly got me killed.'

'Bad planning. Better luck next time, eh?'

Despite herself, she smiled. 'Damn it, Müller. I thought that with those fake bikers, we'd seen the last of *The Semper* around here. Know what? I don't much feel like eating out any more – especially not with a dressing on my shoulder. Let's just have something at the hotel.'

'I agree. Graeme Wishart's favourite restaurant can wait.'

They got into the Explorer, and Müller dressed the wound. She watched him as he worked.

'You've got gentle hands, Müller,' she said as he was finishing.

'Bet you say that to all the—'

His mobile rang.

'You always get saved by the damned bell, Müller.'

'Must be that luck of mine ...Yes, Pappi,' he said into the phone.

'Enjoying Oz?' Pappenheim's cheerful question had been preceded by the sound of a long drag on his inevitable cigarette.

'We've been having some "enjoyment". The most recent episode just a few minutes ago.'

'You've just grabbed my interest by the throat.'

'Miss Bloomfield has been shot—'

'*What?* How is she?'

'Very lucky.'

Pappenheim paused. 'You'd better give me your news; then I'll give you mine.'

Müller gave him a rapid but full recounting of all that had happened during the day, leading up to the moment that Carey Bloomfield had been shot. He could hear Pappenheim puffing continuously at his Gauloise as he spoke.

'Busy,' Pappenheim said when Müller had finished. 'So who's the likely suspect for the shooting? Someone on that cruiser?'

'The more I think about it, the more that possibility seems the favourite option. It was practically dead in the water at the time.'

'Taking his shot. A sniper could have been positioned anywhere on that boat, and you would not have spotted him ... or her.'

'Something might show up in the picture. I framed the shot so that it was within it.'

Müller was aware that Carey Bloomfield was staring at him, but he ignored her for the time being.

'Then we might have some luck,' Pappenheim said. 'I'm certain the goth can work her magic on it. If anything worth seeing is on there, she'll find it.'

'My very thought.'

'And, of course, you'd like me to see what I can find on that dead American...'

'As ever, you've read my mind.'

'And his Aussie pals?'

'As comprehensive as you can make it. Liaise with the Federals through your something-in-diplomacy friend in Perth. See what he can dig up. And on our biker friends.'

'Talking of which, do you think the red-headed goddess might take up your offer?'

'She's a hard one, but even the hard ones need to survive. She might give that serious thought. Let's wait and see. It might also be an idea to check any possible links with the wolfhound – especially to do with illegal arms dealing. You never know...'

'I'll enjoy that,' Pappenheim said with eager anticipation. 'Which brings me neatly to the man himself. I'm building quite a dossier on him.'

'Such as?'

'Drugs for money – *big* money. It's a neat triangular trade ... and I'm not talking about slavery, although more on that later.'

'Arms/money/drugs ... loop in any order...'

'Got it in one, or three.'

'And what was that about slavery? I'm assuming you don't mean historically.'

'I don't. I'm talking about movement from countries east of the current EU borders. I'm talking specifically about a girl moved west against her will, committing suicide after becoming pregnant...'

'I can't wait...'

'Yep. The wolfhound was the proud father. Seems she was a hospitality present...'

'My God.'

'I want to personally take down that bastard.'

'Not before we're back. If he has confirmable *Semper* links, we want to do as much damage as possible.'

'I can wait,' Pappenheim said, ominously for Wolfgang Melk.

'Anything else?'

'Not so you'd notice. The Great White continues to be conspicuous by his absence. Perhaps he's down in the south of France, spending quality time with his daughter,' Pappenheim suggested in a dry voice.

'His *Semper* pals have got him over a barrel with her – as he knows only too well.'

'And as *we* do.'

'Oh, yes. Give me a call later, Pappi.'

'Any particular reason? I can tell there's something lurking in that brain of yours.'

'Just a hunch.'

'Ah yes. Hunches. I know about them. Any preferred time?'

'Any time after twenty-three hundred, our time down here.'

'Whatever it is you have in mind, you expect it to be over by then?'

'Just a hunch.'

'Aah, those hunches,' Pappenheim said again. 'OK. I'll ask the goth to hang around so she can work that communication magic ... but I'm sure she won't complain, seeing it's for you.'

'Don't you start that.'

Pappenheim chuckled. 'Give Miss Bloomfield my love. Later.'

'Pappi sends his love,' Müller said to her as the call ended.

'I'll reciprocate when I see him,' she said. Her expression was the kind that said she knew he was holding out on her. 'Alright, mister. Give. What is it about that boat?'

'You heard?'

'Not enough to get your conversation, but enough to know you've got an interest in it. You believe I was shot from there?'

'I can't say that. It's all circumstantial. It was in the right place, and the timing was right. But the shot could just as easily have come from land. Plenty of places – especially in the fading light – to hide, and from which to take a shot...'

'But a boat has the better getaway from the scene.'

Müller hedged. 'It's a balance.' He glanced around. 'Getting dark in many of the possible hiding places. No need for an immediate getaway.'

'But there would have been plenty of opportunity for another shot.'

Müller nodded.

'So it looks like the boat, then,' she said.

'It increasingly looks like it.'

'The bastards could be anywhere by now.'

'They could indeed.'

'I know that tone you've got on, Müller. But...?'

'There's a "but"?'

'With you? Always.'

Müller started the engine. 'Let's get you back to the hotel.'

He turned on the lights. A swarm of insects danced madly into the beams.

'Bugs,' Carey Bloomfield said. She did not add the 'ugh', but it was there in her voice. 'Look at them. They can't resist it.'

'Like some humans.'

They were halfway into the return drive to Broome when the radio squawked.

'You there?' came Wishart's voice.

'We are.'

'Going to eat?'

'Change of plan. We're heading for the hotel.'

If Wishart wondered about that, he gave no

indication. 'That's handy. I'd like to meet you there.'

Müller glanced at Carey Bloomfield. 'Oh?'

'Seems your bedside charm worked,' Wishart informed him.

Müller knew what he meant. 'An offer taken up?'

'You judge. Wishart out.'

'The redhead?' Carey Bloomfield asked as Wishart signed off.

'It would seem like it,' Müller replied. 'The real questions are: "what does she expect?", and "what is she offering in return?"'

'And my question is, are we going to get to eat? I'm beginning to feel hungry.'

'We'll eat.'

She looked at him as if she did not believe it. 'You've got some bug buzzing round in your head, Müller. You asked Pappi to call you back at twenty-three hundred. Do we get to eat before? Or after?'

'Can I take the Fifth?'

'You're not American.'

'Ah well.'

Night had totally fallen by the time Wishart knocked on the door to Müller's suite, five minutes after he and Carey Bloomfield had arrived.

Müller opened up.

Wishart had a companion. Still in handcuffs, Sharon stalked into the room ahead of Wishart. Despite the handcuffs, her manner gave the impression that Wishart was the prisoner.

She looked about her. 'Very nice. They give Berlin coppers a year's salary in expenses?'

Müller looked at her, but ignored the comment.

She gave Carey Bloomfield a passing glance. 'What happened to your shoulder?'

'I fell.'

'She was shot,' Müller corrected as he closed the door behind them.

Both Wishart and Sharon were surprised. The way they expressed this was, however, very different.

Sharon tried to pretend she wasn't. 'They missed? Too bad.'

Wishart looked shocked. 'How? Where?'

'Gantheaume Point,' Müller replied.

Wishart gave Sharon a hard stare. 'Just how many *more* of your people are there in my shire?'

'Little point asking her,' Müller said. 'She has no idea, although she's pretending otherwise. She is as surprised as you are to hear that Miss Bloomfield was shot at by someone else. Your employers are not a trusting lot, Sharon. They sent backup – without your knowledge. The people who took that shot at Miss Bloomfield could well be hunting you, too. Since you have come here with Inspector Wishart, at your own request, I am assuming you have something worthwhile to say to me. Please take a seat.'

She did so.

Everyone else remained standing.

'Have you killed many people, Sharon?'

'Have you?' she countered.

'I'm a policeman,' Müller said. 'I only shoot people who are trying to kill me, or others. What is your excuse?'

She took a long time replying. 'I've never killed anyone...'

Carey Bloomfield made a scoffing noise.

'It's *true*,' Sharon insisted, glaring at her. 'I've ... roughed people up...'

'Bet they enjoyed that.'

'Look!' Sharon got to her feet. 'If I'm going to have to—'

'Sit down!' Müller ordered. He did so in a quiet voice, but the look in his eyes, and the manner in which his words were spoken, shook her. She stared at him, mesmerized.

Even Wishart looked warily at him.

Sharon obeyed, the look on her face indicating that she was astonished by her own acquiescence.

'I'll ask again,' Müller said to her. 'How many people have you killed?'

'None!' she answered. 'I've told you! My job was to...'

'Do the strong-arm stuff?'

'Yes! It helped being a woman. No one expected it. They were always ... surprised.' She looked at Carey Bloomfield. 'You know what I mean.'

'Don't look to me for support ... *girlie*,' Carey Bloomfield said in a cold voice. 'This isn't a good-cop-bad-cop routine. This is all bad cop.'

'So tell me, Sharon,' Müller said to her, 'on whom did you use the strong-arm stuff? How much damage did you do? A bone here, a bone there? Or was it full-blown bodily harm?'

'Mainly on—' Sharon stopped abruptly, and looked at each of them, but focused on Müller and Carey Bloomfield. 'Mainly on people who work for the same people I work for.'

Wishart was staring at Müller. 'What is she talking about?'

'I would like to know that myself. And what is your position with these ... "people", Sharon?' Müller went on to the redhead. 'If that is your real name...'

She ignored the remark about her name. 'I'm one of the ... you could say ... foot soldiers. Most of my ... correction jobs were aimed at those people who had screwed up in some way...'

'So you were yourself already well aware of the penalties for failure.'

'You never expect to fail—'

Carey Bloomfield gave another snort.

Sharon glared at her, but did not take up the challenge.

'So, somewhere along the line,' Müller said, 'a "corrector" or "correctors" will be looking for you, and for Gino. That can't be his real name, can it?'

'I don't know his real name. As I told you, we only teamed up a few days ago...'

'To find us.'

She nodded.

'To kill us?'

She shook her head. 'Only to locate you.'

'Did you know others were on the same job?'

'No. We all work independently. That way, one team can't say much about another, if caught.' Sharon looked at Wishart. 'I can't tell you how many there are around here, even if I wanted to.'

'So you have no idea, whatsoever, just how many teams may be roaming around out there?' Müller said, looking as if he did not believe it.

She shook her head. 'No.'

He still looked as if he did not believe her. 'Well ... Sharon, not much you can tell us, is there?' Müller glanced at Wishart. 'After your Federal colleagues are finished with her, tell them I recommend that she and Gino be released. I—'

Sharon got to her feet quickly. 'Look, I can—'

'*Sit down!*' Müller snapped with such quiet ferocity that she sat down again as if slammed into the chair. 'If you have nothing worth saying, we are finished here!'

She glared back at him, but kept her mouth shut.

'Well?' Müller demanded. 'You can do ... what?'

'I can give you our communication link.'

'And?'

'And I can tell you about Gino...'

210

Müller's expression was impassive. 'I thought you knew nothing about him.'

'I knew nothing about him before we met. But Gino likes to talk.'

'He certainly does,' Müller commented, grimly remembering.

'He also likes to boast,' she went on. 'He was trying to impress me.'

'Ah yes. The legs of steel.'

Sharon's mouth turned down. 'He was whistling into the wind.'

'That's one way of putting it. So who relayed the fact we were at Gantheaume Point? You? Or Gino?'

'It certainly wasn't me. Gino must have done it.'

'Why was he taking photographs of us?'

'To upload, as proof. We have – had – a satellite-capable palmtop...'

'That's true,' Wishart said. 'Found it on their bike. The Federal team are all over it.'

'That won't help them,' Sharon said. 'The terminal dies the moment anyone without the entry code plays with it, and there's no way of finding out the destination of any upload that might have been transmitted before. I can give you the code, but it will only be of use to you if they haven't already killed the palmtop by trying to make it work.'

'So Gino's message about our location might have alerted that cruiser...'

'What cruiser?'

'Never mind.' Müller looked at Wishart. 'Let's hope your colleagues have not yet

211

played with the palmtop.' To Sharon, he continued, 'Tell us about Gino.'

She paused for a few seconds, as if trying to decide whether to say more.

'It's too late for second thoughts,' Müller reminded her.

'Gino has killed,' she said after some moments. 'He boasted about it to me. He's killed at least two cops – according to him. But that could have been just another boast.'

Müller's mouth tightened briefly. 'That weapon he carried is a German police-issue pistol.'

She nodded. 'I know. He took it off a policeman called Hammer ... Hammer–something...'

Müller's voice was sharp. 'Hammersfeldt?'

Sharon was staring at him. 'You *know* him?'

'I *knew* him,' Müller corrected. His expression was cold as he remembered what Hammersfeldt had done. 'At least he got his just desserts.'

Wishart, almost morbidly fascinated by Sharon's revelations, asked Müller, 'A dirty cop?'

'A very dirty cop, who got "corrected". Deservedly. He killed his own partner, in Berlin. He had infiltrated us, for the same people, I suspect, that Sharon has told us she works for.'

Carey Bloomfield stood by, watchfully silent, intrigued by what Sharon had to say.

'What about the other police officer?' Müller asked.

Sharon glanced at Wishart. 'She was one of yours...'

Wishart stared at her. '*She?*'

'According to Gino,' Sharon replied. 'I can't tell you for sure if it's true. But he took such pleasure in telling me that I think it could be. He bragged about how great he was, making love to her. Full details. He really thought that would impress me...'

'Now there's a man who is in love with himself,' Carey Bloomfield said with distaste.

'I couldn't agree more,' Sharon said.

'Hey!' Carey Bloomfield snapped. 'This is not a sister solidarity pact. You're not talking to a friend.'

The pale-green eyes widened at Carey Bloomfield, as if storing something in there for future reference. But the red-haired goddess made no retort.

'What...' Wishart began, with some hesitation, to Sharon. 'What happened to the officer?'

'He killed her – according to him. She was undercover...'

'Jesus!' Wishart exclaimed softly. 'That's one of the two agents the Federals lost.' He looked at Müller. 'There is no way you're going to persuade them to turn him lose after this.'

'I would not even try,' Müller said. 'Gino, or whatever his name is, deserves all he gets. Just like Hammersfeldt.' He threw a sudden question at Sharon. 'Why do you carry a gun?'

'Self defence.'

A disbelieving smirk appeared on Carey Bloomfield's face.

Sharon darted a poisonous glance in her direction, but spoke to Müller. 'The palmtop will give you plenty of information. I'll take your offer. I hope you'll keep your word.'

Müller looked at Wishart and, as if suddenly thinking of it, said, 'A word with you outside?'

Uncertain of what to make of this, Wishart said, 'Er ... yes.'

'Watch her,' Müller said to Carey Bloomfield.

'You got it.' She took her gun out of the bag.

Sharon watched with interest as the two men left, before turning with a speculative look to Carey Bloomfield.

'So?' she began. 'Something there with him? Back at Gantheaume Point, I told him he wasn't my type – but I could be wrong. Gino told him I had legs of steel. Gino was in a fit of wishful thinking. But I do have legs of steel ... for the right person.'

'Rules, Miss Whoever-you-are,' Carey Bloomfield snarled at her. 'Keep your trap shut, and I don't talk to you. Agreed?'

'Touchy.'

'I take it,' Wishart said, 'you don't trust her.'

'I'd feel safer with one of your mulgas in a sleeping bag.'

'That's putting it straight.'

They were sitting in Wishart's vehicle, looking at the speckled lights of a cruise ship

214

moving on the far horizon of the darkened ocean.

'Does that mean you've changed your mind about letting her go?' Wishart continued.

'No.'

Wishart was surprised. 'But if you don't trust her...'

'She's told us a nice little story. She offered us Gino like a sacrificial lamb. He quite probably did do the things she's said, but telling some truth within your tale gives it a mantle of fact. It is what's underneath that really matters.'

'But the information in the palmtop...'

'She is quite certain your Federal colleagues have already had a go at it. But it does not matter if they have. The suddenly co-operative Sharon is feeling secure in the belief that the palmtop has been scrambled beyond recovery. Back in Berlin, however, we've got someone who can dig things out of dead electronics. Don't ask me to explain. I just know that whatever is done works wonders.'

'So you'd like to take the palmtop back with you.'

'It could be a powerful weapon...'

Wishart was probing beneath his seat. 'Well ... the Federal crew did not get the chance to ... screw it up.' He dragged something out. 'A weapon that looks like this?'

Müller stared at the palmtop. 'Graeme, you're a wizard. How did you...?'

Wishart grinned. 'I grabbed it before the Federals could get their hands on it. I had an idea you might want to see it. It's alive. No one's tried to turn it on.' He handed the palmtop to Müller. 'Nice little piece of high-tech – for a pair of jobbing bikers.'

Müller was almost reverent as he took it. 'I'll not forget this.'

The palmtop felt solid, and was of a comfortable weight. In length, it reached from the base of his palm to the tip of his middle finger, and was about four fingers in width. It would fit neatly into a side pocket.

'Just keep the heavies off my back,' Wishart pleaded. 'That's all I ask.'

'Consider it done, and more. From now on, you're a protected species.'

'Talking of species, what do you think our redhead's up to?'

'I believe she may be trying to get into our witness-protection system. Perhaps to identify to her employers the people who are being protected, and those doing the protection. Perhaps even to find out how the system works.'

'She's not going to love you when you dump her.'

'I can live with it.'

'Let's hope you don't die by it. I think she knows how to use that gun of hers.'

'So do I. I am also certain she has used it before. What passports are they carrying?'

'Gino has Australian ID documents in the name of Gino Rossini. She's got a Brit passport, and an Oz work permit. The name on the passport is Sharon Wilson. If those documents are fake, they are very good fakes.'

'They will not be fakes in the accepted sense. The people responsible for supplying alternative identities will be as good as those who supply new IDs for our own protected witnesses. Those documents will be perfectly real. Only the identities are not.' Müller stared at the ship on the horizon. 'If you wanted to inspect a ship in the port tonight, how would you go about it?'

'The hard way would be to get a search warrant – which could use up valuable time.'

'And the not-so-hard way?'

'Reasonable suspicion, or a customs ... er ... "visit", with the police tagging along, if you understand me.'

'I do understand.'

'I had a talk this arvo about something else, with the bloke who was on duty. They usually close up shop at four thirty p.m. But he's an old mate. I'm certain something can be arranged. Got a boat in mind?'

'As a matter of fact, I do. That cruiser I mentioned ... I believe the person who shot at Miss Bloomfield was on it.'

'If you're right, I'd think it would be long gone.'

'Not necessarily. These people are so confident, they can hide in plain sight. That is their strength. The cruiser could be moored in the port right now. I'll know it if it's there. Once you know what you're looking for, it is unmistakable. A sudden "visit" should take them off guard.'

'What do you expect to find?'

'A rifle similar to the one the sniper who killed Jamie Mackay had with him.'

'When do you want to do this?'

'How long will it take to organize?'

'I'll take Miss Redhead back, then come back to get you when everything's ready.'

Müller nodded. 'Alright.'

'The two of you coming? Or just you?'

'Considering who got shot, what are the chances of my being able to persuade her to stay behind?'

'A big fat zero.'

'There's your answer.'

Wishart made a tiny, rueful sound in his throat. 'I'm not going to believe you've left Broome until I see your plane in the air.'

'I had hoped for a quiet evening,' Müller said in his defence.

'No rest,' Wishart observed. 'You must be a wicked man.' The dry comment was accompanied by a chuckle. 'And talking of wickedness, both Sharon and Gino overheard a conversation between colleagues. It would seem that you and the colonel have come all this way for nothing. You could not find what you came here for. There is a strong certainty that you're searching in the wrong state, perhaps even the wrong country.'

'An "overheard" conversation. Some people just can't stop being curious.'

'Yeah. Nosy people.'

In the gloom of the police vehicle, Müller's faint smile was invisible. 'Do you think they went for it?'

'I'm sure they did. Two of my colleagues – they're looking after our guests in the cells – grumbled among themselves about a Berlin copper making them run around like jackasses looking for something that doesn't exist. I thought that made things more believable. Sorry. No offence.'

'None taken. Coppers grumbling about an outsider trampling all over their turf is very believable. Stroke of genius doing it that way.'

Wishart cleared his throat. 'And that cruiser...' he began, switching subjects hastily. 'Can you describe it?'

'I can. I had a very good look.'

Müller described the boat he had seen. 'She looks more like a small, fast frigate than a motor cruiser, and bristling with radar and communications gear.'

'Sounds like the *Aphrodite Rising*,' Wishart said. 'She is ... well, she *was* in port. Arrived a day ago. A rich boat, with very rich people aboard. According to my Customs mate, they are very pleasant, polite people – which he didn't expect from the very rich – and they kept to themselves. None of that I've-got-the-money-and-I'll-show-it-off-and-you're-all-peasants. Are you sure you've got the right boat?'

'Interesting name. If I've described it well enough for you to recognize, I have got the right one. Whether it has a sniper aboard is another matter. But the people we're dealing with would behave exactly as you have

219

described. They do not bring undue attention to themselves. They show their true nature only when they feel threatened. And I *am* a threat. I was sleeping, and they woke me,' Müller finished in a hard voice so low, he sounded as if he had spoken to himself.

Wishart shot him a glance accompanied by a slight frown; but Müller took no notice – or was unaware – of it.

'On second thoughts,' Müller said, as if thinking aloud, 'no inspection. When you've got your mate ready, just come and get us.'

'Don't know what you're up to,' Wishart said, 'but we'll follow your lead.'

'Whatever that is,' Müller said, still thoughtful.

'Ah ... something you might be interested in.'

Müller waited.

'We're giving a party on the beach for Jamie Mackay, at Cape Leveque. That's over two hundred kilometres from here – dirt road. It's a notorious road, so you need to give yourself plenty of time to get there. It's a car-wrecker if you try to take it too fast. The party will start in the arvo, and go on till it stops going on.'

'Are you inviting me to the party?'

Wishart seemed to pause for thought. 'Many of Jamie's friends will be there – especially those who knew him for years. You might like to meet some of them. There's a dirt airstrip, but don't fly in. Drive. The party will be about a five- to ten-minute walk from there. You'll need this, if you're interested.' He handed what felt like a map to Müller. 'Directions, the date, and two phone numbers – mine. One's private, the other is my direct line at the police station.'

Müller took it without a word, and put it into a pocket.

'If you are interested,' Wishart said, 'call me. I'll make sure your suites are booked. I'm assuming Carey will be with you. I can also have a four-wheel-drive waiting ... perhaps even the same one you've got now. Accommodation could be a slight problem, as it's around the time of the festival. But you'll be OK ... if you're interested. If you're worried about the security of the call, we make it short. Just say "It's on" and I'll know. I'll expect you to arrive in Broome the day before, so you'll be fresh for the trip to Cape Leveque the next day – the day of the party.'

Müller understood the code. 'Thanks, Graeme. I could be interested.'

In the hotel suite, Sharon was getting impatient.

'What are they doing out there?'

Carey Bloomfield looked at her stonily, but said nothing.

'Why the look?' Sharon continued. 'I'm being co-operative. You should be happy. I'm giving you good information.'

Carey Bloomfield remained silent.

'Look...' Sharon began.

'Don't piss me off!' Carey Bloomfield snapped, eyes lacking any warmth. 'Next time you open your trap without my addressing you first, I'll shoot you in the shoulder, just so you know what it feels like. In case you make the mistake of thinking I'm joking...' She held the gun with two hands, pointing it at Sharon's left shoulder.

The pale-green eyes widened, not wanting to believe it; but she wisely kept her mouth firmly closed.

At that moment, Müller and Wishart returned. They looked at the two women with curious expressions.

With undisguised relief, Sharon was the first to speak. 'She's mad!'

'You must have done something to annoy her,' Müller said to her calmly. 'I did warn you. Alright, Sharon,' he continued. 'The inspector will take you back. I'll arrange things in the morning.'

She gave Carey Bloomfield another of her wide-eyed looks as she got to her feet. Again, it was a look that seemed to be committing things to memory. She went over to Wishart, her walk deliberately languid.

Carey Bloomfield, gun lowered, returned the look unblinkingly, and in silence.

Wishart took his prisoner out.

'What went on between you two?' Müller asked after they had gone.

'She annoyed the hell out of me.'

'I can see that. But how come?'

'I don't trust her.'

'Snap,' Müller said.

'You too, huh?'

'Me too.'

'So what did you and Graeme Wishart talk about?'

Müller told her, then took out the gleaming grey palmtop. 'And I got this.'

'Oh wow!' she exclaimed. 'That is a beauty. We have nothing that looks like that.'

'The lack of cutting-edge technology is not one of *The Semper*'s problems,' Müller said. 'To use Wishart's own words, it's alive. And remember Sharon kindly told us that it's satellite capable. The Federals never got their hands on it. He grabbed it first, reasoning I'd want to see it. '

'Smart man,' she commented with approval. 'Have you opened it?'

'No. And I won't even try, until we're back in Berlin. I'll give it to the goth to work on. She'll be able to bypass any defences they've got in there. Judging by the communications suite on the *Aphrodite*, I'm willing to bet this little unit can talk to it.'

'So if that boat's what you think it is, it could be a relay station to any *Semper* base ... anywhere.'

'It certainly could.'

'Neat. But what if you're wrong?'

'Then I've got egg all over my face, and it's back to the drawing board.'

'But you don't think you are.'

'I'm keeping an open mind.'

'Not that again, Müller. Am I coming on this little trip tonight?' she added.

'Do you want to?'

'Would you try to stop me?'

'No.'

'Good. Now do I get to eat before the inspector comes back? My blood sugar needs a refill.'

'I shall order immediately,' he said with a straight face. 'Let me put this in the safe.'

'OK.'

There was a small combination safe in the suite, well hidden behind a panel in the large double wardrobe. The camera he had taken from Gino was already there. When the palm-top had joined it, he went to the phone and ordered room service.

'You said when "we" get back to Berlin,' she said when he had finished the order.

'Don't you want to come? Or are you thinking of heading straight back to Washington?'

'You inviting me to that palace in Wilmersdorf you call an apartment?'

'Would you accept?'

'Hey, isn't it great, talking in questions? Besides,' she went on, 'I haven't seen your Hammonds in a while.'

Eight

They had just finished their buffet dinner when Wishart's knock sounded.

'He's got great timing,' Carey Bloomfield said.

Rising to his feet, Müller asked, 'Blood-sugar levels fully restored?'

'Are you saying I eat too much?'

'Now where, in that question, did you hear that?' he asked as he went to the door.

'Just checking. Sugar levels restored.'

Müller shook his head slowly as he opened the door.

'Billy Johnson's waiting in the car,' Wishart greeted. 'He's been warned not to be nosey. So we're ready, if you are.'

'We are. We'll just put the empty dishes outside the door for collection, and then be right with you.'

'Right-oh. I'll wait with Billy.'

Müller nodded. 'Alright.'

He picked up the gun-carrying camera bag, and slung that across his chest in the usual manner. Then he and Carey Bloomfield put the dishes on trays.

'Ready?' he said.

'For whatever the night brings – including bullets.'

'That should not happen...'

'We didn't expect it at Gantheaume Point. Boy, was I surprised...'

'Point taken.'

'Ooh. That was a bad one.'

They left the suite, put the laden trays outside the door, then went to find Wishart and Johnson. They saw the police car waiting out of the hotel's direct lighting, and went up to it. Johnson, a man who seemed as big as Pappenheim, Müller thought, was in the passenger seat.

They climbed into the back.

Wishart commenced the introductions. 'Billy, *Hauptkommissar* Müller from Berlin, and Lieutenant-Colonel Bloomfield from Washington. Billy's an old vet. He was a sergeant. Tough as old boots, he keeps telling me.'

Johnson grinned in the gloom of the vehicle as he turned in his seat to shake hands.

'Jens,' Müller said.

'Howdo.'

'And it's Carey.'

'Howdo, Carey. Wish they had colonels that looked like you in my day.'

'Flattery, Billy, will get you everywhere.'

'I like her already,' Johnson said to Wishart. 'Graeme says you don't want an inspection,' he added to Müller.

'No.'

'So how are we going to do it?'

'By ear.'

'That should be interesting. I know the

Aphrodite,' Johnson continued in a deep baritone of a voice. 'Boarded her when she first came in. Beautiful boat. I've seen some boats in my time – Spain, South of France, Miami, the Bahamas, the Keys, Monaco, Sydney, Freo, up by the Whitsundays – but this boat makes them look like also-rans. She's not big, if you compare her to some of the bigger boats, but she more than makes up for it in class. As for the people aboard, I hope you're wrong about them, Jens. From what I've seen, they are some of the best I've met in this job; not like some yachting yobbos I could tell you about.'

'Is the *Aphrodite* well equipped?'

'"Equipped" does not do it justice. Some navies would die to have the stuff she has on her bridge.'

'That good?' Carey Bloomfield asked.

'Better. She's not a boat. She's a spaceship. Navigation, communications, radar, safety equipment ... that bridge is all monitors. Hardly a dial in sight. From time to time, when boats come into this port, we check the foul-weather status of their gear. The *Aphrodite* exceeds it all.'

'A boat prepared for anything,' Carey Bloomfield said. She gave Müller a fleeting glance.

'A boat that can go anywhere,' Johnson said, 'and at any time. Fast, and very high-tech. Even the screens on the bridge darken according to the glare intensity. And the bridge is raked so steeply, it looks made to slide through the air.'

'A spaceship indeed,' Müller remarked. 'Who owns it? And how many people aboard?'

'The owner – who is also the captain – is called Martin Laurentius. He is an Estonian national, but the boat is registered in Norfolk...'

'Virginia?' Carey Bloomfield asked more sharply than she'd intended.

In the twilight of the vehicle, Johnson stared at her. 'Why, yes. So you know the *Aphrodite*?'

'No. A thought just crossed my mind. Sorry. Please go on.'

Johnson looked momentarily uncertain, then continued. 'There are six people aboard. Passengers and crew. That is, the passengers *are* the crew.'

'Just the captain and five passengers to look after a boat like that?' Müller asked.

'I wondered about that myself, considering they don't all seem to be the kind of people who could handle such a vessel. But that's the beauty of the *Aphrodite* – a boat that's been well named, if you ask me. She is so high-tech, she can be sailed in complete safety by just two people. Laurentius told me himself. He and his wife do most of the handling, and the others make themselves useful by doing various small jobs. Computers sail the boat, if you ask me. God knows what it cost to build. A couple of fortunes are riding on that keel.'

'If they are who I think they are,' Müller said, 'money is the least of their worries. You said they don't all seem to be sailors.'

'Ah ... what I mean is that two of them seemed ill at ease on a boat...'

'You mean seasick?' Carey Bloomfield asked.

Johnson nodded. 'Could have been anything, of course. But they seemed a bit pale. I think they had just joined the boat. Man and woman. Sexy in a tough way, the woman.'

'Are you thinking what I'm thinking?' Carey Bloomfield asked Müller.

'I am. But I don't think it can be the same two. They were tanned...'

'Oh, they were tanned,' Johnson put in. 'When I said "pale", I didn't mean from lack of sun, as if they just came down from Europe, or the northern US. I meant pale and peaky – seasick kind...'

'Does the woman have red hair?' Müller asked in a studiedly mild voice.

'And the man a droopy moustache?' Carey Bloomfield added for good measure.

Johnson's surprise was almost comical in its wonder. 'But how did you...?'

'As a Customs man,' she said, 'don't you sometimes look at someone who appears outwardly inoffensive, yet you know in your gut that he or she's carrying something you'd like to check?'

'Many times.'

'There you go.'

'We have seen both the man, and the woman.' Müller did not explain further. 'When you were aboard, did you see a motorbike? A big one, like a Harley Davidson?'

'No. I didn't, but that doesn't mean there wasn't one. People carry all sorts on their boats, for use ashore. It all depends on the size of the boat, or how rich the owners are. I've seen skates, rollerblades, skateboards, bicycles of just about every type, mopeds – and, yes, motorbikes too. On a boat like the *Aphrodite*, they could have had a Harley on there somewhere...'

'Could they hide it from a Customs inspection?'

'My honest opinion?'

'As honest as you wish.'

'Easily,' Johnson said.

A silence descended upon them.

Then Johnson said, 'Sometimes people have bikes, or cars, waiting at pick-up points...'

'There is that possibility,' Müller agreed.

'That seasick couple,' Johnson went on, 'will at least have a doctor on board to look after them.'

Müller peered at him. 'Someone on board is a doctor? How do you know?'

'None of them is down as a doctor,' Johnson replied. 'It's just something I saw on the boat that made me think that one of them could be.'

'What did you see?'

'A book someone had left lying around. Didn't take much notice.'

'Can you remember its title?'

Johnson thought about it for a few moments. 'Bio-something. Bio ... biometrics. Yes, I'm sure. Dennison Biometrics.'

Carey Bloomfield shot Müller another glance.

Their silence made Johnson ask, 'It's not a medical book?'

'It is a medical book,' Müller said. 'Of a kind.' As with Sharon and Gino, he did not explain further. 'I must resist the temptation,' he added.

'To do what?' Carey Bloomfield asked.

'To go out there and confront them, just to see their faces. I hate to admit it; but that's what I would like to do. So, change of plan. Billy,' Müller went on to Johnson, 'you have given us more than you know – and we would have been none the wiser, if Graeme hadn't called you out.'

'I didn't do much.'

'It's not the quantity. It's the quality of the information you have just given us.'

'So you're not going in?' Wishart asked.

'No. Part of me wants to, just see how they would react. But far better to let them wonder what I'm up to. It keeps them wrong-footed.'

'If we're not going in,' Johnson said, 'I'd better get on home. Old dog like me, I need my sleep.' He twisted round to hold out a hand. 'Colonel, I wish I'd known you when I was younger.'

'What would you have done, Billy?' she said as she shook the hand.

'Got into trouble for trying to fraternize

with an officer.'

'Not if the officer didn't talk.'

'Watch her,' Johnson said to Müller, as they shook hands. 'She's dangerous.'

'I know.'

'Whatever and whoever you two are chasing, I hope you succeed.'

'Thank you, Billy. And thanks for coming.'

'Glad I could help. I'll go over to my car, Graeme,' Johnson said to Wishart. 'I'll leave you youngsters to it.'

'Right-oh, Billy. Thanks for coming out, mate.'

'No worries.'

Johnson got out and walked away with a slight wave that was suspiciously like a salute.

'A nice man,' Carey Bloomfield said, watching him.

'Salt of the earth, is Billy,' Wishart said. 'Salt of the earth. So I finally get an early night?' he added drily to Müller.

'You finally get an early night,' Müller said.

'And what do I do about the red-haired Sharon?'

'Turn her loose in the morning ... after we've taken off.'

'She'll probably bust a gut when she realizes.'

'And the rest,' Carey Bloomfield said.

'And do I still leave Gino to the Federals?' Wishart asked.

Müller nodded. 'They need him more than I do, and they're welcome to him. He's already been sacrificed, thanks to his loyal friend, Sharon. He was the price she was prepared to pay, in exchange for her trying to con me into believing her little act.'

Müller and Carey Bloomfield climbed out, and went over to the driver's side.

Müller held out his hand. 'Graeme, thank you for everything. Sorry to have brought all these troubles to your patch. And do remind the Hargreaves they can reach me, if they wish.'

Wishart's grip was firm. 'No worries, mate. I'll tell Jack and Maggie when they're back. Just keep the brass off me.'

'Count on it.'

Wishart shook hands with Carey Bloomfield. 'Carey, you keep this fella under control ... And, please, don't shoot anyone else until you're both well out of Australia.'

She smiled in the gloom. 'No worries, mate,' she said in a passable imitation of an Australian accent.

'Make an Aussie out of you yet.'

Wishart started his vehicle and, with a parting wave, drove away.

'It will be an interesting day for Sharon tomorrow,' Müller said, watching as Wishart's police 4WD turned a corner and went out of sight.

'I hope she enjoys it,' Carey Bloomfield said with unbridled vitriol.

At 10.10 the next morning, Müller looked down upon the Broome peninsula as their aircraft winged over in its turn for Perth, just

233

over 2200 kilometres and five minutes short of three hours away by air.

Their guns, together with the palmtop and Gino's camera, were in the special canvas bags that Pappenheim's diplomatic contact, Peter Waldron, had arranged for transport of their weaponry. The bags would be handed back to them on their eventual arrival in Berlin. There would be no stopover in Perth, as they would be catching a connecting flight out.

Next to him, Carey Bloomfield was making herself comfortable in her seat.

'It makes one come to terms with the size of this country,' he began, 'when you realize that Lisbon is actually some kilometres closer to London than Broome is to Perth.'

'Well … whatever,' she said. 'Wake me when it's over. I'm going to have a pleasant dream about Sharon being pissed off when she finds out.'

Sharon was not only pissed off. She was flaming.

Her pale-green eyes glared at Wishart. 'What do you mean you're releasing me? He gave his word!'

'If I remember correctly,' Wishart said, in a frustratingly calm voice, 'he said he would arrange things in the morning.'

'And this is it? I get *released*? He dumps me in the middle of nowhere, on my own, after all that I gave him?'

'This isn't the "middle of nowhere". It's

234

Broome—'

'It's the middle of bloody nowhere!' she spat. 'Where is the bastard?'

'At his hotel, I expect.' Wishart maintained his calm, which outraged her even more. 'I trust all your personal belongings have been returned to you?'

'Piss off!' she snarled.

Wishart just looked at her.

'Right,' she raged. 'Let's see what he has to say about this!'

She stormed off, leaving Wishart staring neutrally after her.

'Have fun,' he said, after she had gone.

She walked all the way from the police station. Outwardly, she seemed perfectly normal, even smiling at the people she pass-ed. But within the pale-green eyes, something murderous was lying in wait.

When she got to the hotel, she was sweetness itself.

'Hi,' she said to the receptionist. 'I'm meet-ing some friends ... Names of Müller and...' Her voice faded as she saw the receptionist's expression. 'What? What's wrong?'

'I'm so sorry. They've checked out.'

'Checked out? When?'

'This morning. You've missed them by about an hour...'

The receptionist stopped talking when she realized there was no one to talk to.

Still hanging on to her outward calm, but boiling inside, Sharon took a taxi to the port. She got out and began walking away.

'Hey!' the cab driver called.

She whirled. 'What?' she barked at him.

He was almost afraid to say it. 'You haven't paid.'

'Oh.' She came back, and handed him more than was necessary. 'Keep the change.'

He took the money as if worried it would bite him. 'Thank ... thank you...'

But she was already striding off.

She got to the *Aphrodite* and climbed aboard, going straight to the bridge, where Martin Laurentius looked at her in surprise.

'What are you doing here?'

'You screwed up, Laurentius!' she barked at him. 'Get ready to leave.'

'What? I...'

'Do it!'

'But Gino...'

'Is where he deserves to be. Are you going to get this sick bucket moving?'

Laurentius saw the look in her eye and decided upon discretion. 'Alright.'

'You were supposed to kill Carey bloody Bloomfield!'

'Something happened when I took the shot. She moved out of the scope...'

'She fell! That's what happened. Why did you take so long? I thought you were good.'

'Look. The boat was on a gentle swell. Have you...'

'I don't need your excuses! Everything was well prepared. Now we've got a *complete* mess! And now that we haven't even got *girlie* Lieutenant-Colonel Carey Bloomfield, the

236

whole thing's gone *completely* wrong. Müller's been chasing his backside looking for people who are not even in this state – perhaps not even in the country. We have a shooter who's gone missing ... and ... and ... and ... And you couldn't even shoot the girlie! What else is going to go wrong?

'Have you any idea of the damage you've done with that missed shot? I ought to shoot you myself! Now get this thing moving and out of here before that country copper wakes up. I'm going to my cabin. I *hate* sailing. I don't want *anyone* to talk to me on this piece of floating shit! Got it?'

'Got it.'

She brushed roughly past the supposed wife of Martin Laurentius, who had come to see what the yelling was all about.

She stomped down to her cabin, hissing to herself in her rage. 'The bastard! He knew I was setting him up, and he set *me* up! I'll get him for this, if it's the last thing I do. But I'll get his *girlie* first.'

It was a vow.

She had left her naturally red hair loosely bound that morning but now, as she stood before a mirror, she very deliberately freed it, letting it hang about her shoulders. For some moments she turned her head this way and that, letting the hair swirl about her face. She stopped and stared at herself. Her expression softened and, for the briefest of moments, it seemed as if a different person stood there.

Anyone watching would have been shocked

to realize that someone quite beautiful was hiding behind the mask. Then she removed all her clothes. It was easy to understand why Gino's libido had rocketed into the stratosphere.

'I could do much more for you than your girlie, Müller.'

Very slowly, she drew her hair tight and began to plait it, all the while keeping her eyes on the mirror. When she was finished, she wound the plait into a bun and secured it. By now, the pale-green eyes were again blazing with a murderous fire. The brief flash of beauty was gone.

She stared at the familiar face – the true one that had little to do with beauty – in the mirror.

A soft tremor went through the ship as its powerful engines were started; then it began to move. She stared up at the cabin ceiling.

'Can't you stop this puke bucket from rolling?' she yelled. 'All this money and it still wallows more than a bloody dinghy!'

Which was, to put it very mildly, an exaggeration of the highest order. *Aphrodite Rising* had been designed and built with faultless precision. It was one of the most rapid yet most stable boats that had ever put to sea.

In her current mood, to the woman who identified herself as Sharon Wilson, movement of less than a millimetre would seem like a giant swell.

She returned her attention to the mirror. 'Yes, Müller. Your girlie goes first. How will that feel?'

The killer in the pale-green eyes stared back at her.

'Someone's thinking very hard about me,' Carey Bloomfield said.

He gave a mild chuckle. 'Must be the red-haired goddess. Anyway, I thought you were asleep.'

'Something woke me up.' She frowned un-certainly.

'Don't frown.'

She frowned even more. 'Strange,' she said, and closed her eyes again.

Müller watched as a few strands of hair fell slightly forwards on to her cheek. It gave her a look of vulnerability that made him want to pass his hand gently along it. She had positioned herself so that she favoured the wounded shoulder.

He looked up suddenly and saw a flight attendant smiling at him. She mimed a ques-tion, clearly not wanting to wake Carey Bloomfield. He mimed no to the offered coffee, and the attendant moved on.

She met a colleague in the galley. 'There,' she whispered, 'is a man in love if I ever saw one.'

'Which seats?'

The attendant told her colleague. 'She's sleeping,' she said, 'but the look on his face said it all. I went to offer coffee, but for a while he didn't even know I was there.'

'If he's the one I'm thinking of, some

women have all the luck.'

'Ain't that the truth.' The attendant gave an exaggerated sigh. 'Back to the pilots then.'

They smiled knowingly at each other.

One hour into the flight, Carey Bloomfield was still blissfully asleep.

Far below the aircraft, and heading as fast as it could out of Australian territorial waters, *Aphrodite Rising* was cutting a spectacular dash as she raced across the Indian Ocean. She had a maximum speed of 50 knots, and could outrun virtually any fast patrol boat in the world.

She was nearly at her max as she sought to put as much distance, as quickly as possible, between herself and Broome. Normally, she cruised at the relatively sedate speed of 30 knots. From her navigation database, destination co-ordinates 2106S 5536E had been selected. The destination was an island off the east coast of Madagascar.

She was heading for the French island territory of La Réunion.

At infrequent intervals, bursts of code were sent from her communications suite. They did not all go to the same recipient.

Müller was thinking about a conversation he'd had with Greville, Aunt Isolde's long-lost-believed-dead first husband who had turned up out of the blue after an absence of close on thirty years.

Aunt Isolde had been completely ignorant

of the fact that Greville, ostensibly an army officer, had actually been a deep-cover British agent, working mainly in the Middle East.

The conversation had been the stuff of nightmares, and Billy Johnson's remark about the book he had seen on the *Aphrodite* had brought the nightmare back.

'Greville,' Müller remembered himself saying, '*think back. Have you ever heard of Primary Specimen Zero?*'

Greville had paused for so long, Müller had felt a chill descend upon him.

'*Greville?*'

Greville's voice had been full of shock. '*My God. They're trying again, after all these years.*'

'*Trying?*'

'PSO,' Greville had said. '*That's for Primary Specimen Zero. It's the culprit that alerted our lot in the first place. It was the template for the monster I'm wearing ... or is wearing me. But PSO by itself was not working. Something was missing. It took them a long time to identify the missing ingredient, so to speak. That little gem was christened PS-01. Primary Specimen Zero-One. Call it the nightmare genesis. From that source, all manner of variations could be produced, to target specific DNA. You could decide to eliminate only redheads, or blondes, or men, or women, or people of a specific age group, ethnic group, the entire range of skin colour, and so forth. To cut a long nightmare tale short, dear boy, the variations were potentially endless.*'

'*Jesus...*'

'*Well you might. When I nabbed the original*
241

PS-01, I shut Pandora's Box but, as you know, ended up carrying it meself. I am, if you like, now the source code. The destruction of the lab meant they needed to start, literally, from zero. It's taken them years, but they're trying to open the damned box again. A plague on their houses!'

'But can they make progress?'

'Progress is always possible. But the original maker of the nightmare has long departed the mortal coil. His work was destroyed with the lab. That was our intention.'

'Are you saying that without what you're carrying, they are stuck where they are?'

'Let's put it like this, old man. Progress is always possible, as I've just said. But, given how long it took the man who managed to make the original PS-01 live to do so ... PS0, by itself, is a dead end. Should they, however, discover for certain that I am the bearer and do manage to get their hands on me – or my body – then, dear boy, they've got the goldmine. That thing must have refined itself in me by now, and is quite possibly ready and willing to share its dark secrets, and proliferate. It has lived within a human body, almost symbiotically, but it is also killing its host ... stealthily. Rather like our pals with a penchant for medieval symbolism. In fact, I would say PS-01 is their viral equivalent.'

Müller had known Greville could only have meant *The Semper.*

'Strange thing is,' Greville had gone on, 'although it is killing me, I have the bizarre feeling that it is also prolonging my life. Making me healthier, while carrying on its deadly work.

Can't explain it. Must be something to do with my own DNA. Perhaps there's a bit of tiffin in there it likes. Makes the entire damned nightmare even more horrible.' Greville had paused again. *'Did the name you mentioned earlier lead you to this?'*

'Yes.'

'I won't ask how. What did you do?'

'Killed what we found.'

'You were able to do that?' Greville had been impressed, and not a little relieved. *'Mightily chuffed, old boy.'*

'Of course, they could have made copies...'

'If you reached the PSO, you will have found the current source. They may well have outsourced bits of it, but without PSO itself, the "outsourcee" might as well be playing with putty. In the days when I went to that other place, things had to be written down, or printed. These days, it all goes into the computer – easier when you can watch your nightmare take root and the risk of papers floating, about to fall into the wrong hands, is lessened. Of course, disks can be made, but that too, is fraught with potential for security breaches. Safest to keep no copies, and hide behind a rigorously secure electronic barrier. But this is also a two-edged sword. Once your data is gone, it's gone. I do hope for all our sakes, Jens, you really did kill it.'

'So do I,' Müller had said fervently.

And the name that had brought the nightmare back had been the name of the book that Billy Johnson had seen on the boat: *Dennison Biometrics.*

They were still trying to reopen the bloody box, Müller now thought, despairing of mankind's seemingly eternal stupidity.

How many nightmares, he wondered, had escaped from labs all over the world – either accidentally or by design?

Carey Bloomfield came slowly awake. It was the second hour into the flight.

Müller looked at her with some amusement. 'Sleep well?'

She stifled a yawn. 'How long was I out?'

'A good two hours.'

'Gawd, Müller!' she hissed. 'Why didn't you wake me?'

'Why? You obviously needed the sleep. How's that shoulder?'

'Believe it or not, it feels OK. And what did you do while I was out?'

'Some thinking.' He glanced out of the window.

'What about?'

'Mainauer. I'm wondering whether he will ever be found.'

'You haven't been thinking of him for all this time.'

'I was mainly thinking about Pandora.' He kept his voice low.

'You mean that book on the boat.' She kept her own voice low too.

He nodded. 'Let's talk about this later. We'll soon be landing.'

'Sure.'

One of the bursts of code from the *Aphrodite* had gone through a procedure that eventually culminated in a phone call received by retired General Sternbach. He was already awake, but still in his bedroom and wearing his dressing gown. He had just taken a cold shower.

Sternbach did this every so often, irrespective of the time of year. It may have been the secret that kept him looking far younger and fitter than his years would suggest; or perhaps not. But he had kept up the routine ever since his first year of military service.

Face impassive, he went to the phone and picked it up. 'Sternbach.'

'It's a washout,' the caller said immediately.

Sternbach waited, with the controlled calm of the general officer he had once been. There was also something in his predator's eyes that had the chill of implacability.

'We are down five people,' the caller went on. 'Adelmann, Renton, and Niles, our American colleague. Then Rossini...'

'*All* dead?'

'We still don't know about Mainauer ... but as he has not reported since we last heard, it must be assumed he is dead, or lost somewhere out there. It's a wilderness that one can easily get lost in...'

'I don't need a lecture about the Australian outback.'

This brought a short, cold silence, before the caller continued, 'Rossini was taken with

245

Wilson—'

'And?'

'And the attempt on Colonel Bloomfield was again unsuccessful.' The caller seemed to enjoy saying that.

Sternbach's face appeared to have been fused into stone, and he spoke with a calmness that gave no hint of the anger within him. 'So what is the status of Rossini, and our seasick-prone Miss Wilson?'

'Rossini is in the custody of the Federal Police. I don't think he'll be a free man this century. Wilson carried out her mission, sacrificing him.'

'As intended. And has Müller taken her into safe custody as expected?'

There was another silence, which lasted pointedly longer.

'*Well?*' the general demanded with some impatience.

'Müller did not act as expected.'

It was the general's turn to be silent. He gritted his teeth so tightly, the outline of his jaw seemed in danger of tearing through his skin.

'Where is she now?' he finally asked.

'On the boat.' The caller appeared to find some humour in this. 'She'll be in the foulest of moods when she finally gets off it. Useful.'

Sternbach did not think it funny, but he agreed about the potential usefulness of Sharon Wilson's burning anger. 'She now has a real grudge that requires paying. Ways can be found to channel it. Now, give me a full chronology of this debacle.'

When the caller had finished the tale of woe, the general could not resist shutting his eyes, briefly allowing the anger and frustration he felt to betray itself. He wanted to yell at the caller, but did not. The caller was not a subordinate.

'At least he has the palmtop,' the caller said, 'and he has no idea what it really is.'

'How can you be certain he's got it?'

'Wilson disclosed more than enough to ensure he would want to get his hands on it.'

'But he has also got the camera.'

'In war, there is attrition. This *is* a war, let us not forget...'

'I do not need reminding.'

'Of course. This was not the intention. At least,' the caller went on, 'Müller failed to find whatever – or whoever – he was seeking out there. So he comes away empty-handed.'

'And so do we,' the general said tightly. 'We still need to know what he was really after.'

'He will lead us where we want him to.'

'In war,' the general said, 'over-confidence can lead to defeat.' He hung up on the caller.

He stood next to the phone, staring at it as if it would give him some answers.

'Like father, like son, Müller. Like father, like son. As in life...' Sternbach left the rest unfinished. He knew what he meant.

He decided to break routine, and have another shower.

A very hot one.

★ ★ ★

247

The plane landed on time, and Müller and Carey Bloomfield found Pete Waldron waiting for them with a welcoming grin.

'Home are the hunters,' he said. 'Well, not quite home...' They shook hands.

'Hi, Pete,' Carey Bloomfield greeted.

'Peter,' Müller said.

'Your ... er ... special bags will be on your connecting flight.'

'Thank you for everything,' Müller said as they went to Waldron's car.

'No worries. Glad to have been able to help. Things go OK with you and Graeme Wishart?'

'Graeme was brilliant. I want him covered, Pete. Look upon him as a protected species.'

'You don't want the brass giving him a bad time?'

'I want him totally insulated. Lay any problems about that at my door, if necessary. I'll take the blame, but Graeme Wishart smells of roses—'

Waldron chuckled. 'Ease up, mate. I've got the picture. Inspector Wishart is untouchable.'

'Thank you,' Müller said with relief.

'Find what you were looking for?' Waldron asked.

'No,' Müller answered. 'But we did find what we were *not* looking for.'

'Ah yes. People the Federals have been waiting to get their hands on for years. Cut their careers short. You've earned some brownie points in some quarters for that.' They were

248

now at Waldron's car. 'Enough about work for now. You've got at least four hours to kill before you board your next flight. I know a good little restaurant for a perfect lunch. I recommend the chef.'

'You just started singing my tune,' Carey Bloomfield said.

The 'little restaurant' turned out to be Waldron's magnificent apartment overlooking the Swan River.

'No guessing about the chef,' Carey Bloomfield said, looking about her. 'I can't believe we were here just four days ago.' She sniffed. 'Mmm! So what's cooking, chef? Smells like ... shellfish.'

'Cape York crayfish,' Waldron answered with the smile of someone who knew a special secret. 'Hope you two like shellfish.'

'I overdose on the stuff, given the slightest chance. I love crawfish.'

'These are not your southern crawfish,' Waldron told her. 'These are ... well, come see for yourselves. Jens? You do like shellfish, I hope. You can't come to Oz and not like the best thing to go on a platter...'

'I don't quite overdose, but I'm close.'

'Thank God! Come have a look, children.'

He took them into the kitchen. Three large steamers were on the huge cooker.

'*Three* pots?' Carey Bloomfield exclaimed. 'Just how many of those things have you got in there?'

'Three.'

'You've got to be kidding me. What kind of

249

craw— crayfish...?'

Waldron carefully opened one of the steamers. Carey Bloomfield peered in at the crustacean inside.

'Jesus! This is a *crayfish*? It's a giant lobster!'

'Yes ... Big specimen, isn't it? It is a crayfish, also called a rock lobster.'

'I'll never eat all of that by myself! Müller? Can you?'

'I can.'

'You would.'

Berlin. 0720, local

Pappenheim was already in his office, and was approaching the end of his fourth cigarette of the day. A mug of half-drunk black coffee was on his desk, next to the ashtray into which he now stubbed out the cigarette. A small cloud rose briefly in response, and spilled over the edge.

Pappenheim peered into the mug to see if any specks had landed in there. It would not have been the first time.

He grunted when he saw that none had. 'Missed.'

He was just about to pick up the coffee when one of his phones rang.

'Carlton Niles,' the contact said as soon as he had lifted the receiver.

'Who's he, when he's at home?'

'The mystery man your friend met on the lonely highway. Former colonel, US Marines. Long history of dirty tricks in many countries

250

– globally – whose regimes were not on the Christmas list. In, and out of uniform. You name it, he's done it.'

Pappenheim did not ask how the contact knew about what had happened on the Great Northern Highway. 'Officially?'

'Officially, semi-officially, and sometimes – many times – none of the above. Sometimes, a mixture of all three at the same time.'

'So for country, and mammon.'

'In recent times, mammon got most of his loyalty. Money makes the world go round.'

'I thought that was love.'

'Throw away your fairytale books, Pappi.'

'What a thing for a woman to say.'

'Haven't you heard? We are smarter.'

The call ended.

Pappenheim put down the phone with a smile that went deep into his fond memories. 'I've known that for years.'

Aphrodite Rising was making good time.

The Indian Ocean was behaving itself, and only the barest of swells disturbed its surface. To a boat like the *Aphrodite*, this was motorway conditions. Sometimes having a high-speed dash up to 40 knots, she was averaging 30 knots an hour. It would take her five days and seven hours to cross the 3814 nautical miles to La Réunion.

Laurentius sat in a high-backed chair at the controls. The chair, which could be swivelled, was itself on a solid pedestal that was adjustable for height. His right hand gently held the

251

side-stick controller with which he steered the boat. He made the barest of control movements. Banks of highly specialized computers acted upon his inputs within nanoseconds, and translated his commands into infinitesimal corrections that steered the boat with remarkable precision. The *Aphrodite* sliced across the surface of the water as if on ice skates. The boat's transit was so smooth, it would not have disturbed a glass of water filled to the brim.

In her cabin, Sharon Wilson did not think so. To her, every nuance of the boat's movement was a continuing nightmare.

'This bloody boat!' she screamed. 'Bloody Müller! Bloody girlie Bloomfield!' Then she got up hurriedly. 'Aargh! I need to puke!' She staggered to the en-suite bathroom.

Moments later, she began to retch violently.

When she was at last finished, she flushed the results away, rinsed her mouth, then splashed her face with cold water. She had long refused the pills Laurentius had offered to ease the symptoms.

'I'm not putting any of that shit into my body,' she had said. 'I already take one pill, and that's bad enough.'

Now she groaned slightly. 'Nearly five and a half days of this. Five and a half days! I *hate* you, Müller! And your little girlie too. I'm coming for you both, no matter how long it takes! This is not a job any more. This is *personal.*'

Then she felt another heave coming.

Nine

'I can't believe I ate it all!' Carey Bloomfield said. 'Pete, that was ... sick!'

He grinned at her. 'Well, you did tuck in.'

'Müller! He's calling me a pig.'

'Then there are two of us. As you can see, my own lobster has vanished. I second the accolade, Pete. Great, great cooking.'

'Take that as a real compliment, Pete,' Carey Bloomfield said. 'The guy can cook. I hate guys like you.'

They had eaten on Waldron's large balcony, which had a superb view of the river.

'Well, next time I'm up in Berlin, Jens, you can return the compliment.'

'And I shall.'

Waldron glanced at his watch. 'Hate to spoil the party, but I'd better get you to the airport, or it's another night for you here.'

'I wouldn't complain,' Carey Bloomfield said.

'Nor I,' Müller agreed. 'But...'

'Work is work,' Waldron finished.

'Our unforgiving master.'

'Too right. Well, you'll be in Berlin before lunch, local time, tomorrow. When you two decide to come back for that six-month drive-

253

about, you let me know. We might just join you.'

'Hey,' Carey Bloomfield said. 'That would be great...'

'As long as we guys did the cooking?'

She looked at each of them. 'You shouldn't be so good at it.'

'Is this what they call being hung by your own petard?' Waldron said to Müller.

'I would definitely say so.'

'Women have got us beat, mate. They're smarter.'

'It was ever thus,' Müller said.

He got to his feet and went to the edge of the balcony. He placed both hands upon the guard rail to look out across the river and down towards the Narrows, and Fremantle beyond.

'I'd like to see this again soon,' he said. 'I should get something for Pappi,' he continued, turning round. 'But I don't want to get some touristy stuff at the airport. Do we have time...?'

'I have a better idea,' Waldron said. 'Give me a mo...'

He hurried inside and, a short while later, returned with nothing that they could see. Then he took something out of his pocket. A set of keys.

'Car keys?' Carey Bloomfield said with one of her frowns. 'You're giving him a car?'

'To Pappi, this will be better than any car; and I'm sure he doesn't need one. These are the keys to my old Volkswagen combi, which,

254

alas, is long gone. I've kept them as a reminder of that night when he hauled me out of the Thames and saved my life. Considering we had both enjoyed the company of several jars of the amber, I'm still amazed he made it. I think this rightfully belongs to him.'

Waldron handed the keys to Müller with something approaching great reverence. It was more of a presentation.

Müller took them with respect. 'I'll make certain he gets them, Pete.'

Waldron cleared his throat awkwardly. 'Yeah, 'kay.'

In Berlin, Pappenheim picked up a phone and called Hermann Spyros's department.

'I know you don't want to talk to me,' Spyros said before Pappenheim had uttered a word. 'I'll get the boss. For you, Miss Meyer,' Pappenheim heard Spyros say to the goth.

Pappenheim smiled thinly.

Then Hedi Meyer was on the line. 'The Rogues' Gallery?'

'As soon as you can.'

There was the slightest of pauses. Pappenheim imagined her looking at Spyros, who had clearly given in gracefully. 'I can.'

'I'll meet you there.'

'Yes, sir.'

'Give me Hermann, will you?'

'Here he is.'

'Hermann...' Pappenheim began smoothly.

'You're smiling,' Spyros accused. 'I know your smiles, Pappi. That's when you're at your most dangerous.'

'Hermann, Hermann. I was going to be nice to you. How many drinks do I owe you now?'

'I can set up a taverna.'

'That many?'

'More.'

'I promise you we will have them, and I'll drink you under the table.'

'You'll lose.'

'Oh ho! A challenge. You are definitely on.'

'Be prepared to be made a pauper.'

'Don't be ridiculous. I'm already one.' Pappenheim kept his smile on as he hung up. 'I'm slipping. I owe someone more favours than are owed to me. Hmm.'

He lit a cigarette, took his time enjoying it, then went out to meet the goth.

She was already waiting outside the Rogues' Gallery. She was dressed in vibrant blue, with blue nails, and blue eye shadow.

'Something wrong?' Pappenheim asked as he tapped in the entry code. 'Why all blue?'

'Nothing wrong. I just fancied blue today.'

'Ah. I see.' The door swung slightly open. 'After you.'

He followed the goth in.

She went directly to the computer and powered it up. 'When is he back?'

'They'll be here some time tomorrow.'

'They? I *knew* I was right to wear blue.'

Pappenheim thought it wiser to say nothing.

'Do I launch the simulation?' the goth asked without turning round.

'Yes. We need to send a message to the man with the beacon.'

She launched the flying game. 'Ready.'

'Send ... Carlton Niles.'

'Just that?'

'Just that.'

The message, in block capitals, appeared on the left multifunction display of the simulated jet fighter.

'Now we wait ... er ... you wait. I'll be right back. Call me if anything happens before I return.'

'Enjoy the cigarette,' she called, again without looking round.

Pappenheim paused at the door. 'You are in a bad mood, aren't you?'

'No I'm not.'

Pappenheim went out, shaking his head.

He returned thirty minutes later, after two satisfying cigarettes. There had still been no response.

'I've been flying a long mission,' the goth said, 'but nothing's come back from him. Perhaps he's ... Hold on. Something coming in ... Yes ... here it is.'

On the left MFD was the reply.

DANGEROUS, DANGEROUS, DANGEROUS!

'Send ... Deceased, deceased, deceased,' Pappenheim said. 'Let's see how that hits him.'

She sent the message.

The response came immediately.

HOW?!!!

'Shot,' Pappenheim said. 'By friends. His.'
Hedi Meyer sent it.
DESERVED appeared on the MFD. Then,
WHAT DO YOU NEED?
'Anything useful,' Pappenheim said.
The goth sent the response, followed by
another wait.
Then came a single word: PRINT.
The goth turned on the printer. It soon
began to chatter. When it had finished, five
sheets of paper – including one with a series
of photographs – were in the tray.
Pappenheim took them out with undis-
guised anticipation. He went over to the
table, spread the sheets out, then scanned
through them rapidly.
'Ooh, yes,' he remarked softly. He then
checked the photographs. 'Oh, definitely *yes*!
Miss Meyer, send him my thanks.'
She did, and a single word came back:
ENJOY.
'Oh, I will, I will,' Pappenheim said, un-
ashamedly gleeful. 'Miss Meyer, I'm off to
attend to these. Fly for as long as you like, if
Hermann Spyros won't burst a blood vessel.'
'I'm working on something for him. I think
it would be wiser to go back to it.'
'Perhaps you're right,' he said.

Müller and Carey Bloomfield had said their

goodbyes to Waldron at the airport, and were checking out the shops. Their business-class tickets gave them some flexible time before boarding.

'I'm going to sleep for most of the flight,' she said. 'That lobster dish—'

'Crayfish—'

'*Lobster*,' she insisted, 'was wicked. Pete's a mean chef.'

'He certainly knows his cooking,' Müller agreed.

She paused suddenly, staring at a display window. 'Will you look at that? It's beautiful. Very individual.'

'That' was a coned shell of quite spectacular colouring. It was mainly bright blue, but with black, green, and red twists within it, near the coned tip. It was about eleven centimetres from coned tip to the slightly belled end; which was perhaps five centimetres across. It stood out among the other shells on display.

'But is it real?' Müller said, seeing it as a tourist trinket. 'Or a plastic replica?'

For a brief moment, he thought she had brought attention to the shell because she had seen him take the small blue example from beneath the potted plant at Woonnalla. But he knew she could not have done so.

'It *is* real,' someone from inside the shop said.

A young woman came out, smiling at them. She had a small badge with the name Luara upon it.

'It's the only one we've got,' Luara said. She noted Müller's expression. 'You don't believe me.' She went back inside, took the shell out of the window, and came back to hand it to him. 'See for yourself.'

Müller took the shell. It was real, and smoothly exquisite. He passed it to Carey Bloomfield. 'What do you think?'

She inspected it closely. 'You know what I think. It's beautiful. Unusual.'

'It's one of a kind,' the young woman with the Luara badge said, looking at Müller. 'I won't put another one in there if you take this, because there's not another one. We've had it a while, but no one seems to want to buy it. They all take the more ordinary shells. Guess it's too unusual for them. This one was found near Broome.'

Neither Müller nor Carey Bloomfield reacted to this.

'Why don't you take it?' she said to Müller.

Thinking she wanted it for herself, he said, 'Alright.'

Luara beamed at Müller. 'It's going to a good home.' She took the shell inside to pack it.

Carey Bloomfield mimicked her silently. 'It's going to a good home.'

They entered the shop to make the purchase.

'Your receipt,' Luara said, still beaming at Müller.

'Thank you.'

'Have a nice flight.'

'Thank you,' Carey Bloomfield answered sweetly.

They left the continuously beaming Luara, and headed for their boarding gate.

'Do you think she knows how to spell her name?' Carey Bloomfield said when they were out of earshot. 'I half expected the corners of her mouth to reach her ears. You have a strange effect on some women, Müller.'

'Ouch,' Müller said. He held the package out to her. 'Your shell, madam.'

'That's not for me,' she said.

'What? But I thought...'

'It's for the goth. *I* thought you should get her something. She'll like it. Bet you. But don't tell her I found it. She'll want to kill you instead. I would.'

He shook his head in helplessness. 'I give up.'

'So what else is new?'

But a tiny smile he did not see fled across her lips.

At 1400 Berlin time, Pappenheim got a phone call.

He had studied the information on Carlton Niles several times, and was still engrossed.

'You have been a busy little man,' Pappenheim murmured, allowing the phone to ring. 'And just look at some of the company you kept.'

He leaned back in his chair, drew on the inevitable cigarette, squinted at the photographs of Niles, and let the phone continue to ring.

It did not stop.

Pappenheim stubbed out the cigarette with a weary sigh. 'Alright, alright.' He snatched up the phone. 'What?!'

'Do you always answer your phone like that?'

'Aah! Wolfgang! Sorry. But I was rushing back from the toilet...'

'Happens to us all. The phone always rings when you don't want it to.'

'Always. Like the tram that never comes when you're waiting on a cold day, but as soon as you rush off to a kiosk to buy a paper...'

'It turns up while you're waiting for your change.'

'I can see you've been there. So ... what's the reason for this pleasure?'

'I was just wondering whether you've got further thoughts on my proposal. Müller is still unavailable, I take it?'

'Unfortunately. Busy man. But I have been giving your proposal serious thought...'

'Sounds encouraging,' Wolfgang Melk said, eagerness stealing into his voice. 'If I can help...'

'I know you can. What can you tell me about Carlton Niles?'

Melk was so stunned by the unexpected question, he actually gasped in shock down the phone. A long silence followed within which Melk's breathing could be clearly heard.

Pappenheim waited, a patient fisherman who knew he had hooked a big one, and would not let go.

At long last, Melk spoke, voice tight with a toxic cocktail of malevolence. 'You have just made a very bad enemy.'

'There you have a problem,' Pappenheim said, dangerously calm. 'You made one when you tried to bribe me.'

'*Don't* challenge me, Pappenheim. You'll lose.'

'How little you know.'

The resultant click was so loud, Pappenheim held the phone away from his ear.

'He actually banged his phone down,' he said, a dreamy look in his eye as he replaced the receiver. 'Wonder if he'll need a new one.'

He returned to his study of the Niles photo gallery. The one that currently held his attention showed Niles falconing somewhere with a hot climate, and high sand dunes.

His companion, was Wolfgang Melk.

'You said nothing to Pete Waldron about Mainauer,' Carey Bloomfield said to Müller on the plane. Their sleeper seats were reclined, and there was no one close enough to overhear. 'Don't you trust him?'

'Being cautious. Besides, I would not like to have *The Semper* sniffing around him and his family. The less he knows, the better for him.'

'He's a "diplomat" ... if you know what I mean.'

'It does not mean he knows anything about *The Semper*. True, he knew about those three on the Great Northern, but only as criminals of interest to the Federal police. Interesting to see if Pappi has been able to dig up anything on the American.'

'I've been trying to recall whether I've seen him anywhere before ... but nothing jogs.'

'Pappi might have something by the time we get back.' Müller held out the map Wishart had given him. 'Take a look at this.'

A question in her eyes, she took it and spread it open. On one side was a large-scale area map of the route to Cape Leveque. On the other was a larger-scale map of the area around the airstrip, showing the beach. A red circle on the beach had the caption PARTY written next to it. In a rectangular box at the airstrip was written PARK HERE. A dashed line showed the route from the parking area, to where the party was being held.

She looked at him. 'Who gave this to you?'

'Graeme Wishart.'

'And the party's on the date on here?'

Müller nodded. 'It's a beach party being held in Jamie Mackay's memory.'

'Why would he give this to you?'

'It seems many of Jamie's friends will be there. He made a point of saying that friends who had known Jamie for years will attend.'

Her eyes widened slightly. 'You mean...'

'I see no other reason for his emphasis. He even suggested that he would book my suite, *and* have a 4WD waiting ... if I were inter-

264

ested. That's his private phone number on there, plus the direct line to his office.'

'That date's less than two weeks away. You going to do it?'

'If I do decide, do you want to see how this turns out?'

'I don't think you'd be able to stop me.'

'I'll be going as a private citizen. No warning, no Pete Waldron – so no gun.'

'I'll find a way to bring mine, in case we need one.'

'*If* I decide to go.'

'Naturally.'

In Berlin, General Sternbach received another unwelcome call.

'Pappenheim has connected me with Niles!' Wolfgang Melk told him.

'How is that possible?' The general was shocked.

'If I knew,' Melk said impatiently, 'I would be doing something about it! Wherever he gets his information from, it must be from a person, persons, an organization, or organizations with excellent access...'

'Are you suggesting there are those among us—'

'I'm "suggesting" nothing. I am stating a fact. Pappenheim and Müller have a route – or routes – to information that most of my political colleagues don't even have.'

The general gave a short bark of a laugh that was conspicuously devoid of humour. 'Since when did politicians know anything of value? Do you really believe we can trust them with anything beyond their immediate career needs?'

'I am a politician.'

'You are more than a politician. You are one of us and, as such, you must neutralize your foes. They have refused to accept your offers of promotion. That is their concern. In our interests, it is a matter of survival. Nature's most implacable law.'

'Are you telling me that I should take direct action against those two?' Melk sounded as if he did not want to hear what the general was saying.

'As I said earlier to someone, the carrot has been offered ... and now that it seems to have most certainly been refused, it is time for some of the stick. I expected a refusal,' Sternbach continued. 'Though pleased if they had accepted, I would still have been disappointed...'

'Disappointed? You *admire* those two?

'Learn something about warfare. It is not amiss to admire the qualities of your enemy, even if you violently oppose all he stands for. It makes you understand him, and his motivations, far better. This gives you clues on how to tackle him. The biggest cardinal sin of all is to underestimate him. There lie the seeds of your own eventual defeat. You misjudged them.'

Melk said nothing to this.

'The grotesque irony,' the general went on, 'is that both Müller and Pappenheim possess the kind of qualities we could use. Unfortunately for them, they are diametrically opposed to us. Pity. Now see if you can devise ways to neutralize them. It is either that, or they *will* destroy you.

'Our organization – our Order – has been in existence for decades. We have infiltrated widely, both here and abroad. We did not last this long without certain skills in the art of survival. We have control of, and access to, a remarkable amount of high technology in many fields. This takes extreme patience, and ruthless action when necessary. To succeed, you must obey the highest law of all: that of survival. Destroy before you are destroyed.'

The general hung up, almost before Melk.

Pappenheim dragged the goth away from Hermann Spyros for the second time that day. In the Rogues' Gallery, he went to the cabinet where all the sensitive material about *The Semper* was stored. He took out the mini-disc that Grogan had passed to Müller during the time of the killings of former Romeos.

That disc contained a mine of information and clues that were slowly falling into their proper places. Both Pappenheim and Müller had often wondered how Grogan/Vladimir had managed it without being killed.

Pappenheim now went over to the goth, who had long since powered up the computer, and handed her the disc. There was a very private and secret reception scene on it where many well-known faces from all walks of life and nationalities had been present. And that was before the Wall had come down.

'Call up the scene at that reception. Let's see who else we can spot among those strange bedfellows.'

'Are we looking for a particular face?'

'Carlton Niles.' Pappenheim glanced at the faces in the photograph on the sheet of paper he was holding.

The goth had glanced round at that moment. 'Is there another one?'

'Wolfgang Melk,' Pappenheim said after a brief moment of hesitation.

'Sir! That's the minister's...' The eyes of changeable colour stared at him.

'I know. See if he's in there.'

She turned back to the computer and began to call up the scene. When it had appeared, she put a fine grid over it, then began to expand each square.

'Is there a photograph on that sheet that shows the two together?'

'Yes.'

'Then it's going to be easy. The photos, like the other information, are in the memory. I'll just call up the photos.'

A new window appeared, showing all the photographs that Grogan had sent. She selected the one with both Niles and Melk, then copied it into the grid. The computer began to do a rapid search for a match. Within moments, two of the squares on the grid began to blink.

'They're both there!' she said.

'So I see,' Pappenheim said in a soft voice. 'Can you expand?'

'I can fill the whole screen with each at a time. I'll adjust resolution until both are nice and sharp.'

'Let's see what you've got.'

The faces were younger, but in the end there was little doubt. Both Niles and Melk were *Semper*.

'Well, Wolfhound,' Pappenheim said quietly, 'you can stuff your promotions. You could before this, anyway.'

'Promotions?' The goth did not look round as she tapped at the keyboard. 'You're being promoted, sir?'

'It wasn't worth it,' he said.

'You *refused*?'

'I would like to think you would have refused under similar circumstances.'

'Ah. One of those.'

'One of those.'

'And if you tell me to forget what you've just said, I'll stamp on your foot. There's no need to tell me.' She still did not look round.

'I'm not brave enough,' Pappenheim said.

Woonnalla Station, Western Australia. 2000, local

The photo-electric lighting of the airstrip normally operated automatically when the Hargreaves were at home and planned to fly, or were expecting someone to fly in. But, in their absence, the main power supply had been switched off.

Now Peter Lysert turned it back on. Immediately, two rows of lights bordering the airstrip came on. The normal lights of the station were already on. Lysert scanned the night sky, looking for the navigation lights of the Cessna 337. His brother was still away, driving as far as possible to find a suitable spot to dispose of the sniper's body and vehicle.

Ten minutes later, the unmistakable sound of the centreline twin sang upon the night. Soon, the navigation lights could be seen.

Lysert watched as the aircraft set up for a straight-in landing. In minutes, it had touched down immaculately.

Lysert shook his head in admiration. 'Every time, any time of day. Wish I could fly like that. That was a Maggie landing.'

He waited until the aircraft had taxied to a stop before going out to meet the returning Jack and Maggie Hargreaves.

'Everything OK, Pete?' Hargreaves asked as they climbed out.

'Everything's OK, Jack. Evening, Maggie.'

'Pete.' She looked towards the house. 'And in there? Any visitors?'

'That Berlin copper came round,' Lysert replied. 'He had this looker of a Yank sheila with him. Real beaut. Graeme came over with them.'

'Did he ... say anything?'

'The Berlin copper? Nah. He looked around, though.'

Maggie shot a glance at her husband. 'Did he take anything, Pete?'

'Not that I could see. Why would he do that, anyway?'

'Oh, nothing. Foolish question.' She turned to her husband. 'Jack, you and Pete see to things. I'll ... I'll just go in and see if...'

Hargreaves seemed to understand what she was trying to say. In the glow of the airstrip lighting, his face was impassive.

'Yes. You go on, Maggie.'

She hurried away, as if there was something very urgent she had to do.

He watched her all the way, until she disappeared into the house.

Maggie Hargreaves rushed frantically through the entire house, checking everything minutely. After each check, she seemed increasingly relieved that nothing had been altered.

She finally went out on to the terrace. She put on all the lights, so that every corner was lit. The first thing she did was to check the card under the flower pot. She saw the pen that had been left deliberately.

She looked at what had been written on the card. She kept the card, and the pen.

Something seemed to be pushing her on. There was an intense – and at the same time worried – expression upon her face. She kept looking. It was as if she already knew what she would find. She came to the plant pot.

And saw that the little blue seashell was missing.

'Oh, God forgive me,' she said in a small voice. 'He knows.'

At that same time, it was three hours into the flight from Perth.

Müller felt in his pocket, and touched the little shell he had taken from beneath the plant.

'It will help it to grow,' he whispered to himself.

Almost with a sense of guilt, he flicked a quick glance in the direction of Carey Bloomfield in the adjoining sleeper seat. She was dead to the world.

She certainly seems to need her sleep, he thought.

Relieved, he settled back to wonder what the Hargreaves would make of it when they returned.

'Seasons of change,' he said quietly.

He did not see Carey Bloomfield open an eye to look at him.

In Berlin, Pappenheim had been poring over the information about Carlton Niles.

Something almost unobtrusive had jogged his memory, but he could not remember what. He looked over the sheets of paper one by one, checking every single word. Whatever it was, it still eluded him.

'What the hell was it?' he asked himself past the cigarette stuck between his lips. 'What was it ... What was it?'

Then he stopped. He had been looking only

at the printed letters; but faint handwriting, like an annotation, had been scribbled in a margin. It had not printed out clearly, but enough had been copied on to the paper to enable it to be read without much difficulty.

Dennison Biometrics.

There was no other annotation, but it was enough.

'Well, Carlton Niles,' Pappenheim said, barely breathing the words. He stared at the scribble, squinting through a wreath of smoke. 'In what capacity did they employ you?'

Carlton Niles, Wolfgang Melk, Dennison Biometrics, and *The Semper.*

'Pro killer, hungrily ambitious politico, maker of nightmares, and the nightmare organization itself.' Pappenheim grunted with satisfaction. 'I have you, Wolfhound ... by the balls, and by the time I let go, you'll be a eunuch squealing for mercy. Trying to bribe me was the worst mistake of your miserable life, and now, I have enough to stop your career dead in the water. But I will not squander my ammunition. Using it sparingly will have the best effect. And the most damaging,' he added.

He took a long drag on the cigarette, and blew out a satisfying trio of smoke rings.

The phone rang.

'Not now!' he said. But he picked it up.

'Sir!' came a strained voice.

Pappenheim was astonished to realize it was Hedi Meyer. He was certain he had detected a tinge of fear.

'Still in there, Miss Meyer? What's wrong?'

'Sir ... just come over. I'll explain when you get here.'

This was a very unusual goth he was listening to.

'On my way,' he said, and hung up.

He killed the cigarette as he got to his feet, wondering what could possibly have agitated her so completely, and hurried out.

As soon as he entered the Rogues' Gallery, Pappenheim noted the tightness about the outer corners of her eyes, and that she seemed paler than her usual ethereal self.

Wordlessly, she pointed to the printer tray as if it carried the plague.

'After you left,' she began as Pappenheim went over to pick up the three sheets of paper in the tray, 'I called *Kommissar* Spyros and suggested that I work here on a small program that I'm developing. I wanted to run a simulation, and this computer is much more suitable for what I wanted to do. He agreed. While I waited for him to send me the data on the LAN, I went online to check if my friend was OK for a flight. She was busy, so I came off. That was when the man with the beacon sent this.'

'This', as Pappenheim discovered to his astonishment, was a highly confidential memo from Dennison Biometrics.

'How the hell did he get his hands on...' Pappenheim stopped, as he began to silently read the chilling memo.

EXTREME CONFIDENTIAL

To all sections concerned. Global.

Dr Lewis Markham, leader of the global team responsible for the development and evolution of Primary Specimen Zero-One from Primary Specimen Zero (PSO–PS-01) committed suicide a few days ago. The reasons were easy to find. The entire database for the development and evolution of PS0 into Primary Specimen Zero-One (PS-01) was destroyed. The system was hacked into and, despite a rigorous, multi-level password defence, it was penetrated. The data was accessed and irrevocably deleted. The storage area was then systematically sanitized. There is no way to retrieve even scattered bits of data that might have been left behind. It was a clinically efficient attack.

The essential questions are:

Who gave the information?

Who is capable of mounting such an attack?

Who is/are the hacker/hackers?

What is to be done?

What does this mean for the Order?

There are many other questions, but these are the current priority.

1. **Who gave the information** – this requires a root and branch investigation. If any member of this Order is found to be a traitor, or an infiltrator, I recommend to the Order that he or she be eliminated. Many years ago, the Order suffered a particularly

damaging attack by someone who had successfully penetrated us to the highest levels. Action was taken to neutralize the person concerned. Permanently. The Order must be as ruthless with anyone found to have been involved in this attack.

2. **Who is capable of mounting such an attack** – there are many who would like to prevent us from achieving our goal. None is so inimical to our interests as the son of that high-ranking traitor. But has he the capabilities? This, I would suggest, appears doubtful. We must search elsewhere ... but he should not to be overlooked. All avenues must be pursued.

3. **Who is/are the hacker/hackers** – again, find the source, and we find the hacker, or hackers. Finding the responsible party will be difficult. They were extremely clever. No trail was left to follow. Had the data not been destroyed, there would have been no way for us to discover that we had been compromised. Whoever did this is a genius; but there should be no doubt about the action to be taken, when those responsible are found. Members of the Order come from all walks of life, and control or belong to, many civil and military organizations. It is within our capabilities to do what is necessary.

4. **What is to be done** – self-explanatory.

5. **What does this mean for the Order** – bluntly, this is a catastrophic setback. We must again start from scratch, as was the case with the destruction of the first laboratory,

years before. Our one hope of regaining the considerably lost ground would be to find the original sample. It is believed that someone among those who destroyed the lab was infected. His DNA would be the perfect source, as PSO would have had time to evolve within its host. What stories it could tell! However, this unknown person is most likely dead by now. His remains would still yield sufficient material to make further development highly viable. We may even find that PSO has evolved in ways far beyond our expectations. The search continues for the likely resting place of his remains. It is to be hoped he was not cremated. Cremation destroys all vestiges of PSO. There are organisms which can survive extreme temperatures. Dr Markham planned to pursue that route, to see if PSO could be made temperature-proof. It is tragic that he took his own life. Regarding carriers, several possible, living candidates were taken. All proved negative, and were eliminated.

I would respectfully suggest that all sections of the Order, globally, make finding those responsible for the attack – and the search for the carrier's remains – twin priorities to be dealt with as a matter of continuing urgency. Without PSO, we have null chance of restarting the program. Without it, the most efficient weapon ever devised by man will have ceased to exist. Can it be restarted from scratch? No doubt someone else will eventually rediscover how to make it work ... but no member of the Order currently alive will live long enough to see that happen. At least, not in the form we were so close to perfecting. Let us not forget that we have lost a program that was commenced in the Fifties.

We do not have another fifty years within which to wait.

Dennison.

A signature, presumably Dennison's, was above the name.

Pappenheim looked up from the memo, face still. 'My God,' he uttered softly.

The goth was looking at him with the eyes of a child seeking assurance. 'They're looking for me.'

Pappenheim's baby-blue eyes fixed themselves upon hers. '*Nothing* is going to happen to you. Jens would never forgive himself if anything did ... And while this may not hold the same cachet for you, neither would I. They will have to go through Jens, most of the colleagues here, *and* me, before they got to you. And they won't. That's a promise,' he finished in a firm voice that was full of the reassurance she sought.

She gave him a tiny smile, and nodded.

'OK?'

'OK,' she said.

'He considers you a genius,' Pappenheim went on. 'Praise from the enemy.'

'Doesn't make me feel better.'

'I can well understand. You do take your

278

gun home, I hope?'

Again, she nodded.

'Don't be afraid to use it if the time ever comes. Your record says you're a good shot. Remember that. Always. And remember what I've just said. Nothing is going to happen to you. That's a promise.'

Ten

Berlin, the next day. 1200, local

Müller and Carey Bloomfield made their way towards a taxi. Müller had left his own car safely in the underground car park of his police unit, on Friedrichstrasse.

The day was bright, with a cloudless sky.

'Well, Müller,' she began, 'you're home again. How do you feel?'

'Different,' he replied. 'Seasons of change.'

'"It will help it to grow",' she quoted. '"Seasons of change". "A million miles away". Are you going to explain these cryptic sayings to me, Müller? Or will I have to guess?'

He gave her a strange, almost detached look. 'You've been listening in.'

'Hey, I wasn't snooping. I guess I'll have to wait.'

A tolerant smile flitted her way as they neared the first cab. Then lights flashed once, to their left.

Müller looked and saw the familiar, big, gun-metal grey BMW 645csi coupe. It was a confiscated *Semper* car once driven by one of their killers and it had, understandably, never been reclaimed. Pappenheim still made use of it.

'We're being picked up,' Müller said to her.

'Where?' Then she saw the car. 'Pappi! Now that's what I call service.'

The cab driver had been about to get out, and looked disappointed as they began to turn away. Müller gave him a shrug to say sorry.

The driver looked back at him stonily, then re-entered his car.

'Yes,' Müller said drily. 'I'm definitely home.'

They went to where Pappenheim was waiting.

'So you're back,' Pappenheim greeted as he got out.

'I'm back.'

They shook hands.

'Hey, Pappi,' Carey Bloomfield said to him.

'Hi,' he responded.

She gave him a hug, which brought a suspiciously pink tinge briefly to his cheek.

'I'm surprised you can reach around me,' he said, covering his pleased reaction.

'Don't you always say you're cuddly?'

'I do?'

'Yes.'

'Don't spar with her, Pappi. You'll lose.'

'There speaks the voice of experience,' Pappenheim remarked. 'In, children. Let's get out of here.'

They put their travel bags into the boot. Their guns, along with the palmtop and Gino's camera, had arrived safely in their own bags. They kept those as they got into the BMW, Müller getting into the back.

'How did you know?' Muller asked as Pappenheim started the car and moved off.

'Flight schedules. I checked those I thought you'd most likely to be on. I decided to wait out here. Less conspicuous.'

'It's almost as warm here as down under,' Carey Bloomfield said.

'We're having a very good August,' Pappenheim said, glancing at her. 'You look as if you've caught some Aussie sun. You too, Jens.'

'It was a bit warm,' Müller admitted.

'Talk about understatement,' Carey Bloomfield said.

'Plenty to see down there,' Müller went on. 'Not enough time – by a long way.'

'That's sounds like a prelude to going back,' Pappenheim said.

'I'll definitely go back.'

Pappenheim shot Carey Bloomfield another glance.

'Don't look at me,' she said.

'Perhaps you should tell me about it,' Pappenheim said over his shoulder to Müller.

'Have I got something to tell!' Muller responded.

'And I have something for you.'

'First stop the Rogues' Gallery?'

'The very place. Will we need the goth?'

'Yes. But not immediately. Seen anything of the Great White?'

'Still conspicuous by his absence.'

282

'Perhaps we should send out a search party.'
They both laughed.

Berlin, Friedrichstrasse

The wide, blast-proof door began to roll upwards as Pappenheim drove on to the gentle slope of the descending ramp. The garage lights came on as the car passed beneath the door which again began to lower, as soon as the BMW came off the ramp and on to the garage floor.

Pappenheim parked next to Müller's gleaming, seal-grey Porsche Turbo.

Carey Bloomfield looked at it as she climbed out. 'This car continues to look as brand new as when we first met, Müller. What have you got on it? Something that frightens dirt? You should see my old Bimmer on a bad day.'

Müller gave her one of his tolerant smiles as he got the travel bags out of the boot of the BMW and put them into the Porsche.

'I'll meet you in the Gallery,' Pappenheim said, seemingly in a hurry. 'Just shut the doors when you're done. It's already locked.'

Müller nodded. 'See you there. Did you notice anything?' Müller added to Carey Bloomfield when Pappenheim had gone.

'No. What?'

'No smoke in the BMW. He certainly did not smoke in there while he was waiting.'

'Now that you mention it ... Poor Pappi. He must be gasping.'

'I gave up trying to get him to stop a long,
283

long time ago. He's happy with it. I still tease him about it, of course.' Müller picked up his gun bag. 'Got yours?'

'Right here.'

'Well ... let's see what Pappi's got waiting.'

Having had his quick fix, Pappenheim arrived at the door of the Rogues' Gallery just as they got there.

Müller looked at the thin folder Pappenheim was carrying. 'Interesting things?'

'Oh, yes. Youth before age,' Pappenheim continued as they entered. 'Then you can read these, and be pleasantly alarmed.'

The door shut solidly behind them.

'And what do you call "pleasantly alarmed", Pappi?' Carey Bloomfield asked.

'There's some good news, and some bad news. The bad is very bad.'

'Clear as mud.'

'All will be revealed.'

After filling in a few more details about the news he had already passed on to Pappenheim, Müller told him about the *Aphrodite*, and Sharon Wilson's attempt at infiltration. Müller said nothing about his own strange feelings at Woonnalla, nor about the seashell he had taken. There were other things he wanted to do first. But he mentioned the party for Jamie Mackay.

He caught a few questioning glances from Carey Bloomfield, but chose to ignore them.

'Now you're fully up to date,' Müller finished. 'The camera and the palmtop are in there.' He indicated his gun bag. 'We'll need the goth to look them over before we attempt anything with them.'

'She's already on standby,' Pappenheim said. He looked at Carey Bloomfield. 'And the shoulder?'

'It's OK. It felt a lot worse than it really was at the time. The snake thing, you know...'

Pappenheim nodded. 'I can only imagine. You were very lucky. You'll see why when you've read this.' He tapped at the folder. 'Things have turned a little hotter since we last spoke,' he went on to Müller.

He put the folder on the table, and took out the last page – the one with the photographs of Carlton Niles.

'Does the name Carlton Niles ring any bells?' he asked Carey Bloomfield.

Her eyes widened slightly. 'The US Marine colonel?'

'So it does.'

Müller listened with sharp curiosity, but decided to remain silent for the time being.

'Sure. He was under investigation some years ago. Illegal arms, drugs – among others...' She stopped. 'Why?'

Pappenheim pushed the sheet with the photos towards her. 'Is that face familiar?'

'My God! It's *him*! That's the guy from the highway ... the Great Northern. I didn't recognize him because I've only seen bad pictures of him in an official report about the investigations. But that is definitely the same guy. The investigations, and the report, never made it into the media.'

'What a surprise,' Pappenheim said.

'Who's that with him in this picture?' She pointed to the one with Wolfgang Melk.

'Ah ... well ... this it where it gets really tasty. Jens,' Pappenheim said to Müller, 'your turn.'

Müller picked up the sheet. His eyes narrowed, and grew cold. 'Melk.'

Carey Bloomfield stared at him. 'The guy who offered you promotion? The guy in there with Niles?'

Müller's grim expression was reply enough.

'Jesus...' she said. 'So he really is *Semper*.'

'And right next to the Minister. Marvellous, isn't it?'

'Not for very much longer,' Pappenheim commented smoothly. 'At this moment, he must be considering his options. I haven't even told him the rest.'

'Pappi,' Carey Bloomfield began, 'you're telling me you called the guy and told him you knew about this? Are you suicidal?'

'Not the last time I checked. And I did not call him. He called to ask me if we had thought further about his offer. I told him Jens was still away, but that I had given it some hard thought. He mistook that for a positive sign. Since he was in such a good mood, I asked him if he could tell me anything about Carlton Niles. Innocuous little question...'

'"Innocuous". Sure. Bet that made his day.'

'It made it several degrees colder. He actually warned me about going against him.

286

Imagine that.'

'Bet that made you see your favourite colour.'

'Now, now, are you calling me a bull? I know my girth is ... generous...'

Carey Bloomfield was shaking her head slowly. 'You two are crazy.'

'Well, this crazy man is going to leave you travellers to it for a while. Read what the other pages have to say about Niles, then follow that with the *pièce de résistance* waiting patiently in the folder. Then feel the chill. Everything in there is courtesy of our friendly man of mystery, Grogan.'

Pappenheim went to the door.

'Enjoy the smoke,' she said to him.

Pappenheim was cheerfully unrepentant. 'I've already had that parting shot from the goth. Yesterday.'

Müller began reading through the first page as Pappenheim left. Wordlessly, he passed it to Carey Bloomfield, and picked up the second page.

They read the four pages in total silence. Only the soft, ambient noise of the room and the rustle of paper disturbed the comparative quiet.

When she had read them all through, Carey Bloomfield put them into a neat little pile on the table. She did so with particular deliberation.

'That guy was truly a nasty piece of work. He even did jobs for some people I know,' she said to Müller. 'I never imagined they were so borderline.'

'Military? Or civilian?'

'The department I'm thinking of is a mix of both. Jesus, Müller ... Could *they* be *Semper*?'

'Not necessarily. He might just have been a contractor...'

'Müller, this guy offed a high-ranking politician who was opposed to a regime that was in favour. These people...'

'You know this happens. It isn't right, but it happens. In your kind of job, you must know that...'

'That's not the point I'm making. The guy he was sanctioned to kill had a case running against a company called Sunburst Enzomes – that's a merging of rhizome and enzyme...'

'Aptly named,' was Müller's dry comment. 'One spreads roots, the other is a biochemical catalyst.'

'Sunburst wanted to use a large section of rich land, to set up GM crops,' she continued. 'The regime welcomed it. The politician made a lot of noise, denouncing the decision.'

'You're going to tell me that Sunburst have a connection—'

'To Dennison Biometrics, who have a connection to—'

'*The Semper*,' Müller finished, 'by any other name.'

'Give the man a cookie.'

'Tentacles, and yet more tentacles,' Müller said. 'Are you ready for Pappi's *pièce de résistance*?'

'No, but let's give it a shot.'

Müller took out the Dennison memo. He stared, riveted, when he saw what it was.

'How, in the name of all that's holy, did Grogan get hold of *this*?'

She was staring at him as he read, then saw his face harden and go pale. She resisted asking him what was wrong. He got through the first page, then handed it to her without saying anything.

He began the second page. As he read, his lips tightened, and a slight tremor went through him. He finished the page, and passed that to her.

No words were exchanged between them.

Müller came to the third and last page. Again, he read it through silently, then passed it on to her. He waited until she had finished.

A long silence fell. Carey Bloomfield looked as if she was not certain what to say. Müller stared into nothing.

'Jesus,' she at last said. Her voice was a whisper.

Müller said nothing.

'You OK, Müller?'

'I'm fine.'

He did not sound fine, she thought.

She tried again. 'That ... "traitor" he talks about...'

'Yes. He means my father.'

'And he more or less says they'll be hunting you...'

'They've been doing that already. That attack on you at Gantheaume Point was a continuation, and was meant to be a warning.

If they had succeeded, it would have been meant to teach me a lesson; to tell me that they will force an attrition rate upon me that I could not take. They are not afraid to attack anyone close to me. They tried it on Pappi. In the very beginning – which you saw – they would have killed Aunt Isolde. They murdered the first *Schlosshotel* manager in the attempt. They tried to kill you in Washington, and they have already killed some police colleagues. So this is not new. What *is* new, is that it will no longer be random. It's coming to a head. I would keep an eye out for Sharon Wilson, Gino's red-haired goddess. Wherever she is, she will try to get to us. And you will be first. This is the way it will go. The seasons are changing – in many ways.'

'I can look after myself, Müller.'

'I know you can. But at Gantheaume Point, one accurate shot off that boat would have done it. The shot *was* accurate. You have plenty to thank that rock for.'

She made a rueful sound. 'A soft piece of rock, and a fall: the difference between life and death. That was a close call, Müller. I was caught in the headlights.'

'Sometimes, we do need that stroke of luck. It came your way out there.'

'I'm glad it did. The person they would like to find most of all,' she went on, 'is Greville, isn't it?'

'They would ... if they knew what he is; but they have no idea what he is carrying. They expect, as you have seen in the memo, that

290

the carrier is already dead. To discover that he is actually alive and kicking...' Müller let his words hang. 'They must never find out,' he went on. 'They would go to any lengths to secure him, particularly now that we have killed the core data for the PSO variants, and would risk a bloodbath at the *Schlosshotel*, if they ever found out. I will make certain this does not happen.'

'Would they be crazy enough?'

'Not crazy. Ruthless. We expected the destruction of that data to enrage them; but there is also a clinical ruthlessness in what they would do for their own survival. I am a threat to that survival. That puts me, and all close to me, in the firing line.'

Müller paused. 'I've come to a decision about two things. Any doubts I may have had have been removed by what Pappi just gave us about Niles and Melk and that memo. I'm going down to the *Schlosshotel* today, and I am going to Jamie Mackay's beach party at Cape Leveque.'

'I had you down for the beach party ever since you told me about it. And before you ask, of course I'm coming. This memo changes nothing for me. If I'm in the firing line, then I was there the moment that bastard killed my brother. I'm coming to the *Schlosshotel* too. It will be nice to see Aunt Isolde and Greville again.'

'Then it's settled. I'll let Pappi know.' Müller went over to the phone. 'I might as well tell Graeme Wishart about my decision. It's early evening over there. He might be home.'

He quickly dialled one of the numbers on the map that Wishart had given him.

Wishart was home. 'Graeme,' he answered.

'It's on,' Müller said.

'Good-oh.'

They hung up together, having deliberately kept the conversation extremely brief. If anyone had tried to intercept the already secure line, there had simply not been sufficient time to even begin.

Pappenheim, fresh from a double cigarette fix, entered at that moment. 'Enjoyed the good news?'

'It's good news for us about Melk,' Müller said. 'Bad for him. As for that memo ... we know where we stand. Warn Berger, Reimer, and the others that they must not leave themselves exposed.'

'They'll be told,' Pappenheim said. 'The goth was shaken by it.'

'Nothing's going to happen to her.'

'I've already told her.'

'It's all coming to a head, Pappi,' Müller said, glancing at the folder.

'It began all those years ago,' Pappenheim said, 'before any of us was born. It had to arrive at this point one day. We just happen to be in the way.'

'Not a good place to be.'

'Ah well...' Pappenheim let the words fade.

Müller opened his gun bag and took out Gino's digital camera and the palmtop.

'Saving these for last,' he said to Pappenheim. 'Time for the goth to do her stuff. But before we call her, I've got something from Oz for you. Hope you like it.'

'Oh, you shouldn't have...' Pappenheim jokingly mimicked the familiar stock phrase.

Müller reached into his pocket to get the keys for Waldron's old combi. He kept his hand closed around them.

'Hand out, Pappi.'

Pappenheim gave him a cautious, sideways look, then glanced at the smile that had come to Carey Bloomfield's face. He did not extend his hand.

'OK ... what are you two up to? If this is some fiendish Australian creature hiding in your hand, I'll...'

'Hand, Pappi.'

Pappenheim finally held out the hand, looking at Müller closely. 'This had better not be some horrible insect...'

Müller opened his own hand, and dropped the keys into Pappenheim's.

Pappenheim stared at them as if he really did expect them to crawl off his palm.

'My God,' he at last uttered softly, quite clearly moved. 'The keys to Pete's combi.'

'He's been keeping them for all those years. He felt they rightly belonged to you.'

Pappenheim was at a loss for words. 'I'm ... I'm...' He stopped. 'He shouldn't have told you about that.'

'Why not? To him it is something that has defined his life, which you gave back to him. Jumping into the Thames to rescue someone when you're both drunk was no small thing...'

'I only did what anyone else would have,' Pappenheim said gruffly.

'I doubt that, Pappi.'

Pappenheim stared at the keys for a while longer, then closed his fist over them. 'It was the last time Silvia and I were in London together. Thanks for bringing them.'

'I am glad I was the one to do it.'

Pappenheim nodded slowly. 'Who would have thought Pete would have kept them all those years? He's surprised me ... That Aussie lunatic...' Pappenheim opened his hand, and looked down at the keys. 'Memories.' Slowly, he put them into a pocket.

Müller thought of the little blue shell he had taken from Woonnalla, and of his own memories.

Then Pappenheim roused himself. 'I'll get the goth,' he said, and went to the phone to call her.

The goth arrived in a flaming-red outfit that just escaped being diaphanous, and which reached to her ankles. She wore blue eye-shadow, blue fingernails, and red flat-soled trainers with blue side stripes. The attire accentuated the power of her eyes.

She carried what looked like a tool bag.

'You're back,' she said to Müller, smile full of warmth.

'I'm back.'

She turned the changeling eyes upon Carey Bloomfield. 'Colonel.' The drop in the temperature of her voice was just subtle enough to prevent it from being seen as hostile.

'Hedi.' Carey Bloomfield's expression remained studiedly neutral.

'So,' the goth said, looking at them as if about to teach a class. 'Who do I have to ... er ... what do I have to kill?'

'First,' Müller said, 'I would like you to print me a second copy of that memo. Then,' he pointed to the camera and the palmtop, 'see what you can extract from the camera, and that palmtop. Be very careful with the palmtop. I have not opened it. It may have defences. If we can break through them without damaging any data in there, we might find some very useful information about the people that memo belongs to. It's been used as an in-the-field communicator, so there may be a small goldmine in there.'

The goth nodded, placed her bag upon the table and studied each item closely, without touching them. She went over to power up the computer, and printed out the second copy of the Dennison memo. She then returned to the table, as Müller removed the new printout from the tray.

She gave the palmtop and the digital camera another close scrutiny. Then she opened the tool bag.

The others watched her go about her work, fascinated.

She took out a small scanning device that looked like a torch, and plugged it into the computer. She tapped at the keyboard. A window that looked like an infrared screen came up. A perpendicular bar, segmented in different colours, was tucked to one side.

The goth passed the scanner over the palmtop. Instantly, an image of its interior showed onscreen. The miniature keyboard and monitor screen, overlaid, showed up sharply, as did the motherboard.

'That's an x-ray scanner?' Pappenheim asked.

'Very low level,' the goth replied, not looking round. 'But it's much more than that.' She did not explain. 'Sir ... could you hold the scanner just as I've got it, please?'

Pappenheim obeyed with a brief, amused raising of his eyebrows.

'Thanks,' she said, and took her seat at the computer. 'Don't move it. Just keep it right there.'

'Yes, sir,' Pappenheim said.

She ignored him as her fingers flew over the keys.

Something odd was happening to the image of the palmtop. It kept expanding, zeroing swiftly to a point on the motherboard. A red pinpoint now began to expand until a full circuit diagram filled the computer's large plasma screen. A series of numbers and letters appeared to one side, scrolled swiftly upwards, then stopped.

'What the hell's *that?*' Carey Bloomfield asked.

'That, Colonel,' the goth replied, as if to a student in her class, 'is a listening and tracking device.' She swivelled her chair to look at Müller. 'This is just an ordinary palmtop. By that I mean, apart from the fact that they used it to bug you, it's nothing more than an ordinary palmtop. Whatever they used to communicate, it was not with this. Good thing you did not open it to have a look. That was the activating switch. As long as you had it with you, they could have tracked your whereabouts, and listened to everything you said. Not in here, of course, because this place is shielded. But anywhere else, and you might as well have been using a megaphone.'

Müller was staring at her. 'Are you certain?'

The look in the changeling eyes said it all. 'Of course.'

'Peace, Hedi. I just want to be absolutely sure.'

'OK.' She turned back to the computer. 'What that scroll of code can do for us, though, is give us an idea where the information about you would be going. But we can't know ... unless we activate it.'

'Do I still have to hold on to this?' Pappenheim asked her.

'Oh, no. I've got all I need.'

'Thank you, Miss Meyer.'

She ignored his dry remark, and glanced back at Müller. 'Do we activate it? It won't get anything through from in here, but as soon as you take it out it will broadcast to wherever it's meant to. We can piggyback, right to its destination. But everyone will have to keep silent.'

297

'What's its listening range?'

'You won't like this.'

'I can take bad news.'

'If you drew a circle around it,' the goth answered, 'the entire area within that circle would be live – three-hundred-and-sixty-degree coverage.'

'And how far out does that circle go?'

'One kilometre.'

'*What?*' came the chorus from Müller, Carey Bloomfield, and Pappenheim.

'And everything within it could be picked up, from wherever its controllers happened to be. Anywhere in the world.'

'Jesus,' Carey Bloomfield said.

'It gets even better,' the goth told them calmly. 'It's got voice recognition. It can zero in on a particular voice and filter everything else out. If it's locked on to your voice,' she said to Müller, 'or all three of your voices, that's what it will transmit. The people listening can select whose voice to record, and as many as they choose. It is quite a piece of kit, for a palmtop.'

'Thank you, Sharon Wilson,' Müller said.

'Who's Sharon Wilson?' the goth asked.

'Someone you would not like to point a gun at you.'

'I don't want anyone to point a gun at me. Do we activate?' the goth asked again.

'We can definitely make use of it,' Müller said. 'Let me think of a way to give us the best advantage. Meanwhile, we'll leave it in here – unopened.' To Pappenheim, he added, 'It goes into the cabinet for now.'

Pappenheim nodded.

'Now for the camera,' Müller went on to the goth.

This time she did not use the scanner. Instead, she took a cable from her tool bag, and plugged the camera directly into the computer.

'Ha!' she exclaimed, as the camera gave up its secrets in a series of codes. 'Very clever.'

'What?' Müller asked.

'This is what they used to communicate. It's got a defence that would have fused everything in there if anyone tried to dig into it. But I'm not "anyone". I've killed it. So it's wide open to us. It's still a camera, but it's got added functions. Listen...'

'They're heading for Gantheaume Point,' came a female voice. *'We're following...'*

'That, Miss Meyer,' Müller said, 'is Sharon Wilson.'

'There's something wrong with her voice,' the goth said.

'What do you mean?'

But Gino's redheaded goddess was speaking again. *'Can't you keep this bike straight?'* It was a scream of intense irritation.

'Yep,' the goth commented. 'She's not all there. You're right, sir. I would definitely not want her to point a gun at me. Do you want to hear more?'

'No need. We know what happened next. Wait. Run on until someone answers.'

The goth fast-forwarded. 'That sound you

299

heard in the background when she was speaking is the bike. Sounds like a Harley. Or a copy. But a copy wouldn't have sounded like that. It's a Harley.'

Carey Bloomfield glanced at Müller. 'How do you know it's a Harley?' she asked the goth.

'I know about bikes,' came the reply.

'That tells me.' Carey Bloomfield shot another glance at Müller.

'Here's something,' the goth was saying, ignoring Carey Bloomfield's remark. She let the recording run through.

'*This is* Aphrodite. *We read you. Let us know when we can take the shot.*'

Carey Bloomfield paled. 'My God. They were setting it up!'

The goth, hearing the horror in her voice, turned to look. 'Setting what up, Colonel?'

'My assassination,' Carey Bloomfield replied with a suppressed anger that was directed at Sharon Wilson and her cohorts. 'A sniper on that boat – the *Aphrodite* – took a shot at me. He missed because I slipped off a rock and fell. He was still good enough to graze my shoulder. If I hadn't fallen, I'd be dead.'

'It also helped,' Müller said, 'that by then, the *Aphrodite* no longer had them to act as spotters. The sniper had to work solo.'

Despite the rivalry she clearly felt, the goth's eyes widened with genuine shock. 'The luck was with you. I'm glad.'

'Thank you, Hedi.' Carey Bloomfield was

pleasantly surprised.

'And anyway, it wouldn't be fair.'

'What wouldn't?'

The goth turned back to the computer, and did not explain that either.

Carey Bloomfield looked at Müller and gave a puzzled shrug.

He responded in the same way.

A tiny, secret smile played at the corners of Pappenheim's mouth.

'How about the pictures?' the goth was saying. 'Shall I run them through?'

'Let's see what they took,' Müller said. 'We might find something useful.'

What came onscreen were many shots of Sharon Wilson, clearly when she was not looking. One was of her nude, on a red patch of ground. The camera also had a semi-video function. It lingered.

'Well, it wasn't Sardinia,' Carey Bloomfield remarked drily.

'Australia,' Müller said.

'Our man with the camera liked to spice his stories up a little.'

'Who's the one with the obsession?' the goth asked.

'Someone called Gino,' Carey Bloomfield answered. 'He had a thing about her. She didn't have one about him. She would have shot him as soon as look at him. He's lucky she didn't spot him doing this.'

'Perhaps she did,' the goth said. 'She was biding her time.'

'Knowing what we now do,' Müller said.

'She took her revenge.'

'Never mess with a woman,' the goth said to no one in particular. 'More pictures?'

'Let's see what else,' Müller told her.

There were shots of the *Aphrodite*.

'That,' the goth said, 'is a *beautiful* boat.'

Many pictures of the *Aphrodite* scrolled past, then members of the crew came on-screen.

'Ah!' Müller said. 'More for the gallery. Can you enhance and save them?'

'No problem,' the goth replied.

She gave high definition to all pictures of the people on the boat. There were no more of Sharon Wilson.

Then came shots of Müller, and Carey Bloomfield.

'Hmm,' the goth said. It could have meant anything. 'Shall I save those too?' There was a sharply pointed sweetness to the question. 'You're right, sir,' she continued before Müller had said anything. 'I'll delete them. There. Gone.'

Pappenheim found something of great interest in the ceiling.

Müller and Carey Bloomfield were heading from his office towards the lift.

As they approached the door to the Rogues' Gallery, he said, 'Let me check if she's still in there. Good time to give her your present.'

'*My* present?' she hissed. 'I suggested it, but it's *your* present. All the better now, after seeing that stuff in the memo. I'll wait by the elevator.'

'Hmm,' he said as she walked on.

He stopped at the door and tapped in the code. He entered as it swung open. The goth was still there, working on one of her many programs.

'With your incredible skills,' he said to her, 'you could make a fortune in industry.'

'So you keep telling me,' she said without looking round. 'And I keep telling you that working anywhere else does not interest me. Do you want something, sir?'

Müller went forward and put the neatly wrapped box on the desk, next to her right hand.

'Just a little thing from Oz. Take your mind away from that memo.'

She stared at the box for some moments, then picked it up, and began to unwrap it. She gasped with real pleasure when she saw what it was.

'Oooooh. It's beautiful! What amazing colours!'

'I ... er ... thought it would fit with your ... er ... cool periods, and ... the others.'

'How thoughtful of you, sir. This really is a wonderful thing to do. It's so beautiful,' she repeated. 'I know exactly where I'll put it. On my desk. Now go before I do something to embarrass you ... and me.'

'What? I ... um...'

'Go, sir!' She kept her back to him.

'Um. Alright.'

'Men,' she said when the door had closed

behind him. 'They understand nothing.' She looked at the shell. 'You are beautiful,' she said to it. 'And he thought about me.'

She smiled.

The lights in the underground garage came on as they entered.

'Hot in there, was it?' Carey Bloomfield said as they went towards Müller's Porsche.

'What?'

'You haven't said a word, Müller.'

'Oh. Thinking about Greville.'

'Greville? I see. So?' she persisted. 'Did she like it?'

'You were right. She did. It was a very good choice you made.'

'Sure. I might live to regret it one day.'

He unlocked the car, and Carey Bloomfield got into the passenger seat.

'Hi,' she said to the Porsche, and patted the dashboard. 'Remember me? Love your smell of leather.'

Müller got in, a tolerant look upon his face. He turned the key. The powerful engine barked into life.

'And your sound makes the hairs on my arms stand on end,' she told the car.

'You're talking to the car?'

'I like its conversation.'

Müller shook his head slowly as they drove up the ramp, and out beneath the rising door.

Eleven

The *Schlosshotel* Derrenberg was a little over 300 kilometres from Berlin.

Müller drove at speed.

'Feels good to be doing some real speed again?' Carey Bloomfield asked.

'Am I going too fast for you?' He began to slow down.

'There are ways of interpreting that question, Müller, and speed would not come into it. But no. You're not driving too fast. I've grown accustomed. And besides, I like the song of the car.'

He increased speed once more.

'So when do you plan to return to Oz?' she asked.

'I suggest we arrive the day before, have a good rest, then head for Cape Leveque in the morning. Graeme said the road – unsealed virtually all the way – is a vehicle killer if you take it too fast. Those two hundred or so kilometres will take us several hours. A lot longer than it will take to get to Aunt Isolde's. The party starts at fourteen hundred. I'd like us to arrive just after that.'

'Sounds good to me.'

They were a hundred kilometres into the

journey when the central console pinged, and Pappenheim's number showed on the display.

'Yes, Pappi.'

'Is there anything you want to tell me?'

Müller glanced at Carey Bloomfield. 'And this is code for?'

'We've known each other long enough, Jens.'

Müller thought about it. 'Just some thoughts running through my head,' he eventually said. 'I promise I'll tell you when the time comes. As you've said ... we've known each other long enough. You know I'll do as I've said.'

'OK. But if anything's troubling you and I can help ... don't hesitate.'

'I won't. You know that.'

'OK,' Pappenheim repeated. 'Can you hear me, Carey?'

'I can,' she replied.

'Watch his back.'

'You got it, Pappi.'

'OK,' Pappenheim said for a third time, and ended the call.

'Now what was all that about?' Müller asked.

'Do you want an answer? Or was that rhetorical?'

'Rhetorical.'

'I'll give an answer, anyway. A loyal friend who's worried about you.'

'You don't have to tell me about Pappi. I do know his value.'

'Well, just keep remembering that there are

a lot of people who care about you.'

He nodded. 'I know.'

His voice was quiet, thoughtful, and seemingly talking about something far distant in time.

The Porsche hurled itself along the autobahn, its engine roaring a challenge to a host of unseen enemies.

'What will you do about Melk?' Carey Bloomfield asked some kilometres later.

'For now ... nothing. Pappi has already given him a jolt. That will make him realize we're not going to roll over. We are steadily accumulating the kind of information that we can use effectively as weapons against people like him, when the time comes. Melk has many dark secrets he would not like to see the light of day. He made a bad mistake when he tried to divert us with the obvious bribe of promotions. He got our interest. In the Rogues' Gallery, the evidence continues to mount against *The Semper* ... but there is much left that we need to do. As for Melk, when the time is right, we will sink him. His friends will dump him very fast when they realize he has become a liability. They are not very loyal when their own interests are at stake.'

'No honour among thieves.'

The general received another phone call and, again, it was not good news.

'The unit is still not responding,' the caller said. 'He must have decided not to open it as yet.'

'With Müller,' the general said, 'anticipating his actions is a high-risk strategy. He does not play according to any rules but his own. He appears to do things that defy common sense but which turn out to be more logical than at first appeared. If the unit is still not operating within the next twenty-four hours, he is either sitting on it for reasons of his own...'

'Or?'

'Or he has discovered what it really is. Or he has it somewhere that blocks transmission.'

'The first is not possible. The second probable.'

'All things are possible.'

The medium-sized mansion that was now the *Schlosshotel* Derrenberg had gone through some rough years of neglect, during its days in the old DDR. A former seat of a branch of the von Röhnen family, it had been appropriated by Party élites at the end of World War Two, and had been left derelict and overgrown through years of misuse.

Aunt Isolde had inherited the sad shell, fortunate enough to find and regain family property that had at least been still standing, after the Wall had come down. Spotting a ready and waiting niche market, she and her second husband had restored it to its former self. It had been like a virtual reincarnation, and had become a mix of family residence and luxury hotel.

The building had more than enough space

to accommodate the two. Its main structure, plus its right wing, became the hotel. The left served as the owner's fully independent residence with its own secure entrance, and a large garden and courtyard behind a high wall. The thickness of the separating inner wall between the residence and the hotel section was such that nothing of either establishment could be heard through it.

Business had thrived and continued to do so, and the place had become almost too popular for its own good. There were always several cars in the guests' parking area; and the hotel's MPVs were always busy, taking guests on tours of the local Thuringian sights.

Within the vast main gardens were ground-level spotlights that had been positioned in unobtrusive locations. At night, they flooded the building with light, and illuminated the gardens. A much prided natural feature of the *Schlosshotel* was a stream that appeared placid, but which could turn into a raging torrent during heavy rainfall. Flood defences of raised banks of an earth and concrete mix had been constructed to protect against flooding.

The stream, forming a natural border between the manicured gardens and the wooded section of the huge grounds, was currently flowing at a pace that was seductive enough to entice someone to stand at the bank, simply to listen to it. Its route took it past the rear of the hotel. Its eventual destination was the River Saale, a kilometre or so further. A small wooden bridge, leading from the gardens to the woods, arched across it.

The man dressed in the wide-brimmed hat, white shirt and trousers and desert chukkas standing by the stream looked far younger than his years. This was Greville, Aunt Isolde's first husband, who had long been presumed dead. Greville, ex-Honourable, ex-major, ex-spy, ex-Sandhurst graduate, and ex-dead husband – ex-everything as he sometimes deprecatingly put it – had spent most of his adult life faithfully serving his country, sometimes in places few knew about, and frequently in situations of great danger. The fact that he was still alive was a tribute to his prowess. He had lasted over thirty years, where some had barely made it through thirty hours. He had never been back in all those years to the country – and thus the southern county of England – to which he belonged.

His rhythms of speech were sometimes eccentric, seemingly locked in a time when he first left the shores of his native land.

Standing by the stream at that particular spot was a favourite pastime. It appeared to give him a kind of solace. At those times, his piercingly pale-blue eyes looked into a far distance, perhaps remembering, perhaps looking forward. One could never be certain. As they stared down at the water, the pale-blue eyes seemed startling in a countenance darkened by thirty years of sun.

At such moments, when he appeared to retreat into a world inhabited by old demons,

Aunt Isolde tended to leave him to it.

She had been both shocked and overjoyed to see him again. He had appeared one day in May, seemingly out of nowhere. The husband she had married in his absence – believing Greville dead – had himself died years before. Seeing Greville again had made her realize that she had never stopped loving the man who had so abruptly vanished out of her life.

'The Honourable Timothy Charles Wilton-Greville,' he now said to the stream. 'Major. Ex-everything.' He looked up from the stream, head cocked, listening. 'I know that sound.'

He turned as the moving Porsche passed the trees at the far end of the grounds. Then it came into full view.

'Aha!' Greville said, and began to hurry back from the stream. He arrived at the main entrance to the building just as the car came to a halt.

'Dear boy!' he greeted as Müller climbed out. 'Back from the travels, eh?'

'Back from them, Greville.'

Greville shook his hand warmly, clasping it in both hands, then looked round to see Carey Bloomfield get out. 'And the beauteous colonel too!'

'Hi, Greville.'

He went up to her and gave her a quick embrace. 'And how's he treating you?'

'Same as usual.'

'Don't know when his luck's in, that man.'

'If you two are quite finished...' Müller said.

311

'See?' Greville said to her. 'Jealous. Says plenty.' He gave her a smile full of mischief. 'Come on. Let's go to Isolde. She'll be tickled pink to see you. My word,' he went on, looking at the car. 'Every time I see this beast ... and in that unusual colour ... what do you call it again?'

'Seal grey.'

'Ah, yes. Slight air of menace. Said that before, didn't I?'

'You did. Last May.'

'Say it again. Says something about you too. There is menace in you. An asset in these times. Said that too, I think.'

'In a different way ... but yes.'

Greville looked at Müller, suddenly interested. 'Anything wrong?'

'I think we should move,' Müller said. 'The hotel guests are getting curious.'

'Of course. But that is not what I meant.'

'I know.'

'Take Carey in, shall I? While you drive through?'

'I'll open the gate for her. You wait here.'

Greville's pale-blue eyes took on a thoughtful look. 'Right, old boy. I'll wait.'

Carey Bloomfield, carrying her bag containing her gun, accompanied Müller to the pedestrian gate, which was next to the tall, sliding vehicle gate. He tapped in the code on the keypad, and the gate popped open to swing inwards.

'You know the way,' he said.

She gave him a quick glance, then went

312

through.

He waited until the gate had swung shut again, then returned to Greville. 'Your favourite spot?'

'All very mysterious, old boy,' Greville said as they began walking back to the stream. 'What has happened?'

'Many things.'

'Found what you were looking for in Australia?'

'Not what I was looking for ... but I may have found something else. I'm going back to find out if I'm right.'

Greville again cocked his head to one side briefly. 'There is a certain intensity in your demeanour. You have changed a little. What happened to you down there?'

'Ghosts.'

'Now you *do* intrigue me. Care to shed some light?'

'I have no light to shed.'

'Ah. You're still groping around.'

'That's about it.'

'Must be of great importance, if it's dragging you back to make that long flight so soon after this one. Need to get it out of the system?'

Müller nodded. 'Yes.'

'Can I help?'

Müller shook his head slowly. 'Sorry. No one can help. This is not self pity.'

'Wouldn't dream of thinking so, dear boy. Not your style.' Again, Greville paused. 'There's something else.'

313

They had reached the stream.

Müller looked down at it, then reached into an inside pocket of his lightweight jacket. He pulled out an unsealed envelope, and passed it to Greville.

After giving him a curious look, Greville reached into the envelope, and took out the stapled sheets containing the Dennison memo.

He began to read, face seeming to freeze into immobility. He read the memo through in complete silence. When he had finished, he carefully folded the sheets of paper, put them back into the envelope, and handed it back to Müller.

'*Damn* these people!' he said with quiet savagery. 'Why won't they leave well alone?'

'The good thing is,' Müller said, 'they have absolutely no idea who the carrier is. As you've seen, they expect the person to be long dead. They are not looking for you specifically. You are as safe here as you would be anywhere else.'

Greville gave a slight nod, more to himself. 'I assume you do not want Isolde to know of this memo.'

'You assume correctly.'

'I approve. So, dear boy, the hornets are working themselves into a frenzy. Storm's a-coming.'

'Yes.'

A silence fell between them. The stream murmured to itself.

'Don't forget your promise, Jens. If ... anything should happen ... whether I die naturally – as naturally as this thing inside me allows – or unnaturally, remember I must be cremated. I will not be responsible for taking this plague into the world. And also remember, my ashes in the Healey, driven the length of the Green Hell at Nürburgring.'

'I'll keep my promise.'

They found Aunt Isolde in the large kitchen with Carey Bloomfield. Carey Bloomfield was enjoying a choice of excellent sandwiches that Aunt Isolde had made.

'I'm hungry,' she said defensively to Müller, in answer to an amused look. 'And besides, I love these English sandwiches Aunt Isolde makes.'

Aunt Isolde, tall and elegant, gave a welcoming smile as she went up to Müller to give him a gentle kiss on the cheek.

'Hello, Jens. How was Australia?' She spoke the Sandhurst English she had absorbed from Greville all those years ago.

'Not enough time to see much of it. But what I did see has encouraged me to go back.'

Her eyes looked almost through him. 'And what are you not telling me?'

'Usual police thingy.'

'"Thingy"?'

'You know how it is.'

'I do know how it is. That's the problem.' But she said this fondly.

Carey Bloomfield noticed that Greville was looking her way, eyes telegraphing a message.

She grabbed another sandwich and stood up.

'I think,' she said, 'Greville wants to show me the garden. If I may be excused, Aunt Isolde...'

'Of course, my dear.'

Aunt Isolde watched them leave. 'Now if that is not a set-up, I don't know what is.'

'I said nothing to Greville. This was all his own initiative.'

'He must feel you wish to talk to me.'

'I'm not sure I do, Aunt Isolde...'

'But on the other hand?'

'I'm confused,' Müller said after a while.

'You? Confused?' She sounded as if she considered such a possibility unthinkable.

Müller paused for a long time, while she watched him anxiously.

'Do you remember, when I was six,' he began at last, 'I found a pretty little shell when you, Mina, and I went to Brittany? Father was away at the time.' Mina had been his pet name for his mother, when he was a child.

She looked puzzled. 'Yes, I do remember. It was blue. You were fascinated by the colour. It was so different from all the others. You took it home. Then you did a strange thing. You put it into a plant pot. For some reason, the plant was ailing. You said the shell would help it to grow. We were all astonished when, a few days later, the plant actually began to recover. Perhaps it was something in the shell. Perhaps there were micro-organisms in it that helped the plant. Whatever the reasons, that plant got well again. To this day, I don't know why.'

'And do your remember what Mina did with it?'

'She always took it with her when she travelled without you. "Her good luck piece", she used ... to say...' Aunt Isolde looked distraught. 'Oh, Jens. Why now? Why do you bring this memory back? It's not going to help after all these years.'

He did not tell her about the shell in his pocket.

'Don't worry,' he said to her. 'I'm not cracking up. It's just something to do with the case.'

'But what does the shell have to do with it? She had taken it with her on the flight. It must have been smashed to smithereens in the crash.'

'I know. I know.'

She came close, and put her arms about him. 'What you need, my boy, is a holiday. Stay here with Carey for a few days. Enjoy the wonderful scenery, and let me pamper you both.'

'It's a great offer, but she's returning to Washington, and then we're going back to Australia...'

'So soon? You only just had that long flight...'

'There's something that has to be finished up down there. It really is important for the case. And talking of pampering, how are the two colleagues? Getting in the way?'

'Not at all. We hardly know they're there.'
Aunt Isolde looked amused. 'They do what
they call "sweeps". They check things all the
time, usually out of sight. They spend a lot of
time checking through the woods. As they
never show their guns, the guests just see
them as staff.'

'I'll have a talk with them later.'

'Are you staying the night?'

'If that's alright...'

'Jens Müller, this is your home. You can
come and go as you please...'

'We'll stay the night,' he said quickly.

'I should hope so too. Carey can have her
usual room. I know she loves it.'

'When she first came here, I asked her if she
liked her room.' Müller smiled at the memory. 'She answered that you don't just like a
room like this. You love it. You wear it.'

'She has her way of saying things.'

'She certainly does.'

'She's good for you, Jens,' Aunt Isolde said.

'Now, don't you start, Aunt Isolde. There's
a dear.'

'And have you noticed she does have a
slight resemblance to Mina? Very odd.'

'Oh, no. Not the every-man-looks-for-his-
mother-in-a-woman hoary old chestnut. I
never knew she existed until Kaltendorf
dumped her on me that day, remember?'

Unrepentant, Aunt Isolde smiled. 'Got
under your skin, hasn't she?'

'Behave,' Müller admonished. 'Shame on
you.'

Aunt Isolde didn't quite have the smile of the Cheshire cat tacked on; but it was close.

Carey Bloomfield and Greville were on the wide polished landing of the owner's residence. Strewn with searingly expensive carpets from east of the Caucasus, the square landing led to the sweeping, central staircase. Doors to the bedrooms led off the landing and on the walls, in the spaces in between, were hung family portraits. They had paused at the top of the staircase, where pride of place had been reserved for a pair of special portraits. No doors marred this wall.

The portraits were of Müller's parents.

'When I first came here,' Carey Bloomfield said, looking at the portrait of the blonde-haired young woman, 'I thought she was so beautiful. She looks more beautiful every time I see it.'

Greville glanced at her. 'Do you know ... there's a certain likeness...'

'Come on, Greville. We're talking about a beauty here. I'm a pudding.'

'She walks in beauty, and knows it not,' Greville said. 'Refreshing quality.'

'And what's that supposed to mean?'

'That you, my dear, are someone rather special.'

Carey Bloomfield had gone to bed early but for some reason found herself awake at about midnight. She had left the blinds up, and the glow from the hotel floodlights was strong enough to allow her to see clearly.

On impulse, she got out of bed, and went to her door. Very slowly and quietly, she turned the handle, and eased it open. The lights on the landing were on and someone was at the head of the staircase.

In shirtsleeves, and standing with his back towards her, stood Müller, looking at the portraits of his parents.

Very carefully, she closed her door shut again.

'Ever since we went to Woonnalla,' she said as she got back into bed, 'you've been looking as if you've seen a few ghosts, Müller. What did you really see out there?'

The night gave her no answers.

The *Aphrodite* was racing into daybreak.

The ocean was calm, and the rakish boat sliced through the water with ethereal grace. Despite her speed, she was still at least two days from her destination. The air at this time of the morning was pleasantly cool.

Sharon Wilson had decided to come out on deck. She had not left her cabin since the *Aphrodite* had left Broome. Food had been left outside her door, but she had eaten little of it. But now she felt hungry.

She looked out at the expanse of ocean and the beauty of the new day with a baleful expression.

'Water,' she said to herself. 'Bloody water everywhere.'

Laurentius, who was not currently at the

helm, spotted her and approached.

'You haven't eaten much in the last two days. Would you like to try some coffee? It's fresh.'

She nodded. 'If I don't puke it up, I'll see if I can eat. I feel hungry.'

When the coffee came, she tried it, and found it tasted good.

'I'll try some food. What have you got? Nothing greasy.'

'Nothing greasy,' Laurentius said with patience. 'Fresh rolls. Marta has baked some of the frozen stuff. Cheese with freshly cut tomatoes do?'

'I'll try that.'

Half an hour later, she was back in her cabin, bringing it all up.

'*This bloody boat!*' she yelled between bouts of vomiting. 'I hate you, Müller, for putting me through this!'

Schlosshotel Derrenberg the next day. 0800, local.

Müller and Carey Bloomfield were heading towards the autobahn, on their way back to Berlin. They would first be going to the airport, where she would be catching her plane for Washington.

It had been a strange farewell to Aunt Isolde and Greville. Everyone seemed to be holding back on something. It was as if a known secret were being deliberately left unspoken; and that knowledge had left a pall of apprehension upon them all.

'Ghosts that won't speak,' Carey Bloom-field suddenly remarked.

He glanced sharply at her. 'What was that? What did you say?'

'Everyone seemed to have been walking on eggshells ... you, me, Aunt Isolde – even Greville.'

'He does have plenty to think about. He's read the memo.'

'I'm certain he was not thinking about the memo. At least, not when we were saying goodbye. He was watching you in a way that made me think his eyes were ... frowning.'

'Eyes don't frown.'

'You know what I mean, Müller.'

'So why were you walking on eggshells?'

'I'm not sure.'

'Why do you think I was?'

'You can best answer that,' she said to him.

'And Aunt Isolde?'

'That one's easy. She's very worried about you.'

'I'm very worried about her, and Greville. The two officers who are there to protect them have clear instructions about what to do in case of any trouble. They take them both to a place of safety, and hold out until the local force arrives. I continue to hope *The Semper* will never find out about Greville, and that a bloodbath out there can be avoided. It would be stupid and desperate of them to do something so openly, as this would give them the kind of exposure they hate; but it does no harm to be prepared for the worst.'

'Neatly ducked.'

He said nothing to that.

'If the worst does happen,' she said after a while, 'I'd like to be there. I want to hurt those bastards.'

'So do I,' Müller said.

There was a chill in his eyes that she could not see, but the stillness of his face as he drove at his usual high speed was eloquent enough.

They made it to the airport with at least an hour to spare before she needed to check in. They found themselves a spot where no one was close enough to listen in on their conversation.

'So we meet in Broome,' he said.

She nodded. 'Not sure of exact timings, but I'll be there. Don't you dare leave without me.'

'I would certainly not dare.'

An awkward silence fell.

'Damn it,' she said after the pause had become even more awkward. 'I hate good-byes, especially at places like airports. We'll be shuffling our feet next.' Suddenly, she squeezed his hand. 'I'll see you in Broome.'

Before he realized what was happening, she was walking rapidly away.

Ten days later. Tuesday, 2355, local

For Müller, the days till his flight back to Perth and onwards to Broome had seemed to tick by painfully slowly.

He had said nothing to Pappenheim, Greville, Aunt Isolde, or even to Carey Bloomfield about his real reasons for making the long flight a second time within less than two weeks. He was not even sure of his own reasons.

'I'm chasing ghosts,' he said as the 747 lifted off the runway at Frankfurt.

And the ghosts were waiting.

As he settled down for the leg to Singapore, he asked himself whether he had finally lost it. He was making a flight literally into the unknown – into what he believed could easily turn out to be nothing; an overheated figment of his imagination.

Yet something deep within him insisted he was right; that what he intended to do had its own momentum, and there was little he could do to alter the sequence of events that had brought him to this point.

He remembered Pappenheim's thoughtful but worried expression when he had told him about the second trip.

'If you've got to do it,' Pappenheim had said, 'you've got to do it. Avoiding it will make you impossible to live with.'

Pappenheim had grinned too readily; a sure sign of his agitation.

'And here I am,' Müller said in his mind, 'feeling like a child about to open a door that frightens him.'

Pappenheim was in his office, smoking too rapidly even for him, his thoughts on Müller.

'What are you chasing?' he said aloud. 'Why didn't you at least tell me?'

He did not feel upset, or even let down by Müller's reticence. Pappenheim's worries were fuelled only by his anxiety for Müller.

His phone rang. When he had picked it up, it was the female contact who had told him about Carlton Niles.

'This might interest you.'

'I'm always interested in what you have to say.'

'Blatant flattery, but I'll accept it. People who are interested in the whereabouts of your insubordinate friend are worried that they have lost him.'

'How do you know?'

'Let us simply say a conversation was overheard.'

'I shall ask for no further explanation.'

'Good. You won't get it. They seem ... frantic,' the contact went on. 'Whatever he's up to, they seem to expect him to do some damage.'

'He's only beginning,' Pappenheim said.

'You do realize he is declaring open warfare...'

'He declared that from the day they dragged him into this. He was twelve at the time. They started it.'

There was a brief silence.

'We'll continue to support...'

'But you'll deny everything if the brown stuff hits too many fans.'

'You know how this works.'

'Tell me about it,' Pappenheim said with the air of a veteran.

'What do you mean you don't know where he's gone?'

Sharon Wilson had totally recovered from what she continued to see as her ordeal on the dinghy, and was now in Paris. Only one thing was on her mind: the hunt for Müller and Carey Bloomfield. In this, the world was her oyster.

'The *bloody* palmtop should have been working by now. You should have heard at least something that would have given you a clue. I worked hard to get him to take it with him.'

She was sitting at a table of a pavement café. No other customers were close, but her angry tones reached even the furthest, who turned to glare at her.

'What the hell are you looking at?'

Though she was adept at French, she had conversed in English, and had snarled at the offended customers in the same language.

'You should be more subtle,' the voice in her mobile advised.

She actually kept quiet for some moments, but it was not because of the words of caution. She was taking the time for her simmer to boil over.

'You keep your advice to yourself! Just find the bastard. You got that?'

She cut off the call.

* * *

326

The person who had been speaking to her looked at his companion. 'Why do we tolerate this foul-mouthed bitch?'

'Because she's no fool. Because she's very good at what she does. Because she can change her persona when she's not playing the badass ... and because she has powerful backing. Not the kind you would want to go up against.'

'I knew there was a reason.'

Perth. Thursday, 0025, local

Müller's plane landed on time. As soon as he had cleared customs and immigration, he took a taxi to a small hotel near the domestic terminal. He went straight to his room, and bed, and had a dreamless sleep until six a.m.

He awoke refreshed, showered, taking his time about it, dressed and, taking his suiter, went down to breakfast. He took his time about that too, checked out, and caught the ten fifteen flight to Broome.

Now that he was back, his mind was perfectly clear. No doubts assailed him.

The plane landed on time at twelve forty. He took a taxi to his hotel, where he discovered that Wishart had been as good as his word. The same suite had been reserved. A set of keys for the same Explorer – already parked in the hotel car park – was also waiting for him at the reception. It was as if he had never left.

A note with the keys said there was beer in

327

the Explorer. Müller smiled at that piece of information.

He went to his suite to wait for Carey Bloomfield, hoping she would make it.

Within minutes, a knock sounded. Thinking it could be Wishart, he went to the door, and opened it.

'Hi,' Carey Bloomfield said.

He was so happy to see her, Müller felt a sudden wave of emotion flood through him. Almost without realizing it, he grabbed her, squeezed her to him, and began kissing her.

Then he stopped. 'I'm ... I'm sorry ... er...'

'Shut *up*,' she said, 'and continue what you started, mister!'

But she did not wait for him. As if afraid he would revert to his cautious self, still hanging on to him, she pushed him into the room and shut the door in seemingly one motion.

They clutched each other tightly and, when they had at last paused, their breath came in shallow gasps.

'Shit,' she said at last. 'I did not expect this.'

'Nor I.'

'Müller, you know how to spring a surprise. Right ... right now we've got a trip to make; but when we get back...'

'Cable Beach?'

'Who's talking about Cable Beach? I'm talking about the one suite we're going to use.'

The great red swathe of the corrugated, dusty road to Cape Leveque was as bad as Wishart had warned. They saw some of the vehicle casualties lying forlorn, like the ancient remains of strange beasts.

But they also thought the landscape awesomely and frighteningly beautiful.

Carey Bloomfield, as promised, had brought her gun with her. She had also brought an extra Beretta 92R, and a reasonable quantity of loaded spare magazines.

'We may never need them,' she had explained. 'But in case we do...'

'How are you feeling?' she now asked him.

'Euphoric.'

She gave him a warm glance. 'I don't mean that.'

'About what's waiting up there? I'm fine.'

For now, he thought but did not say.

By the time they were about a kilometre from the parking area indicated on Wishart's map, the sun was low on the horizon. It was going to be a spectacular sunset. Jamie Mackay would be getting a royal send-off.

'Look!' Carey Bloomfield almost shouted.

The wide track they were now on took them from behind a screen of trees, and the airstrip had come into view.

And parked at one end was the Cessna 337.

'They're here!' she exclaimed. 'Graeme was right!'

Müller felt his heart pump furiously, but he controlled himself so that she would not detect that anything was amiss. He knew she was glancing at him frequently, but he maintained his outward calm.

'At last,' he said, 'we'll get to know why Grogan sent me here.'

The parking area was not far from the aircraft.

They got out of the Explorer, Carey Bloomfield peering at the ground, and being careful where she put her feet.

Müller looked round to see what she was up to.

'Some things haven't changed, Müller,' she said. 'Snake country is snake country.' She looked up. 'OK. Let's find the party.'

They followed Wishart's directions. First, they heard voices; then, in a short while, they saw a group of people on the pristine white beach. The sun's rays, golden and red at the same time, seemed to make the beach itself glow. The ocean was a sparkling green, and the sky above a riot of colour that merged into the deepest of blues that was almost black. And within it all, the red pindan cliffs seemed to be on fire.

'This,' Carey Bloomfield said in awe, 'is another planet.'

'A million miles away,' Müller said in a soft whisper. His hand was in his pocket, clutching at the small, blue seashell.

It was a while before anyone noticed their presence. They were almost upon the group when Maggie Hargreaves turned.

Carey Bloomfield stopped in shock. 'Oh my Lord,' she whispered to herself. 'I'm seeing a ghost!'

Müller kept walking, putting one foot in

330

front of the other as though afraid that if he stopped to think, he would freeze on the spot. He was aware, dimly, that Carey Bloomfield was not longer at his side; that one by one, the voices were dying out as people began to turn to look at him; that Maggie Hargreaves was staring at him with something akin to fear; that Jack Hargreaves, wondering what was going on, was now also turning to look; that Wishart's mouth hung open; that Jack Hargreaves' eyes widened in disbelief; that Maggie Hargreaves' eyes were now brimming with tears that glistened in the light of the setting sun.

Then the world was back to normal, and he had stopped in front of Maggie Hargreaves. He held out his hand towards her, gripping the small seashell.

Slowly, he opened the hand to display the shell.

She stared at it, the tears falling down her cheeks, unheeded now.

'Mother,' Müller said. 'I smelled your perfume.'